BLOOD NOTES

LIN LE VERSHA

HOBECK

This edition produced in Great Britain in 2021

by Hobeck Books Limited, Unit 14, Sugnall Business Centre, Sugnall, Stafford, Staffordshire, ST21 6NF

www.hobeck.net

A CIP catalogue for this book is available from the British Library.

ISBN 978-1-913-793-51-7 (ebook)

ISBN 978-1-913-793-52-4 (pbk)

Cover design by Jayne Mapp Design

https://jaynemapp.wixsite.com

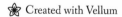 Created with Vellum

BLOOD NOTES

HOBECK ADVANCED READER TEAM

Hobeck Books has a team of dedicated advanced readers who read our books before publication (not all of them, they choose which they would like to read). Here is what they said about *Blood Notes*.

'...a crime story with a bit of a difference...'

'I loved this book, the story, the plot, everything.'

'The reader is immediately hooked.'

For my children, with love

CHAPTER ONE

EDMUND

WE MOVE APART and lie side by side on the rumpled sheets. I turn my pillow over. It cools my neck. The August sun knifes through the gap in the dusty maroon curtains that don't quite reach the sill – the blade slices the dust on the chest of drawers around her old perfume bottles.

She shifts. The bed springs creak.

'How about a cup of tea?' I ask.

'Or we could...' She touches me – there. I slide away from her. I sit on the side of the bed. She strokes my shoulder. She pulls me back down.

We lie. Silent. A spider spins a thread from the lampshade in the afternoon sunlight. She reaches for my hand. Pulls me towards her. Her finger traces the path left by a bead of sweat on my chest. She leans over, catches it on the tip of her tongue.

Lying back, she sighs. 'Yes, tea would be lovely.'

I pull on my boxers, reach for my shirt.

'I'll stay here for a while. You should be working.' She pulls the covers up.

I feel her watching as I tug on my trousers. I turn. She

1

yawns, stretches luxuriously. I pick up her faded yellow silk kimono. I hand it to her.

Sitting up, she takes it, covers her breasts. 'Changed my mind. I'll get up and make supper. Spaghetti Bolognese?'

'Yes, please, Mummy.'

CHAPTER TWO

STEPH

DEREK PEED ON A ROSEBUSH. A prize Queen Elizabeth with the most delicate shell pink blooms. Steph looked around. No one witnessed it. She'd banned Derek from Southwold beach after he'd watered the pale blue handbag of a lady holding a rod for her fisherman boyfriend. How ridiculous – a blue leather handbag on the beach.

'It's the streets for you until we have the beach to ourselves again.'

She fled up the road in case someone overheard her and concluded it was she, not her dog, who was barking. It had been a glorious summer – her first in Oakwood. Weeks of endless blue-sky days and barbecues. Suffolk had been more like Portugal or Italy. Even the east wind had moved out for a few weeks in the solid heat. Bees and butterflies had basked in the endless sunshine, but so had the vicious mosquitoes.

'Ouch! Shitting Henry!' she gasped, as the mozzy bite on the back of her heel became unbearable. She tugged Derek to a stop and told him to sit. He ignored her. She bent down and

3

dug her nail into the swollen lump, attempting to release the maddening gunge injected there.

'Oy! Missus! Your dog peed on my statue! Get him off!'

A grumpy-looking man had been dead-heading the yellow roses on a trellis by his front door. He limped towards her, waving his secateurs.

'I'm so sorry.'

Steph pulled Derek away from the concrete gargoyle-fairy.

'If you can't control him, he should be on a short lead.'

Steph dragged Derek away from the other concrete slab, which resembled a squashed rabbit. Two weeks ago, she'd moved into the ground-floor flat of an Edwardian house with a small garden opening onto fields. The moment she saw Derek, a black-and-white collie lurcher, at the RSPCA, she knew she'd found her ideal dog. She'd never trained a dog, and Derek had never been trained. She now kept him on a lead to avoid blue handbag incidents.

A police car siren in the distance pushed images of her leaving do into her head. She re-played the pathetic affair – a few drinks with a few colleagues. After almost thirty years in the police force, it should have been a bigger party. But they don't celebrate the careers of broken people.

The spiral started. Her stomach heaved. Panic gripped her. She breathed in, counting to seven, held her breath, then let it go. She repeated the technique she had been taught, while concentrating on the number of small panes in a circular gable window. The disrupting images ejected, she breathed out. Oakwood was a new beginning – a fresh start.

The mix of Tudor, Georgian and Dutch-gabled houses led to the High Street. It could be any high street, anywhere. Tesco, Jules and Costa Coffee had replaced the independent shops selling antiques, local pottery and farm produce. She used to drive from Ipswich at the weekends, looking for unusual presents in the little old-fashioned shops. Now she lived here, they'd disappeared.

A midnight blue dress caught her eye in the window of Miranda Modes, where she'd bought her new 'ensembles' – the posh saleswoman's word for outfits. Steph had felt fourteen again under her appraising gaze. She'd emerged with five brightly coloured outfits she would never have chosen by herself, one for each working day. After slobbing around in black tops and jeans for over a year, she could hardly believe the transformation.

She smiled at her reflection in the shop window. Her blonde hair re-shaped into a short, spiky style made her look younger than fifty-three. Her height had always helped her to carry her weight, but now her strict diet had removed her spare tyre and saggy tum. She had a fresh glow and the bags under her green eyes had disappeared. Her doughy skin, developed over the months being housebound, had brightened in the summer sunshine. She would need a second mortgage to pay off her credit card, but it was worth it. Even after a few days, she was enjoying her job as the college receptionist in her new school uniforms.

Derek crouched down low, in attack mode. A tall woman, who appeared to be wearing a long nightdress and walking with a white fluffy cushion on a pink string, floated towards them.

'Hello, Steph – and what's your name?' The woman ruffled Derek behind his ears.

'Derek. Sorry I don't...' said Steph.

'You won't know us all yet – I'm Caroline, Head of Art.'

'Is she a Scottie?'

'No. Norfolk Terrier, aren't you, Marlene? Heading for the common?'

Steph smiled and nodded as Caroline chatted on. 'Such a relief to get out. My partner's driving me bonkers! You know, Margaret Durrant, music teacher?'

Steph wasn't sure. Over the last few days, she'd met about a hundred and fifty teachers and members of support staff. She listened carefully for any clues to identify Caroline's partner.

'Anyway, Margaret's had another row with Harriet, her boss.'

'Really?'

'Margaret was Director of Music until a year ago when she discovered she had Parkinson's.'

'Oh, I'm sorry.'

'She became part-time and Harriet Weston took over. Marlene! Stop doing that to Derek!'

'Can we let them off here?'

Liberated, Derek and Marlene bounced off into the dusty bracken, on the trail of some irresistible rabbit or fox smell. They chased around, leaping over a fallen silver birch tree and in and out of the clumps of ferns, the edges rusty with the first signs of autumn.

'Anyway, the latest row is about changing the timetable for some brilliant cellist.'

Not sure how to react, Steph fixed on a sympathetic smile while nodding in time to Caroline's complaints. They stood side by side as the dogs dashed through the undergrowth in the watery evening sunshine.

'Gosh – is that the time? Margaret will moan if I'm late for supper. Lovely to chat. Come on, Marlene – *Marlene!*'

As Caroline hooked Marlene on her lead and scurried away, Steph realised that what she had thought was a nightdress was an elegant, pink dress in some floaty material. Miranda Modes' saleswoman would have approved of Caroline's style.

The day had drained. The sun had disappeared behind the silver birches, leaving a grey-pink smear across the sky. An early start tomorrow. It was the first day of lessons for the students after three days of enrolment. She turned towards home and supper.

CHAPTER THREE

STEPH

THE PORCH DOOR WAS AJAR. Convinced she'd left it closed, Steph switched on her mobile phone torch and swung the light around the front garden and into the bin store at the side of the house. She pushed the sharpest key between her fingers; she had nothing else. She froze and listened. Silence. No warning growls or barks from Derek. The wind must have blown it open. She must get a lock put on the shared front door.

She turned the key in her front door lock and pushed. She paused again and listened. All fine. Pleased to be home, Derek bounced over to the dog food cupboard, scampered back and jumped up at her.

'Down, Derek! Get down!' She pushed him away, relieved he hadn't snagged her new green skirt. He sat at her feet looking rejected, waiting for her to get his dinner. Leaning against the door, Steph looked around the elegant Edwardian room in the pale streetlight beyond the bay window. Relieved to be away from her old life and the constant hum of Ipswich traffic but now, stood in the gloom, she felt alone. Very alone.

She flipped the brass toggle switch and cosy islands of light from her copper Art Deco table lamps transformed the room. Her mood lifted. This house must have been amazing as one home and now, converted into two decent sized flats, she was pleased she'd bought the one with the garden. When the upstairs flat sold, she hoped she'd have quiet neighbours.

Steph walked around the room, towards the open-plan kitchen. Her hands stroked the dark mahogany dado rail and reached out to the past where Edwardian maids had dusted. The builders had painted the walls on either side with an inoffensive shade of beige recommended by house-porn TV programmes – Cappuccino Foam? Goose Feather? She'd pick up a paint chart tomorrow and choose a colour to make it hers, perhaps a gentle grey to highlight the veins in the marble fireplace. At last, the flat felt like home and for the first time in ages she felt relaxed, re-assured.

Steph stopped and sniffed. What was that smell? Perfume? After-shave? She must be imagining things. Stretching her spine, she took a deep breath, opened the dog food cupboard and served Derek's supper. A floorboard creaked. Must do something about that.

The floorboard creaked again. This time she was standing still. It came from upstairs. Must be the estate agent showing someone around the flat. Silence again. She listened. No cocky estate agent chatter, no striding around admiring original features.

Silence. Footsteps on the oak staircase. Footsteps scraped towards her door. She held her breath. The door handle turned; the door opened – she hadn't locked it! A figure filled the doorway. Steph grabbed a knife from the knife block and gripped it, ready to act.

'Hello, Steph, long time no-see.' He strolled into the room and owned it.

'Carter! What the fuck are you doing? You scared the shit out of me!' She slid the knife on the kitchen island behind her back, hoping he hadn't noticed. He had. He smirked.

Derek bounded up to investigate and Carter chucked a handful of dog treats across the floor. Derek scampered off to hoover them up. Some guard dog! How did Carter know she had a dog?

'What are you doing here? How d'you know I'd moved?'

He said nothing, taking his time scanning the room before staring her out.

'How d'you get in? It's right out of order! Get out now!' Shaken and shocked, she tried to appear strong and in control, but she heard her voice quivering a little.

He ignored her. 'Nice flat. Didn't get an invite to your leaving do.'

'What do you want?'

'Just a chat.'

'What!'

'About your little mate, Sam.' He reached into his inside jacket pocket and pulled out a photograph of a boy in his late teens in blue overalls, standing at a workbench and holding a spanner. He was grinning, confident and looking happy in his own skin.

'Who's that?'

Carter ignored her. He held the photograph in both hands and pushed it towards her. Steph inspected it and shook her head.

'You remember, Sam Odawale. Soon be earning shitloads. All because of you.'

He indicated she should take the picture, but she turned away. It had nothing to do with her. Carter stepped to the side and thrust the photograph at her once again.

'What? Whoever that is, I'm pleased he's doing well. Now piss–'

'Rather than being in the nick, you mean? Smoking spice and enjoying the showers.'

All the usual clichés. But then Carter only had three brain cells. What was she doing joining in? She wanted him out.

'If you don't go – I will – I'll call it in!'

'Don't think you will somehow.'

'Will you get out!' She moved towards the door and held it open. He stood still, stubborn. Her training nudged her. Change tack, de-escalate, get on his side. 'Look, Carter it's me, remember? What's wrong with you?'

'Nothing's wrong with me. I need you to do a little favour for me, like you did for him.' He leaned over her to slam the door, held her shoulders and pinned her back against it, leering into her face. She tried to avoid inhaling his rank breath.

'No idea what you're going on about.'

Carter smiled at her and winked and waited. Without warning, he let go of her and prowled around the room, examining her pictures, picking up her few ornaments. Steph felt invaded and had to get him out. Could she reach the knife on the island? As she edged towards it, Carter swivelled round, beat her to it, swept his hand across the worktop and the knife clattered to the floor. He grinned and moved so close she was forced to breath in his cologne, which failed to disguise the sickly smell of his sweat. Steph backed into the bay. Shuttered light from the street outside threw bars across her face. Carter leaned in further and whispered, 'You thought no one knew. Well, I do, and now you can help me.'

She stiffened to meet his eyes. 'Piss off! Sounds like you're trying to blackmail me! Don't bother. I've done nothing.' She tried to push him away, but he grabbed her wrists and squeezed them tight. She couldn't move.

'Blackmail? No. Just a little favour.' His face so near hers, she could see the dark grey pores on the side of his nose and a tiny drop of saliva just below the left side of his bottom lip. She inhaled his breath; the slight tang of whisky couldn't hide the decay. He needed to find a dentist.

Carter stood solid. His grip tightened around her wrists and hurt. As she squirmed trying to get free, he lunged, twisted her round and propelled her onto the sofa. It creaked as he plunged down beside her.

She felt trapped. Violated. There was nothing she could do or say without admitting her guilt. Admitting she'd crossed the line. Seething with anger mixed with fear, she sat tense. Petrified. Waiting to hear what he wanted.

CHAPTER FOUR

EDMUND

I READ IT AGAIN. Is that first page too shocking? I want you to be there, alongside me. I've polished it as a novelist might, so you can experience every moment with me. Now, at the start of my college life, I have decided to write my memoirs and to share my unique story with you. Home educated, allowed to work on my talent without being distracted by school. Now I'm ready. Ready to step on the stage as a professional cellist. Mummy and I have been preparing for this moment since I was four years old.

In the college library I've found a book called *A Life Worth Sharing – Write Your Memoir in 60 Days*. In it, J. M. Rowe suggests opening with 'a hook – a piece describing a powerful event at the centre of your life story'. Is my first page the J. M. Rowe hook? I see my memoir on a bookshop table. You walk in out of the rain, in your lunch hour. You pick up my book, my story, and flutter through it. Casually, you read the first page. You reach the last line, you gasp! You're hooked. Rowe's right. It stays.

Mummy calls our special love 'cuddles'. She needs them

more now. Now I'm at college. You must wonder about my father? He's gone. He left. I'm not sure why. She won't talk about it and goes quiet if I mention him. I can only remember a gigantic shadow – no features. There are no photographs. Sometimes, I wish I could get to know him. Mummy was a concert pianist until she had me and stopped. She married him but didn't forgive him. After he left, I woke in her bed.

For the last thirteen years we've had a rigid routine. It makes me feel safe. We plan our days – English, maths, history, geography, music theory and practice, practice, practice: five hours' cello practice every day. I breathe my cello. I feel I'm most me when I play it.

I passed all my cello exams with distinction. We would wait apart from the other children in music teachers' dining rooms, which smelled of yesterday's cabbage. After my performance, their eyes always followed me. Mummy would smile and say, 'They think it's a CD they heard through the closed door!' She's always so positive.

I was six when I started playing at music festivals. Again, I sat alone with Mummy. The other children giggled, chatted and complained about their music teachers. We just waited. No distractions. We often won. Actually, that's not quite true – we always won.

You think I had a lonely childhood? Not at all. I had Mummy with me all the time and I had my cello. Now, as I take this next step, I'd like to share my story with you. This is my 'daybook' where, according to Rowe, 'I can reflect on the past, record present thoughts and include short conversations to highlight turning points in my life'.

'EDMUND FITZGERALD TAKES the technical demands for granted and has a vibrant abandonment that makes his music passionate and truly individual. At seventeen, he is a genius cellist in the making.' First place – English Young Musicians' Festival.

I was the youngest competitor, beating some excellent musicians, most of them graduates from music conservatoires. As I walked on stage, I was so nervous, but once I started playing, I lived inside the music. It's always like that.

I met Harriet Weston, one of the three judges who gave me first place, when she came down from the stage to congratulate me. 'You can win BBC Young Musician next year, you know.' Me? BBC Young Musician? 'I've coached others in the past...' She reeled off the names of two finalists and one winner.

Mummy stood up, brushed down her skirt and steadied her handbag on her left arm, like the Queen. 'I agree. Edmund's close, but not ready yet.'

They talked about me. I stood beside them. Taller than both. They made it clear, shoulders turned inward, that I should be silent. Mummy and Harriet negotiated my future while I stood and said nothing. I felt flattered and stupid at the same time.

Harriet – she insists on Harriet – said I should take A Levels at Oakwood Sixth Form College, where she is Director of Music. With my outstanding performance, they will be my passport to the Royal College of Music.

'Edmund needs to maintain his practice regime.' Mummy lifted her handbag further up her body. Harriet held her ground.

'All music students have access to practice rooms, so Edmund may do several hours' practice each day under my supervision and the rest with you.'

Once again Harriet Weston dangled BBC Young Musician – a tasty morsel before the shark, in her blue-grey suit. (Did I really write that? Mummy a shark?) 'Think about it and let me know when you've decided.' She handed a card to Mummy. The handbag jaws snapped shut. Mummy nudged me away. I clutched the trophy as we left, not sure what would happen. I had to wait until Mummy decided.

That night Mummy needed long cuddles.

———

COLLEGE IS SCARY. Yes, at last Mummy agreed to what she called my 'incessant pestering'. I asked her for jeans and a top with a hood. I know that's what they wear; I see them from my bedroom window. Mummy said 'No'. Said I'm different. Do I want to be different? I suppose I do.

Rowe advises re-creating specific moments in your memoirs. 'Reproduce speeches and scenes so the reader can share your life with you.' I had lots of those moments in my first week at college.

I felt very different as I walked into the enormous oak hall, which smelled of floor polish, for enrolment. The old floor was shiny and reflected the sun – a wooden mirror. My blazer, chinos, white shirt and proper shoes made me look different too. Very different. Little crowds squealed and hugged each other as they peered at results' slips. I don't have any GCSE results. My head ached. It's much quieter at home. I stood alone. Had I made the most dreadful mistake? I turned around to go back through the door – back home. I felt sick; my stomach churned. I panicked – I didn't know the way to the loo.

They all looked at me. I felt their eyes as they pretended

not to look. I knew I was a year older than they were, but I felt so much younger. They'd never seen me before. They all knew each other. The same school, the same football team, the same street corners. They were confident and bouncy and shouty. I'm so different.

Harriet smiled as she came towards me across the gleaming hall floor. I enjoyed feeling different then. I felt so special. She had the look of being looked at. She resembles Cleopatra with her black hair framing her green cat eyes. Tutors sitting at their desks around the edge of the hall stopped writing, turned away from talking to a student or just stared as she walked – no, floated – down the length of the hall. I felt so happy to see her.

Looking at the groups of students, she leaned across and whispered, 'Don't be nervous. All the other students are feeling the same. That's why they squeal so much, to show they aren't.'

I must have looked scared or something, as she said, 'Don't worry that you haven't got results' slips. You've got an exceptional talent.'

I said the other teachers might not agree with her. At that she touched my shoulder (my nerves tingle in that place now, as I remember her touch) and said that she would be with me and not to worry.

Across the hall we walked to a desk with a printed notice dangling from the front of it saying, 'All English Courses – David Stoppard'. Behind it sat a well-built man with a black beard that looked like it had been charcoaled on. He's the head of department, which means he runs all the teachers in English. While Harriet explained why I'd taken no exams, how I was older than my year group, what an outstanding cellist I am and how well I will do on his course, he beamed at her, never lowering his eyes. He had that Red Riding Hood wolf's grin and looked as if he'd like to eat her up.

'Call me David' was so helpful. When I told him I enjoy Dickens, Hardy and Austen, he laughed and said I'm better read than some of his new teachers! I don't think I can be.

With that, in the beam of David's gaze, Harriet guided me to a desk at the far end of the hall labelled 'Sam Griffiths – Performing Arts'. Very different to David, Sam has a tiny pale face and all his clothes were black. The sunlight showed up the gaps in his thin blond hair and the sweat marks under his arms. He isn't much older than me. He looked a little scruffy, not what I imagined a teacher to look like. Harriet recited my history once again. Sam looked terrified of her. He pushed a form at me, which I signed, and gave me a list of plays. I thanked him and we walked to the Music A Level desk.

An old lady with grey helmet hair frowned as we approached. Harriet spoke loudly. 'Edmund, this is Margaret Durrant, who will teach you music theory.' Margaret sniffed into a tissue, which she tucked up her sleeve. She turned a list round, so it faced us. I signed in the bottom space.

'Thanks for standing in for me. I need to get Edmund settled.'

Margaret sniffed. 'That's fine, Harriet.' She didn't think it was fine at all.

We left quickly. I felt safe – happy in Harriet's glow. She steered me towards the music centre by touching my shoulder again. I liked that. I didn't mind people looking at us together. The music centre, a modern concrete building, has two classrooms on the right and two practice rooms on the left. At the end of the corridor an impressive recital room and beyond that is an enormous classroom with a recording studio. Harriet told me to meet her there with my cello at ten o'clock the next day.

At home, I tell Mummy about my day. I share the enrolling, the music centre and the teachers – or tutors, they're called. I don't tell her how nervous I was. Or how noisy the college was. Or how it felt to be stared at, like a fascinating specimen in a bottle. I think I can cope with college if I go to my lessons, stay in the practice room and never go to the canteen.

———

WITH MY CELLO strapped on my back, I felt more confident climbing up the hill on my second day. It didn't seem as steep. I walked across Main Quad to the music centre, the way Harriet had taken me, so I didn't get lost and have to ask.

Harriet was waiting for me. Handing me a swipe card with my photo and signature already on it, she said, 'It opens the front door so you can get into the music centre any time to practise.' Then she gave me to a girl called Justine in Year 13, who was in one of the practice rooms, playing her violin. It sounded rather good.

I think of Justine as I write this now and feel happy. I'm reminded of that picture of Ophelia in my encyclopaedia – the one of her floating in the stream and covered in reeds and weeds and herbs. Justine's like that, but she has masses of bright red curls – Pre-Raphaelite red.

That morning was wonderful. For the first time I felt me, without Harriet or Mummy being there. Justine suggested we spend the morning practising. She showed me the Bach sonata she was working on and played it very well. When she finished, I clapped and she made an elegant bow. We laughed. She looked at me, waiting for me to say something.

'That was lovely. Why haven't we met at music festivals?'

19

She lowered her head, looked at me out of the corner of her eye. 'I wasn't good enough.'

'That's not true.'

'It was until Harriet helped me. I'm pleased you like it.'

'Your intonation is great, but...'

'But? Go on.'

'You could lean a little more into those embellishments.'

'You mean the trills?'

'Yes, emphasise the turns and appoggiaturas.' I grabbed my cello. 'Shall I show you how to make them sit on top of the tune – like decorations?'

She sat beside me on the double piano stool. I was so close to her face that when I turned to talk to her, we almost touched. I could smell rosemary; it must have been her shampoo, fresh and gentle like her. 'Now concentrate on my left hand, my third and fourth fingers.' She moved closer. The smell of rosemary became stronger. I pictured Justine washing her hair. I turned the picture off so I could concentrate. I played an extract and showed her how to weave in the delicate ornaments to create the effect Bach intended.

'Let me try it.'

She picked up from the section where she'd had a slight tumble. This time she ran into the turns and trills with no hesitation.

'You see – easy, isn't it?'

'Now it's your turn.' She sat on the edge of the small table to listen.

I closed my eyes and was about to play the opening notes when the door swung open and hit the wall. A boy – Jack or Jake, I think he's called – crashed into the room. He stood still when he saw us together and looked puzzled.

'Justine, coming to the canteen?'

He's spotty and has dandruff. They walked off to the canteen holding hands. They didn't ask me. I left college.

Now the picture of Justine so close to my face keeps coming into my head. We would make a splendid duo. I've written a list of pieces we can play. I'll ask her if she'd like to rehearse with me after the Enrolment Concert – after I've heard her perform in public. I've decided not to tell Mummy.

CHAPTER FIVE

STEPH

'Bye, Miss. Have a good weekend!' Five students walked past the reception desk out into the sunshine, chatting about their plans for Friday night. 'You're joking! He did what?' squealed the Goth girl. The sliding doors cut off further information about his shocking behaviour.

Exhausted after a sleepless night, Steph had struggled through the day, trying to appear as normal as possible. Around two o'clock that morning she'd given up trying to sleep, as a mix of anger, fear and dread for her future whirled in her brain. She sat with Derek, alert and jumping at every creak the old house made in the dark, in case Carter returned. Her brain told her he'd gone, but her stomach insisted he could come back. Chamomile tea hadn't calmed her panic. It was blackmail, pure and simple, and she could do nothing about it. At least being at college had pushed it to the side, but now she had space once again her imagination took over and she felt sick.

Steph grimaced as she pulled off her right shoe. Her feet were killing her. She'd been standing all day. The left one took longer to peel off. Her feet breathed a sigh of relief as she freed them at last. She'd made it. The end of the second week. Most of the students had trooped past to catch their buses or to walk down the hill towards home. The tutors had also taken advantage of the sunny Friday afternoon to leave early. An hour to go and she'd be able to join them – assuming she could get her shoes on again.

Three students stopped by the desk. A dark-haired boy wearing a grey hoodie leaned over and asked, 'Have you found a black backpack, please? It's got my computer course work in it.'

She opened the door of the lost property cupboard. 'Sorry, no black bags. I hope you find it.'

'Thanks, Miss. It'll probably turn up.' He strolled off, blasé about his lost work.

Peter Bryant, the Principal, opened his office door behind the reception desk and stood beside her. 'Well done! Another good week. Coming back for the Enrolment Concert this evening?'

Steph had photocopied the programmes so knew it was happening but hadn't realised she was expected to attend. She had planned an early night to catch up on her sleep after watching some rubbish on the TV, but she didn't want to give the wrong impression. She held eye contact with Peter, so he didn't notice her bare feet.

'Remind me, what time does it start please?'

'Seven thirty. I'll save you a seat if you like. Harriet Weston's transformed our concerts over the last year.'

'Really? Sounds like a good evening.'

'Good. See you in the music centre later. Why don't you turn the phones off now and go? It's been a long week.' With that, he tossed his car keys in the air, caught them and bounced out of the sliding doors into the car park.

23

She looked around reception, her new world, a glass box. The old 1930s building was dark, and the addition of the modern glass structure, which jutted out into the car park, made a good impression on visitors as they entered the college. To the left as they came in was the long, light oak reception desk where she spent most of her day. Behind her, the members of the admin team she managed were hidden beyond a beige screen.

At the very end of her desk the door of the Principal's office in light oak matched the decor, but inside it was like travelling back to the early twentieth century. Opposite was the meeting room where private conversations could be held away from the open space of the reception area. Alongside that, to the right, was the waiting area with two black leather sofas separated by a light oak coffee table. She walked over to check there were no dirty coffee cups waiting for her to wash and straightened the pile of local papers and photos albums of student achievements. She looked down the length of the box to where it joined the old part of the college. The dark oak double swing doors found throughout the college had been replaced here by the lighter shade and led to the staff common room on one side and classrooms on the other. Beyond the traditional 1930s ex-grammar school was a patchwork of modern buildings around two grass quads for the fifteen hundred students who studied there.

Peter had said she could leave early so she would. While she was fiddling to turn off the complicated phone switches for the night, a waft of Jo Malone perfume made her raise her head. Harriet Weston held out an A4 printed sheet.

'I know this is short notice and you've already done the photocopying, but I've had to change this evening's programme. Would you mind popping this through your photocopier, please? One hundred and fifty, double sided.'

'Shall I bring them over when they're done?'

'I'll hang on, if that's OK?'

Steph stepped back to the monster photocopier behind her. The machine was always getting jammed, and she was becoming quite the expert in fishing out bits of paper from its innards. As she loaded the photocopier with a new wad of paper, she watched Harriet, in her designer stiletto heels, click across the wooden floor. She looked so elegant, in a skin-tight black dress, worth at least a month's salary; it proved she must live on lettuce – without the dressing. Seated on one of the black leather sofas, Harriet flicked through the local newspaper, left on the coffee table for visitors.

'It's not fair! I should play the finale. Not him!'

A cascade of bright red curls, on top of an emerald green silk dress, rushed at Harriet, who patted the space beside her on the sofa. The student shook her head and remained standing, a soggy tissue grasped in her hand, her mascara dripping from her eyelashes. She burst into tears.

'Now calm down, Justine. You'll look stunning on stage. I told you that colour would suit you.' Harriet smiled, sounding as if she was trying to win her round.

The student's sobs became quieter. Justine looked a mess. Swollen eyes, a dripping nose and trembling lips contrasted with her stylish gown. Steph dithered, unsure if she had the right to intervene. Just as she was about to ask them to move from reception, she was aware of someone standing in the shadow to the side of the meeting room door. It was Margaret Durrant. She kept out of Harriet's eye-line and listened to the exchange. Breathing deeply, Steph decided not to interfere and retreated to the photocopier to concentrate on the papers flipping into the tray.

'I should have spoken to you earlier, but I've decided that Edmund will play last tonight.'

'It's not fair!'

'Margaret told you, didn't she?'

'But I'm the best in Year 13 – it should be me!'

'You'll open the concert and play before him – two pieces to his one.'

At last Justine got her breathing under control. 'He's good, but...'

'No buts – that's my decision.'

Justine flopped down beside Harriet and grabbed a tissue from the box on the table. She blew her nose loudly. 'Last year you told me I was the best you'd ever worked with. Now you spend all your time working with him.'

'Look, he's home schooled and finding college a real struggle.'

'We were so close – until Edmund came.' She paused, sneaked a look at Harriet, then sat up straight. 'You also spend a lot of time with that new English teacher, David Stoppard.'

Harriet stared ahead.

Justine continued, 'Mr Weston's away at the moment, isn't he?'

'What's that supposed to mean?'

'Nothing really. Just that it'd be a shame if Mr Weston found out about David Stoppard.'

'Right – off you go, Justine. Splash cold water over your face, and next time use waterproof mascara, darling.'

Horrified, Steph gasped at this vicious comment and the shocking exchange. Surely this wasn't how teachers and students talked to each other now? It didn't sound like the conversations she'd had with her teachers.

As Justine ran down the corridor, Margaret positioned herself in front of Harriet so she couldn't get off the sofa without pushing her out of the way. 'That was so cruel. You had no intention of telling that poor girl, did you?'

'I didn't need to. You did it for me. How dare you interfere?'

'Justine's worked hard and deserves to close the concert. Now you've got your ambitious claws into our new musical genius, she's last year's model, isn't she?'

'I couldn't care less what you think. It's my decision, and that's final.' Harriet got up, shoved Margaret out of her way, then turned to face her. 'I can get rid of you like that!' She clicked her fingers in Margaret's face. 'You should accept your illness and retire before the Principal has to ask you to leave.' Harriet snatched the pile of programmes off the desk and marched out of reception.

'You'll regret this, I promise you!' Margaret screamed at Harriet's back.

CHAPTER SIX

EDMUND

FOR THE FIRST two weeks of college, I spent all my free time in the music centre practising. I felt safe there; I belong. Harriet Weston was there whenever I was. When she accompanies me, we fit together perfectly. She'd suggest a stress on that note, to hold back on that phrase, to make a dramatic crescendo in that section. She's so right. Mummy is technically sound, but Harriet has the ear of a performer. Each day the Elgar moved to a new level. I grow with her coaching. She has so much time for me. I adore her!

Other students would stand at the door, listen to us, then leave. Harriet takes no notice of them. They realise they should not intrude. Justine stood and listened for a while, then opened the door and asked for a time to practise with Harriet for the Enrolment Concert.

Harriet gestured towards me. 'Sorry Justine, not now. You can see we're in the middle of this challenging passage.' Justine paused, then left, looking sad.

The next day when she returned, Harriet strode to the door and said, 'Sorry Justine, I'm up to my neck at the moment.

Margaret said she'd love to accompany you and she has masses of time. She'll see you whenever you like.' Harriet looked irritated and her voice sounded sharp. Justine's eyes look watery.

It makes me unhappy that I'm the reason for her sadness. I hope she doesn't blame me. But, having found Harriet, I don't want her to get off the piano stool.

———

As I WAITED in the classroom behind the recital room to play in the Enrolment Concert, I felt at home at last. At the end of those first weeks, I felt tired. So tired of not knowing, of having to ask constant questions and trying to understand the answers. At last I thrive in my own world.

The other students made so much noise. They chattered and jumped around as if they were in a children's playground, not a green room. Two boys, a trumpeter and a tuba player, threw crisps at each other and tried to catch them with their mouths. They showed off in front of a pianist called Grace, who is in my Music and Theatre Studies sets and like me a year older than our year group so not as childish. I think she went abroad with her parents when she was little and started school late. She's tall, with long black hair, but not as pretty as Justine. Several times over the last two weeks, she's tried to get me to talk to her, but I don't want to leave my practice for her.

I found a corner and sat with my back turned to the chaos around me. I checked my strings, rubbed rosin on the horsehairs, tightened my bow and tuned up. No one came near me. No one wanted to talk to me. As I prepared, I became aware of a missing voice, a hole. What had happened to Justine? Harriet had chosen her to open the concert and she should have been there getting ready.

Working with Harriet every day, we dissected the Elgar, then re-assembled it in a new polished state. Now it sounds as if I've written it. Justine too has improved. I heard her when I stood outside the next-door practice room. She's smoothed out her embellishments.

Justine is in Year 13 so I don't see her in lessons, but I hope to work with her again in a practice room. Unfortunately, she's always with that spotty Jake or practising with Margaret, so I can't talk to her. Each day on my way to college, I walk past a Victorian house with a rosemary bush hanging over the front garden wall. As I pass I pick a sprig, squash it between my fingers and breathe in the oil. It lasts me all the way to college. That scent creates Justine.

The noise level rose. No one told them to be quiet. Such poor self-discipline. It must be their nerves. After all, they don't have my experience. I have Mummy to thank for exposing me to public performance at such a young age. I never get nerves. I use the adrenaline to enhance my perfor-mance. Mummy has taught me well.

The door opened, and the room hushed. Harriet scanned the groups of students, now silent, looking for someone. 'Has anyone seen Justine?'

Grace stood up and turned to face Harriet. 'She's in the loo. Sorting out her eye make-up.'

'Thanks,' replied Harriet. She noticed me in the corner and zig-zagged through the students to reach me. She bent down beside me. 'OK, Edmund?' I nodded. Looking at her watch, she stood up and walked through the door that led to the loo.

Seven twenty-five and Justine hadn't arrived. Then she rushed in, red-faced. She'd been crying. I wondered who had been cruel and upset her. Even with a slightly red nose, she looked stunning in her emerald green concert dress. She rubbed rosin along her bow with her head down, her back to me. I couldn't get close enough to smell rosemary. Some students moved towards the door and at last I saw a way through to talk to her. I started walking towards her, but Margaret screeched at us to get into line. Justine moved to the front of the queue, ready to go on.

She opened the concert really well. The Bach ornaments were perfect. I'm pleased that I've been able to help. She's good – but not good enough to play a concerto yet.

CHAPTER SEVEN

STEPH

STEPH ENTERED the recital room and hit a wall of chatter. Peter Bryant, the Principal, calm and controlled as usual, was standing inside the door, smiling at the students and their parents as they entered. Tall, well built, he'd kept the muscle tone developed in his twenties as a Wasps rugby player. Brains and body – not bad for his middle fifties, Steph fantasised, as she looked for a vacant seat.

This was the first of the five concerts held each year in the recital room. Crammed with students and parents, it was impressive. But where was she to sit? Moving towards her, Peter smiled. 'Join me, Steph. It'd be good to have company. I have to sit in the front row, but you get an excellent view.'

They walked down the centre aisle through rows of chatting parents and students. There was an extra buzz as Peter passed. A divorcé in a small Suffolk town walking into a concert with a new woman – the local networks would fizz with gossip!

'These Enrolment Concerts can go on. They're good but

they sometimes put too much on the – oh, you haven't got a programme – have mine.'

'Thank you, that's kind. I understand now how you get so many students to conservatoires. What a wonderful space – the students are so lucky.' The smart tip-up navy seats contrasted with the beech wood on the walls, the stage and the floor. It was a mini-concert hall seating about one hundred and fifty people.

'It's new – about three years old – a self-contained music centre. This recital room leads to the music office and a large classroom with a recording studio. There – through that door at the back of the stage.'

Before she replied, the audience lights dimmed. The hall was in darkness. A procession of talented music students performed their pieces with technical accuracy and striking sensitivity. They had all achieved a high standard, and it mattered so much to them. Harriet Weston must be an outstanding music teacher, but Steph wondered how much Peter knew about her brutal off-stage performances.

Leaning towards Peter, she whispered between a trombone piece by Haydn and the Mozart Clarinet Adagio, 'These students are phenomenal. They are living – no, owning this music. Harriet Weston must be an excellent teacher. That Haydn is tough.'

'I suppose you're right. All the drama's worth it in the end. So, how come you know so much about music?'

'I took an Open University music course when I was off work. It was brilliant!'

The memory of her illness allowed Carter to nudge his way back into her mind once again. His threat infected her enjoyment of the music, the evening and even Peter's company. Her new life had been invaded and she could see no way of escaping the future he had forced on her. She breathed out while counting to seven, determined to give the next piece her full concentration.

A hush spread across the hall as Justine walked onstage to play her second piece. Margaret was flushed and smiled triumphantly as she played the middle 'A' for Justine to check her tuning. Justine raised her gleaming rosewood violin to her chin to play the theme from *Schindler's List*. She captured the rising emotion in the piece perfectly, and the intense sadness of the notes pierced the hall with their purity. As she played the last note, Justine allowed the loss it evoked to fade into silence. Her bow in mid-air, she paused. She dropped her arm. The audience roared their appreciation.

'That was brilliant!' shouted Peter through the applause. 'Right – that's it! We might make it to the pub before closing time, but—'

Steph touched Peter's arm and nodded her head towards the stage as Harriet swept on and sat at the grand piano. Edmund trailed behind and perched on the stool to her left. Steph pointed to the last item on the programme: 'Edmund Fitzgerald'.

'But Justine is our top Year 13 student! Her piece should have been the finale. Why has Harriet put Edmund on after her?' Peter hissed as he plonked himself down again. 'That woman! I don't believe it!'

Should she have told Peter about the change to the programme and the row in reception? Her stomach tightened. Had she got it wrong? Steph took a deep breath. After all, she'd only been a spectator, not involved. She concentrated on the stage.

Harriet smiled across at Edmund. He paused. Nodded. Together they played the opening hushed chord of the Elgar

Cello Concerto. The audience was rapt. The sound dripped off the stage.

His black collarless shirt and smart trousers transformed Edmund from an awkward, shy boy to a good-looking, poised young man. He was over six feet tall and the cello fitted into his body perfectly. He'd removed its spike, so he gripped it masterfully between his thighs and calves. Body and cello swayed together in a sensuous partnership. His elegant fingers scampered along the stave in a relaxed ripple. His expression lived the soul of the music.

In his hands the cello breathed a whimper, followed by a glorious resonant crescendo that mesmerised the audience. He and Harriet were as one. Steph shook herself – aroused by a seventeen-year-old boy? Get a grip, woman, she told herself.

Bang! At the climax – bang! Someone slammed a seat at the back of the hall. Slamming reality into the soulful music. Loud footsteps. The recital room door smashed open, then crashed shut. The noise resonated down to the stage. Steph looked at Peter, who had swivelled in his seat. She too peered into the darkness at the back of the hall, trying to make out who was disrupting this exquisite piece.

Another chair slammed, heavy footsteps, crash! Followed by another. Was someone ill? She sensed Peter taut with tension – not wanting to disturb the recital by going to the back of the room but wanting the noise to stop.

The percussive rhythm of the seats and the banging door competed with the Elgar. Then silence. The seat slamming stopped. Steph felt Peter relax. The students had left the building, smashing the fire escape door behind them. Edmund appeared not to notice and continued to live the Elgar, deep in his own world.

Just as the disturbance appeared to be over, the students

pounded on the outside windows along the left-hand side of the recital room, whooping and shrieking like children playing cowboys and Indians. Their screams and yells echoed across the empty campus. Horrified, Steph looked across at Peter, who was getting out of his seat. Once again, the noise ceased. Steph glanced at him. He looked furious.

Edmund drew his bow across the strings and played the last note. The silence held for five spine-tingling seconds. The audience waited, not wanting to shatter the spell that bound them to this brilliant cellist, his head bowed, exhausted. A cheer broke the silence. Foot stamping. Cries of 'Bravo! More! More!' filled the hall. The audience stood, clapping and cheering. Holding her hand out to Edmund, Harriet gestured to the front of the stage. He lifted his head, opened his eyes and grasped her hand as if being pulled from unconsciousness. They stepped to the front of the stage to acknowledge the standing ovation from the cheering audience.

'Come on, Steph.' Peter, with Steph behind him, was walking towards the stage to congratulate Harriet and Edmund when Mrs Fitzgerald blocked him.

'That was appalling, Principal! A disgusting demonstration! How could they ruin his concentration like that?' she spat.

Steph was amazed that a parent could speak in such a vicious way to the Principal.

'I am so sorry, Mrs Fitzgerald. This is most unlike our students. I can assure you I'll investigate—'

'Such appalling behaviour! It was sabotage! Thank goodness I kept my Edmund away from those – those thugs. Oh – Edmund, my darling...'

Mrs Fitzgerald flew to her son, pushing Peter and Steph

aside. The behaviour of the students had horrified Steph, but she was even more shocked by the rudeness of this parent.

Peter turned to Steph. 'Come on, let's thank the musicians, then get a drink. I need one.'

Steph followed him up the three steps, across the stage, through the door at the back and into the music classroom, where they bumped into Margaret.

'I want to see you and Harriet in my office at break on Monday morning, with the names of all the students involved.' Peter paused. From the music office at the back of the classroom, Steph could hear a screeching female voice.

'Whatever is that awful noise?' asked Peter.

'I think it's Harriet, discussing the concert with Justine in her office,' replied Margaret, rolling her eyes at Steph.

Peter strode to the back of the room, ignoring the violin case he knocked off a table, and stormed into the office. Steph could hear the screaming Harriet perfectly. She turned to look at Margaret to hint that they should leave this embarrassing scene, but Margaret, clearly desperate to listen to the row, blocked the aisle. Trapped between the desks, Steph had no choice; she was forced to listen.

Harriet's voice became louder. 'What? How dare you! Don't play the innocent with me! You organised that to get back at me. You'll be lucky if I let you continue—'

Peter tapped Harriet on the shoulder. She spun round to face him. Steph saw a cowering Justine squeezed into the tiny space between the two desks by a finger-stabbing Harriet.

'Justine, well done. You were great tonight. Congratulations,' said Peter quietly, his voice contrasting with the earlier shouting.

Justine scurried out past Steph and Margaret without a word. She looked like a terrified three-year-old in a grown-up party dress. Her head down, she avoided eye contact. Steph noticed Margaret reach out to stroke Justine's arm, as if she was a distressed dog.

Peter waited until Justine was out of earshot, then spoke very slowly, very clearly, very quietly. Margaret nudged Steph forward so they could hear the exchange. Steph felt uncomfortable listening but had no choice, trapped between the gloating Margaret and the lines of tables. Peter's voice sliced through the silence. Steph decided she never wanted to be on the receiving end of his controlled rage.

'That looked like bullying to me. I don't care what she's done, you do not scream at her like that. For your sake, I hope you didn't touch her. Now calm down. Go home. I'll see you first thing on Monday morning.'

'But—'

'I said, I'll see you on Monday – first thing. Now go home, please.'

Harriet walked out of the office, her head held high. She squeezed past Steph, stopped in front of Margaret and hissed in her face, 'Well done! You stirred that? You'll be sorry!'

Shouldering Margaret as she shoved her out of the way, Harriet strutted out of the music centre. Margaret followed her, stress making the impact of Parkinson's on her walk more obvious. Steph was amazed by such behaviour; she had thought the college was a civilised place of learning, full of grown up and rational professionals. What she had witnessed was more appropriate to a pub brawl, and she'd seen plenty of those.

Steph and Peter followed the women to the front door of the music centre. Margaret had disappeared. David Stoppard's smart red jeep roared into life as Harriet ran towards it. Not her husband, Steph noted. The sound of her slamming the car door bounced off the brick walls. He revved the jeep hard and screeched off into the night.

Steph glanced at Peter, who shrugged his shoulders, sighed and said, 'Are there any more doors in this college left to slam? I knew that boy would be trouble, but I didn't expect it so soon. What an evening!'

CHAPTER EIGHT

EDMUND

MOTHER DOESN'T APPROVE of Justine. I think she must be jealous. After the concert, I told her how well we'd worked together in the practice room, how good Justine is, considering her lack of experience, and how I plan to ask her to form a duo with me. It would give me a new selection of music to play and get me used to blending with other string players.

Mother's lips puckered together in her lemon sucking way. She does that often now I'm at college. We have changed. Mummy has become Mother; it's more grown up. I suppose it had to happen. Mother got angry and said I don't need to learn how to play with other string players as I will be a soloist. That she knew it was a terrible idea to go to the college where I'm getting distracted. That if I want to realise our dream, I must be single minded and concentrate on that. Mother was furious and slammed her fist on the table. A crystal vase fell over and shattered into tiny splinters. She glared at it, as if it had done something wrong, then left to prepare for one of her piano pupils.

I felt bleak. No, worse than that – I can't find a word to

describe how I felt. In a few moments she has squashed me, again. The idea had bubbled up when I helped Justine in the practice room. She picks up new techniques quickly and I can make a difference to her playing. Mother is so negative. I know there is no way she'll let me do it now. It is such a brilliant idea. Justine is good and could get even better with my help, and we'd look great together on stage. That green dress shows off her hair and makes her look beautiful. She is gentle and kind.

The sun sparkled on one of the crystal slices from the smashed vase. I chose a long jagged piece and pushed the sharp edge into the top of my thumb. It left a dip, then a tiny blob of blood escaped. Even though it hurt, it felt good to have control. I pushed it in harder until it really hurt and gave me more blood to suck.

Mother controls everything about me and my life. I don't think I noticed it too much before I went to college. Now I want to do things that the other students do. They have their own money, they have phones to send messages, they have 'gatherings' in houses at the weekends. I don't. Mother insists that life has the same routine as it ever did, except I get to spend the day at college for my lessons instead of with her. I need to have my own life.

I decided Mother was wrong and I would decide for once. I wanted to work with Justine. I wanted it so badly that I ached. I shut the kitchen and dining room doors and went into the hall to phone Justine. She sounded pleased to hear from me and agreed to meet before college on Monday morning to go through an Albinoni piece. She sounded happy and said it was a great idea. I put the phone down; I had made a future with Justine. I heard the dining room door click. Mother had been listening, and I was scared she'd be cross and stop us. I decided not to mention Justine again. I decided to keep it my secret.

The picture of Justine on the piano stool, so close to me, kept coming into my head. I wanted to see her. I wanted to surprise her. I took a bottle of red wine from the cupboard under the stairs and, when Mother was with a pupil, left the house through the French windows. I walked round to Justine's house and rang the bell; she opened the door. The glass lantern in her hallway lit up the back of her hair. It glimmered. I sniffed in the rosemary smell.

I told her I was so sorry for the change in the concert, that it was Harriet's decision and I did as I was told. She should have gone last but I couldn't argue with Harriet. I said I was glad that she'd join me in a duo. I held out the bottle. Her fingers touched mine as she took it. I told her it was to say sorry and also thank you. I wanted her to ask me in so we could share it. Over her shoulder I saw that boy Jake appear from a room. He'd come out to see who was at the door. I waved. He ignored me. Justine thanked me for the wine and said she'd see me on Monday before college. I left.

I stood looking at the front door. I thought she'd be alone, but he was there. There with her. On my way home I stopped myself feeling miserable by thinking that now she's met me, she'll prefer me to him. Surely, she'll find him boring. After all, we have so much in common with our music. Working together, we'll get even closer and I can help her and she'll rely on me. She'll see me as her future and not that spotty, greasy boy. At home Mother was still with her pupil. She hadn't missed me. It will be Christmas before she misses the bottle of wine.

CHAPTER NINE

STEPH

JUSTINE'S BODY lay propped up at an awkward angle. Slumped in a vice between the desk and chair, her head lolled on her left shoulder, her mouth slightly open and her eyes closed. She could have been sleeping, but Steph knew she would never wake up.

In the doorway, Steph was transfixed by the horrific scene. She was familiar with death, but the body of this young student was shocking. It was so out of place in the college. But then, was there ever a right place for death? The irritating slapping of the blind against the open window punctuated the silence, but she knew she must not touch it. The sieved, early morning light flickered across the room. Suddenly sunlight sliced through the skylight, making them jump. The bloodied blade of a knife beside Justine's right hand glinted in the shaft of light. Margaret gasped and started crying again.

'You haven't touched her, have you?' asked Steph, in professional mode, trying to remove herself from her shock and into action.

'Well – yes – I did,' retorted Margaret, now close to hysterical. 'I didn't know, did I? When I arrived, I thought she was asleep. I tried to wake her. I touched her and she fell. She fell like that – just like that.' She stopped, unable to speak through her sobs.

Peter moved to her. 'You did what you thought was best. We'd all have done the same.'

Steph lifted her arm to stop Margaret from going into the room again. Margaret took a step back and caught her breath. They waited for her to continue. 'Then I saw all that – all that blood. I didn't move her. She just fell like that. I had to know if she was ill. She looked asleep.' Peter put his arm around her shoulders.

'Was that window open?' asked Steph.

'I think so. Yes, it was'

They all looked at the window, away from the appalling image before them. Stunned, they stood unable to look at Justine's body yet unable to move away.

'Let's shut this door and go to the music office while we wait for the police.' Steph assumed her old 'I'm taking charge' tone. Peter and Margaret allowed her to herd them into the office. They sat. Waiting. Dazed. Steph phoned the police, succinctly describing the scene they'd found.

'They'll be here in about ten minutes. A senior investigative officer and several uniformed policemen. They will preserve the scene and keep all students and staff out of the way. The forensic team will arrive and take our fingerprints, then we'll need to give a statement. What will you do about college today, Peter? Send them home?'

In response to her question, Peter burst into action. 'Not thinking straight.' He moved to the desk, grabbed the phone and dialled a number.

'Paul, it's Peter. I'm in the music centre. We have a – a

serious incident here. The police are on their way. Meet them at reception and bring them over, please. Find the senior tutors and ask two of them to stand outside the music centre, to keep students away. Send the other two down the drive to tell the students we have an emergency and college is closed today.'

He glanced at his watch. 'Luckily, it's still early and most haven't arrived yet. What's that? ... The staff? Ask them to wait in the common room until I get there. I'll explain when I come over.'

Steph watched intently as Peter slid a pad of paper towards him and scribbled some notes. He looked up at her. 'I need a statement for the staff and students before we find ourselves on social media. We need to control what gets out there, before the students beat us to it.'

He sat at the desk writing. Steph was a little surprised at his calm reaction. She'd attended at least eleven murder scenes as Detective Sergeant – even Senior Investigating Officer in one brutal domestic death in Ipswich. She was used to the full range of reactions: hysteria, fainting, denial and sometimes even business as usual. Peter, it appeared, felt comfortable taking action, while Margaret continued to sniff loudly in the corner. Steph observed them both, noting their behaviour.

Having taken all necessary action, Steph started shaking as the shock hit her. And what if they sent Carter? She held onto the desk to steady herself, then sat down, breathed in slowly, hoping they wouldn't notice, and concentrated on the diagram of an orchestra on the opposite wall. Her years of experience meant that she should be able to deal with stuff like this. She had been able to. No problem. Now – now she wasn't sure who she was.

Sirens shattered the silence. They all stood up. In the middle of this awfulness, Steph realised that she was now on the other side. A different team. Peter and Margaret both looked guilty, and she suspected that she did too. Is that how it happened? She felt shock squared when she saw who stood at the door.

'Good heavens – Steph! What are you doing here? They told me you called it in, but I thought I'd misheard.'

'Hale! I work here now. This is the College Principal, Peter Bryant, and Margaret Durrant, the music teacher who found Justine's body. Chief Inspector Hale, my old boss.'

'Right. Steph, please show me where she is. You both stay here for the moment, please.'

Steph felt Peter following; she turned and shook her head, hoping that Margaret hadn't seen. Peter reluctantly resumed his seat, not used to having someone else take the lead in his college. She showed Hale to the music classroom and recalled the many times they'd worked a scene together. What was it – eighteen months since she'd left? Never did she think she and Hale would meet at a murder scene again. Certainly not at the college.

Hale opened the door of the classroom and paused. He took one step inside carefully, looking down before he did so, and leaned in. He scanned the room. Steph recalled his uncanny ability to pick up the details that provided lines of enquiry. Although it was almost two years since she'd seen him, he hadn't changed much. At fifty-eight he was ageing well and was still fit in both senses of the word. Taller than her, his dark hair fell over his forehead schoolboy-like and made him appear younger than he was. Now spattered with grey, it high-lighted his dark brown eyes that saw everything. She'd always fancied him and had enjoyed the tingle that came from mutual arousal in the office, where nothing went any further.

He breathed in. He sniffed. She noticed the metallic smell

of blood that polluted the sunny autumn morning. Hale turned to her; she'd waited behind him in the corridor, not wanting to assume her earlier privileges.

'What happened here, Steph?'

'Margaret Durrant arrived early to practise and found Justine Dixon, a Year 13 student, apparently asleep on the desk.'

'She wasn't found like that then?'

'No. Margaret said Justine had her arms on the desk with her head resting on them, facing the window.'

'Was it open or shut?'

'She said it was open when she came in.'

'Right. Then what?'

'Margaret went to her, touched her, as she thought Justine was asleep, then she fell into that position. Only then did she notice the blood soaked across the front of her blouse. Justine's wrists were under her chest, so the blood wasn't visible until Margaret moved her.'

Justine's body was skewed in the seat. The crimson stain had soaked a vast map across the front of her white cotton shirt. The path the blood had taken from her wrists, down the sleeve of her shirt to splashes on the grey cord carpet, was now drying dull red. So much of it. She'd bled out.

'No one else has been here apart from the teacher who found her?'

Hale bent down to squint across at the craft knife beside Justine's right hand, stuck to the desk in a puddle of drying blood.

'Well – I have and the Principal – but we stayed by the door.'

'Tell me about – er – Justine.'

'She was a Year 13 student, a very talented violinist. Going

47

to the Royal College of Music in September. Well, she was. Had a nice boyfriend in her year. Popular – very bright. I heard her play on Friday night at the college concert. She was astounding. She had everything to live for. Why would she want to commit suicide? I can't believe it.'

'Thanks, Steph. Really helpful. What's your job here?'

'Receptionist and PA to the Principal.'

'That's good. Ah! Here comes the team.'

Hale and Steph stepped back into the corridor and watched as two technicians emerged from the white forensic van parked outside the entrance to the music centre. They pulled on their white protective suits, surgical masks, goggles and blue shoe covers outside the black-and-yellow crime scene tape that a uniformed police officer had strung across its entrance. He held out a clipboard and asked them to sign in. Fascinated, she observed this meticulous protection of the crime scene, so familiar for so many years, which she'd assumed was in her past.

Hale turned back to Steph. 'Thanks Steph. Please tell the Principal and the music teacher they can go over to the main building with you now. I'll come over when I've finished here.'

'I'll tell them.' Steph nodded, then paused by the door, looking back at Justine sitting like a clown puppet. All elegance gone. The sun shifted and her red hair flamed in its light.

CHAPTER TEN

EDMUND

JUSTINE IS DEAD. She's taken her own life. Why? She was so beautiful. So talented. We would have been sensational together. Why did she do it?

They cancelled college today. I went in early to meet Justine in the music centre. When I arrived, police cars blocked the way in, and we were told by a little man with a squeaky voice called the Deputy Principal to keep away and to go home for the day.

Some other students had come in early too, and we walked across Main Quad and stood around the corner near the old building where he couldn't see us. Josh, in Justine's music group, said he'd come in the back way on Wood Lane as the police were arriving. The classroom window was open and, in the gap, when the blind moved, he could see the back of Justine's head. Nothing else, but her hair – it had to be her. Then when the police white van arrived, we knew she must be dead, otherwise they'd have sent an ambulance.

We stood facing each other, not wanting to leave, needing to be together. No one wanted to go home. Josh kept repeating what he'd seen, and we kept listening to his story, trying to hear something new each time he told us.

They decided that Justine must have committed suicide. One of the girls looked at me and said she wondered if it had something to do with what had happened at the concert. I was horrified! They can't think it was my fault. It was Harriet who decided, not me. They don't know that I took her the wine and suggested the duo. Before they could blame me anymore Mr Bryant came past and told us to go home for the rest of the day. He stood and watched us so we had to leave.

As I walked down the drive, Grace asked me if I'd go into Oakwood with her and bring back some flowers for Justine. She said she would ask Mr Bryant where we could set up a shrine to Justine to show her how much we loved her and that we are sad. I thought Justine wouldn't know now, but I didn't say that.

She must have had a row with that Jake. He trailed after her like a mongrel dog. He wasn't good enough for her. They never looked right together – his greasy hair, dandruff and large spots. He's not even musical – he does science or computing or something. They couldn't have had much in common. I wonder what they talked about. She was so beautiful.

I know that the week before the concert Justine was annoyed at Harriet spending so much time with me, but she wouldn't have killed herself over that, would she? When I saw her at her house, she looked fine and was happy to plan her future with me. It couldn't have been my fault.

Grace, who knows Justine's family ever so well, said that her grandmother, who lived with them, had just died. She could have been sad, really sad after her grandmother died. I've never known my grandparents, but I imagine I would be really sad if one of them who lived with me died.

Mother seemed to know more about Justine than I did. How did she know? She said she was sorry that such a lovely girl was dead, but she wasn't sorry that we hadn't formed the duo. It would have been a distraction from my solo work. Mother can be hard and unfeeling sometimes. She didn't ache as I did.

I shall miss Justine. It was only two weeks, but it felt like months. She's lived in my head since I first saw her. I keep thinking of her playing the Bach and us working together. We could have been so special. My beautiful Ophelia. I picked some flowers out of the garden and took them to the shrine. I stood in the garden by our rosemary bush for a long time.

CHAPTER ELEVEN

STEPH

'Hello again, Steph, is the Principal free please?'

'I'll phone through—'

'Ah, Chief Inspector.' Peter's door was open, and before Steph could make the call, he strode around her desk into reception. 'Please come through to my office.'

There was no handshaking or smiling. Both men were sombre and serious as they faced the grim task of coping with the aftermath of Justine's tragic death. Hale's job was to find out what happened, and Peter's was to support the college students and staff in their grief.

Steph looked around reception and down the college drive. No cars full of students driving down to Oakwood. No groups of smiling kids squealing and laughing at some joke. Justine's death had pushed the pause button. Stopped normal life in its tracks. The students had been told that lessons were cancelled for the day. News of Justine's death had soon got around. Texts, WhatsApp, Facebook: the full range of social media on which these kids survived shared her tragedy in a few seconds.

Justine's death was devastating. Steph had only exchanged

a few words with her but felt, after her emotional and passionate performances at the concert, that she had shared a little of her life. The horrific image of that vibrant, talented young musician, now slumped lifeless on the desk, kept sliding into her thoughts.

What was it that had driven her to suicide? Perhaps she could find out. She wasn't needed here. No phone calls. No visitors. It was about time for her break. A trail of students, lost without their lessons and bound together in shock and grief, had wandered back up the hill into college. In silence, they had trudged past the glass wall of reception to the entrance of the old 1930s building. Steph watched the subdued procession of bewildered students grasping flowers, teddy bears and cards, heads bowed, needing to be with their friends.

Steph asked her assistant, Jane, to cover the phones, turned left out of reception and walked along the corridor to the original entrance hall of the old building. It was typical of the 1930s, with an oak floor, dark oak-panelled walls and an elegant oak staircase. The dignified entrance to academia, designed to impress, had now been succeeded by the modern, twenty-first century glass box – her domain, the new college reception.

The students, prompted by Peter, had chosen the old entrance hall to build a shrine to Justine. A hedge of flowers engulfed the oak table inside the turn of the staircase. Flowers in bright paper from the garage up the road were heaped alongside string-tied bunches in plastic bubbles of water from Stems, the florist in the High Street. Teddy bears, cards, drawings and printed messages punctuated the blooms. She bent down to read some messages. 'Rest in peace, Justine.' 'You can play your violin with the angels now.' 'We shall miss you. Gone too soon.' 'I'm giving you this teddy bear so you can cuddle it in heaven.'

'You are in heaven, Justine – let the bastard who did it rot in hell.'

That last message surprised her. Did the students know something? The message was printed, so no hope of looking at the handwriting. Who was the 'bastard'? What did someone know? If only she'd seen who had placed it there.

Steph looked up from the flowers at the groups of students at the edge of the overpowering, perfumed pile. No one reacted to her picking up the card. Some were weeping, others staring at the blooms or at the floor. There were about fifteen or twenty of them looking lost, not knowing what to do or where to go. The flowers created a focus. Steph replaced the card carefully. One girl sobbed loudly and ignored the snot dribbling from her nose. Steph handed her a tissue from the pack she was carrying.

'Thanks, Miss,' she mumbled, dabbing her nose like a child. She turned, her red eyes swollen, puzzled, confused. 'How could it have happened? Here? To her?'

Before she could reply, another girl hidden inside her navy hoodie emerged, anger and fear mixed. 'What did Justine do to make someone attack her like that?'

'Listen – we don't know what happened yet. I don't know what stories you've been listening to, but you shouldn't go around saying things that may not be true.' Steph spoke slowly and quietly to soothe the girl's scared horror. She handed across another tissue. 'What makes you think someone attacked her?'

'Well, that's what Jake told me and he's her boyfriend.' She blew her nose, but the tears continued to drip down her cheeks.

'Jake?'

The girl pointed to a stooped, dark-haired boy at the edge

of the silent, hugging groups. Jake's hood moved back slightly, and Steph could see his face. He was pale. His eyes swollen. Was it only this morning?

Steph moved round the crowd and stood beside him. 'Jake, I am so very sorry about Justine. Is there anything I can do to help? Would you like a drink? A sandwich from the canteen?'

'No, Miss, I just want to be here. I'm fine.' Jake staggered slightly. Steph steadied him and held him up by his shoulders.

'You're obviously not fine, Jake. Let's go and sit in the air. You must be in shock.'

They walked out of the main building, blinking in the bright sunshine, to the canteen.

Steph kept within reach, as Jake looked as if he might collapse at any moment. They approached a bench in the shade, and she gestured for him to sit.

'You wait here. Tea, coffee?'

'Coffee, please.'

The canteen ladies were subdued and there were fewer than usual making sandwiches for the staff and students who remained on site. The radio, usually blaring Radio 2 pop music while they worked, was now turned off. She walked through the empty tables. All the students in college must be at Justine's shrine. She selected a pack of chocolate biscuits from the basket, poured coffee from the machine, touched her card to pay, then returned to Jake.

He stared ahead at the deserted campus, nibbled at the biscuits and sipped the coffee. Steph sat beside him, waiting for him to feel like speaking. As he finished the biscuits, she took a chance.

'Jake, I'm so sorry about Justine. It's dreadful.'

Jake grabbed some soggy tissues from the pocket in his

tracksuit bottoms and wiped the tears now running down his blotchy cheeks. He spoke through his sniffs.

'We've been together since High School – Year 9. She's my best friend. We just get on and – work so well.' He stopped. Dabbed at his eyes, then continued, 'Going away to uni next September could be tough, but we're both in London... I mean that's what we were... but now...'

Tears poured down his cheeks. Steph gave him a handful of tissues. He blew his nose and looked up. 'Why? Why did she die? I think someone did this to her.'

'What makes you think that?'

'I don't believe she'd commit suicide. That's what they're saying. Did she?'

'We don't know yet. The police will find out.'

'Will they? Will they want to see me?'

'They'll want to see all her friends. Find out if she had any arguments or had got herself in any trouble...'

'Arguments?'

'Yes. Or trouble.'

'What sort of trouble?' His sudden aggression surprised Steph. Did Jake know something? He looked as if he was about to bolt.

'You know. It's just that at your age people sometimes get themselves in with the wrong crowd – or, you know, try out new things – like drugs.'

'Justine never takes drugs. She's going to the Royal College – that's her dream. She wouldn't let anything get in the way. She doesn't drink much and never smoked.'

Steph handed over more tissues. 'Had she upset anyone in college?'

'No – Justine was popular.'

'Has she argued with anyone recently?'

Sullen silence. Jake locked down, his face fixed. It felt as if she'd touched a nerve. There was something here, if only she could get to it.

'Did she get on well with her parents? Her family?'

'They were like – normal. They'll be in a dreadful state. Think of coming home to find out.'

'Coming home? They were at the concert on Friday.'

'Yes, they were. But they went away for the weekend – France somewhere. Normandy? Justine's grandma, who lived with them, died three weeks back. Her funeral was last week – they needed a break.'

'Didn't Justine want to go with them?'

'No, she wanted to stay at home, work on her audition piece. She wouldn't even go out on Saturday. And now...' Jake rubbed his hand beneath his eyes. 'We always got on so well. Must go.' Jake hauled himself up, head down.

'Where, Jake?'

'Back there.'

'Here – some tissues. I'll come too.' She passed him the last of her tissues, and he crammed them into his pocket.

They walked back to the old entrance hall, saying nothing. The sea of flowers now flowed into the corridor. Steph looked at the stunned groups, their lives interrupted, confronted by the possibility of death.

She felt a touch on her shoulder and Peter beckoned her away. Making sure no one could hear him, he whispered, 'The Chief Inspector is now with Margaret Durrant. He wants to see you next. They've taken Justine's body away for a post-mortem, but they're asking some strange questions, like it isn't suicide. I think they suspect someone murdered her.'

CHAPTER TWELVE

STEPH

THERE WAS a peculiar symmetry in seeing her old boss sitting at her new boss's desk. Is there a word for a collection of bosses? It had been a shock to see Hale here, in the college. He lifted his head, raked his fingers through his hair and smiled at her. Deeper wrinkles framed his penetrating brown eyes, but otherwise he was the same Hale. A little more tired, perhaps? She always thought he was bionic – yes, that was the word – bionic. Like that TV programme she'd loved when she was a kid – *Six Million Dollar Man*, was it? He saw right through the lies that wallpapered their world.

'You're looking good. Have you done something different with your hair?' Hale poured water into two glasses. He brought them round to the coffee table, placed one in front of her, then sat down opposite.

'New hair. New clothes. New job.' She smiled across at him, pleased that he'd noticed the change in her.

'New man?' asked Hale, his eyebrow raised, nodding towards Peter's framed Oxford University certificate on the wall behind the desk.

'He's the Principal – my boss!'

'Never stopped you before!'

'The second word is "off", Hale.'

They were back in the familiar bantering tone of the past. She was relaxed, no longer needing the phone voice she'd used since she'd arrived at the college, and they smiled at each other. It felt good. She found she could think with her mouth again.

'I've never been in here before. How many students are there?'

'About fifteen hundred sixteen- to nineteen-year-olds, studying for A Levels, mostly.'

'How are they taking it?'

'As you'd expect – shock, horror, anger. All so intense at this age.'

'Yeah, it is. Any hints about why she did it?'

'Not yet. According to her boyfriend she had a great future planned, was working hard, got on with her parents, had a long-term relationship but... there's something there.'

'Really?'

'There was a strange message with some flowers. It condemned some "bastard" who had done it to her. I couldn't see who'd left it, but I think it was on one of the early bunches.'

'Interesting.' Hale picked up his pen and wrote something in his notebook.

'It could be one of the drama queens; we do have them here, you know. But there's only a few – most students are devastated by Justine's death and are beside themselves.'

Steph wondered where this non-conversation was going. She sensed that Hale was thinking something through. It wasn't like him to dance around the handbags – he usually went straight to the core with his questions. These were going nowhere fast. She waited, but he continued to have that 'should I?' look on his face she knew so well. She prompted him. 'I'm surprised you're still here.'

'Really?'

She pushed further. She had nothing to lose. 'Is there something bothering you about all this?'

He studied his notebook, flipped a page over, sat upright and looked her in the eyes. Whatever had been bothering him, he'd decided.

'Look, Steph, this is in absolute confidence. I wouldn't be telling you if we hadn't worked together for so long.' He pointed his index finger at her to underline the words. 'Not even your new friend Mr Bryant must know at the moment.'

'OK.' She agreed and waited.

'We may be considering a suspicious death here.'

'Why? I mean – the cut wrists, the blood, the knife. It looked like suicide.'

'I can trust you to keep your mouth shut?' She nodded and he continued. 'I think we're meant to think she killed herself, but the divisional surgeon noticed a slight blue tinge on her fingernails – possible drug overdose.'

'Wow! Smart guy,' said Steph.

'Woman actually – Laura McKinnon. Some useful kit developed at East Anglia Uni backed up her hunch. The Intelligent Fingerprint, it's called. A tiny matchbox gizmo takes a fingerprint and can tell from the sweat if alcohol or drugs are present. We'll get a more detailed tox report in four days. At the moment, it appears that Justine had a lot of drugs in her system before she died.'

'Sounds like something out of *Star Wars*. Sweat? Even though she's dead?' Steph pulled the curtain across to the right so that Hale didn't need to squint in the sunshine.

'It works for some time after death – impressive, eh? We'll

need more detailed confirmation, but it gives a strong indication. And we've found it's reliable.'

'I see.'

What was it – about eighteen months since she left? Hale was right. It was pretty impressive that they'd developed a level of technology this high. To get such a quick result would make their job much easier. For a moment she felt as she had done for so many years: a part of the team, her opinion valued, her contribution welcomed. She'd missed this belonging.

'We haven't excluded suicide, but at the moment we've enough to classify her death as suspicious,' said Hale.

'I see.'

'Laura thinks she died about two hours before we arrived – so that would be six thirty to seven o'clock this morning. We'll know more after the PM. The teacher who found her...' He flicked back a few pages.

'Margaret.'

'Yes, Margaret Durrant. Is she usually the first to arrive?' asked Hale.

'Yes. But all the music students can get in the practice rooms any time. I s'pose it's lucky one of them didn't find her.'

'Say that again.'

At last, something that Hale didn't know yet. She explained that all students had swipe or ID cards so they could get access to the practice rooms, even when the music centre was locked. A record of who was in the building, out of college hours, was held on the server.

'Did you see any students in the music centre when you arrived?' asked Hale.

'There weren't any. Peter checked all the rooms after we found Justine's body.'

'I'll need a list of anyone using their card this morning.'

'Yes, of course.'

'We haven't found a suicide note yet – either here or at her home. But we found some crumbs on the desk behind her,' said Hale.

'We had a concert on Friday night. The crumbs could have been from then.'

'Anyway, the lab's got them now. Her parents are on their way back from France. Someone was in the house with her while they were away. You say she had a boyfriend?'

'Jake Martin. I was speaking to him earlier. He's really cut up.'

Hale's question prodded her to ask herself if Jake could have been involved. If he was, how? What was his motive? Jake had been distraught and in a real state earlier. The image of him beside her on the bench, unable to stop himself crying, pushed itself into the front of her mind. Could all that have been a show?

Hale's phone rang. He swivelled in the chair, pulled the phone out of his pocket and looked at the screen. 'Sorry, Steph – need to take this.' He leaped to his feet and went into the corridor. As he closed the door he laughed, 'You're joking!'

The sun had gone in and the room had become darker. She pulled the curtain back and looked at the entrance leading down to Woodbridge Road. It was deserted. The college, so vibrant at the start of term, crammed with students laughing and squealing, was now a quiet, subdued place. The volume had been turned down.

How many murders had she and Hale worked together? Eleven, or was it twelve? Yes – twelve murders over their nine years together, but Justine's death felt very different. Steph was taken aback by her reaction. Now, just as she was constructing a new future, her past had gate-crashed. She hadn't expected crime to follow her to the college, certainly not a murder. Not only that, but this time she found that she was emotionally involved and shared the students' deep sadness at Justine's death.

Could it be murder? Hale seemed to think it could. Violent death could happen anywhere; of course it could. But Justine's death felt so very tragic and out of place in this world of hopeful young lives. If this was murder, why did it feel so different from those in her past? Justine was not just a dead body – Steph had seen her living her life, even if it was just for a couple of weeks. Justine was a gifted girl who had a shining future. Today that had disappeared. Either she had cut her own life short or someone had taken it from her. Either way, life felt unfair, shitty. Irritated and angry, she fiddled with a loose button hanging out of the arm of the red leather chair, trying to twist it back in. She pulled it off.

Hale made her jump when he bounced back in. 'Now, where was I? If someone brought Justine here they must have hit your CCTV cameras somewhere. Where are they?'

'On the three main entrances to college. We don't have cameras outside the music centre, which is in the middle of the campus, nor the pedestrian path. I can have a word with Dick, if you like – he's in charge of the CCTV?'

'No need, thanks, I'll get Joyce onto it. Don't you worry.'

Steph smiled to hide the feeling of not being invited to the party. Hale scanned the last few pages of his notebook, his head down, now engrossed.

'Right, if that's all, Hale, I'll be getting back to reception – you know where I am if you want me.'

'Sorry, thinking about something. Strange to meet like this again. We made a good team, didn't we? And there was always your Mike to make sure we stayed on the straight and narrow. I miss him. We all do. But you seem to be doing well now after your – your illness.'

Sensitive of Hale to use 'illness' rather than 'nervous break-down'. Doctors now call it anxiety or depression. But she'd felt broken down, all right – a weak, shattered failure. Numb depression after Mike's death, then hiding that evidence, sucked her into a bottomless drain. Getting through each hour, then each day, had been so tough. Hale was right. She stood to leave.

'We'll need a formal statement,' he said. 'The Principal and Margaret Durrant are coming down after college. Five pm. And if you hear anything you think may help, you've still got my number?'

'Yes. Thanks, Hale. Good to see you again.'

CHAPTER THIRTEEN

STEPH

WELL OVER FIFTY STUDENTS, heads bowed, hushed, now stood at the edge of the shrine of flowers when Steph joined them. The group had swelled since she was there earlier. Despite their cancelled lessons, they wanted to spend the day in college. They needed to be together. Arms around shoulders and waists, they stood in huddles, sniffing into tissues, comforting each other, fending off the shock of death.

Peter joined her, then turned and handed a tissue to a girl with tears rolling down her cheeks. He touched Steph's arm and they moved to the back of the group. He murmured, 'This is dreadful. That poor girl. Whatever made her do it?'

For a moment she paused and considered her response. Despite Peter's earlier suspicions that Justine's death could have been murder, he appeared to have reverted to suicide. She felt conflicted. Did she tell her new boss all that she knew or remain loyal to her old one? She decided not to reveal the information Hale had shared with her.

'I suppose we'll find out. There were no signs that she might have had problems?'

'None that reached me. Justine was an outstanding student. I suspect it was something outside college.'

'Really?'

'At this age everything is so extreme... final. Unfortunately, with this age group all too often we'll have a fatal car crash with a new driver or a suicide – male, mostly. And over what we might think of as not being worth a life. Last year one boy drove his parents' car into the garden wall, and when they returned from holiday, they found the car on a pile of bricks and their son hanging from the banisters. What a waste of a life!'

'How dreadful.'

Peter sighed and scanned the students. 'I've arranged for a counsellor to be available in the chaplain's room for a couple of weeks. In my experience bereavement is the final taboo for them, especially when it's one of their friends. In personal-social education they get masses on sex and drugs, but they have no idea how to cope with loss and death.'

'I don't think many of us do.'

'You're right. Justine's death will be devastating for many of her friends for weeks and months to come. Look at them – they're confused and lost.'

He glanced towards a group to his left. 'But at this stage there are some who thrive on the drama. Keep an eye on that group, will you? We don't need mass hysteria breaking out. See you later.'

She looked across at the students Peter had indicated. Three girls, dressed from head to foot in black, nudged their way to the front of the group and comforted each other noisily. One of them wore a long black frock with a dramatic Spanish lace mantilla arranged over her head. The two girls either side of her wore black Goth leggings and tops – one turned inside out to hide the slogan printed on it, now a faint shadow. One of the Goths stepped towards long-frock to whisper something, her red converse boots creating a startling fluorescent flash against the sombre mass of black. Those girls were in the year below Justine. If they had known her at all, it was only for a couple of weeks.

Steph watched as long-frock elbowed red-converse, showed her a roll-up she'd pulled from her pocket and swivelled her eyes to the door muttering, 'C'mon babe.' So, they were off for a smoke. Steph cast an experienced eye over the rollie and smiled with relief to see it was weedy – thin, not illegal: more dramatic effect than serious stuff then. The girls moved outside to the smoking area.

A shadow slid beside her as a boy bent down to add more flowers to the edge of the flood of blooms. A string-tied, natural selection of rose-hips, lavender and feathery reeds arranged against a large spray of rosemary, it contrasted with the gaudy greenhouse pinks and purples of supermarket sprays. The boy stood up, stepped back, paused. He bowed his head, as if laying a wreath at a remembrance ceremony. Steph turned to face Edmund.

'That's a beautiful tribute, Edmund.'

'I felt it was right for Justine. She would have liked it, I think.'

A space melted around them as the students turned inward or moved their feet slightly. A couple sneered at his contribution. No one acknowledged him.

'Justine had a rare talent, you know. She'd have gone so far.' Edmund bent down and pushed a sprig of rosemary back inside the string.

'Yes, I was at the concert on Friday.'

'We planned to work together as a duo, you know, violin and cello. We'd made plans, even arranged a rehearsal.'

'Really?'

'We'd have been amazing together. She had a real feel for the music. We might have... and now we can't. Do you know what made her commit suicide?'

'How d'you know it was suicide?'

'That message on the front door.'

'I think it said "Death of a student", not suicide.'

Edmund bent down again to push some rose-hips further into the arrangement. Satisfied, he stood up and turned to Steph. 'Well, the others are saying it's suicide.'

'If it is, do you have any idea why she might have killed herself?'

'I didn't know her that well.' He paused, about to fiddle again with his flowers, then changed his mind. 'Perhaps she had a row with her boyfriend?'

'What makes you think that?'

'What the others are saying. What she said to me while we were practising.' He paused. Steph waited, giving him space. 'Jake didn't like the same things as Justine. She said they were always arguing. Maybe they had a big fall out and she... well... couldn't cope and... What do you think happened?'

Steph decided not to get drawn into his speculation. 'I've no idea, but it is so very, very sad.' Side by side, they watched the flowers drooping.

'Will the police be here long?' Edmund, it seemed, wanted to keep talking.

'As long as it takes, I suppose. They'll find out what happened.'

'Right – yes, of course they will. I hope they do. Poor Justine. Thank you so much, Mrs Grant.' Edmund turned and walked down the corridor. Gazing after him, she wondered at his uniqueness. In his blazer and chinos, he looked so different from the other students, and he didn't seem to notice or to mind. He appeared to live in a single column on a spreadsheet headed 'cello'. He was immensely talented, and that distorted people sometimes.

She noticed that Jake also stared after the retreating Edmund. In his arms he cradled a gigantic bunch of delicate champagne rosebuds. Once again he stood alone. Apart from the others. Hood up. Head down. No eye contact with anyone. Strange; why aren't they cuddling him? Jake's need for comfort must be the greatest of all. Perhaps the students feared touching him in case they caught something. That's what it looked like, as if he had some communicable disease. If they got too close, would they catch death too? Did they suspect he had something to do with it?

Steph edged beside him as he reverently placed the rosebuds so they covered the edge of Edmund's wild flowers. The temptation to investigate was impossible to resist. Hale had wondered if Justine's boyfriend might be involved somehow. Maybe this time she could find out how. It would be worth a try to see if he would talk to her again.

'They're beautiful, Jake.'

'Yes. I got them in town. Justine loved that colour. She wore roses like that on her prom dress in Year 11. That was the first time we went out. Properly went out, you know. That night she looked so...' He burrowed deep inside his grey hoodie to hide his tears, then he exploded into loud sobs and started to shake.

'Jake, why don't we get away from the crush for a while? You look shattered. Take five minutes' break, then come back.'

Unable to speak, Jake looked up and nodded. Too involved

69

in their own grief, the students didn't notice him going. Shutting the meeting room door, Steph turned to see Jake slumped in the bucket chair. He looked empty, as if he'd lost everything – with no future, no dreams.

'Perhaps you should go home and sleep for a bit.'

He looked up, his eyes now bloodshot dots sunk deep in puffy eyelids. 'Have they found out who did this to Justine?'

'You think someone did this, don't you?' Steph prompted him. Jake looked down at the dark blue carpet. Grabbing another tissue, he blew his nose. Silence.

'I know Justine didn't commit suicide – I know she didn't.'

'They're looking at everything, Jake. You want them to do that, don't you?'

'Yes, I do. It's just—'

'What?'

'Oh – I suppose it doesn't matter now...'

'What doesn't matter?'

'What Justine's parents think. Look – I was there, at her house, over the weekend while her parents were away. Well... you know... we were together.'

'Hmm?'

'I went round to Justine's house on Saturday after her mum and dad left for France for the weekend. And we worked – college work. Justine practised her audition piece while I got on with my computing course work. It's due in next week.' He stopped. She waited. 'I sat working in her garden, under their apple tree. I could hear her playing through the French windows. Justine worked so hard. We both did. Until he came.'

'He?'

'That new kid – Edmund.'

'Edmund came?'

'Yes, he didn't know I was there at first. Justine didn't let him in. I could hear them talking at the front door. He said he was sorry for what happened at the concert, that Justine should have gone last, but Weston made him. He gave her a bottle of red wine, a posh one with a flash label, to say sorry. When I went into the hall, he saw me and left.'

'Did you drink it?'

Jake looked at her as if she was suddenly speaking a foreign language. 'Of course we did!' She smiled and let him continue. 'We cooked tea together. Just the two of us. I bought some steak from Millers, the butchers, and we had steak and chips with the wine. It was even fun washing up after. Like we lived there together... you know.'

'I know.' She echoed Jake's words.

'We had breakfast there on Sunday too.'

'Right. Then?'

'I went home to look after my sister, Helen. If only I'd stayed with Justine. I shouldn't have left her alone. If she did... I could have stopped her, couldn't I?'

'You mustn't think like that, Jake. We don't know what happened. The police will find out.'

He shifted in the chair about to get up, then sat back down.

'Are you OK?' Steph leaned forward.

'I keep thinking, why? Why did she have to die? I miss her so much already.' Jake put his hands on the edge of the arms and pushed, but once again sat back. 'I have a really bad headache – do you have any pills, please?'

Steph moved to the door. 'I think you should go home and rest, Jake. Let me tell Mr Bryant, then I'll drive you home.'

'Thanks.' He sat back and closed his eyes. His face drained of colour. He looked so young, so vulnerable.

CHAPTER FOURTEEN

STEPH

As they walked across the car park, Steph raised her face to catch the late afternoon sunshine before it went behind a heavy grey cloud. Jake, walking alongside her, staggered a little. She held him by his elbow, ready to catch him, and supported him to her car.

When she'd returned from getting Peter's permission to take him home, she found Jake had sunk deep into himself. She recognised the symptoms. He was suffering, and if he was alone for long, the hopeless spiral could take over and the temptation to stop the pain might be too great. His sister, Helen, should be back from school, even if his mother was still at work. Steph knew all about loss. As an adult, she had struggled to get through each day. At his age, all emotions were magnified, and he'd be convinced it was the end of his world. For a time, it would be.

In the diluted autumn sunshine, they drove through the common past the duck pond. During the summer drought, it had shrunk to a grey muddy puddle littered with old crisp bags and fag packets. Three children were throwing bread at some shabby ducks, which gobbled the crusts greedily. Two mothers nattered and jiggled the pushchairs to keep their babies asleep.

'Justine and I used to walk this way home after college. We'd sit over there.' He pointed to a seat on the other side of the pond. 'We'd talk about our day. It was great to have someone to share everything with. She was my best friend.'

Steph noticed that for the first time, Jake had used the past tense. It was the start of a very long, very painful process. He would have a tough time over the next year. They came to a part of town she didn't know. She slowed, then stopped at a T-junction. 'Now where do I turn here?'

His eyes had misted over and he looked at the road as if he was seeing it for the first time. An impatient driver in the car behind hooted his horn, and in the mirror Steph could see him waving his hands at the empty road.

She turned left, hoping it was correct, and was relieved when the car behind turned right. She crawled along the road, waiting for Jake to give her directions. They reached the edge of Oakwood, past The White Swan, a scruffy pub where Saturday night fights broke out and ended before the police arrived. They cruised past a terrace of 1960s council houses. The clouds had become solid grey and it started raining, the first time for weeks.

'Here. Left. This is my road.' They drove until Jake pointed to a house. 'It's here.' Jake reached for the door handle as she pulled into the kerb behind a white VW Golf. In the centre of Jake's front garden, a well-tended clump of orange roses still flowered, and the dark green front door looked as if it had been recently painted. How different compared to the house next door, where a supermarket trolley nestled in the long grass alongside old Guinness cans and a broken, pink plastic highchair.

'Thank you.'

'You're welcome, Jake. Is that your mother's car?'

'Yes. She's home.'

'Good. See you tomorrow.'

Jake hesitated, one foot on the pavement. He turned to face her.

'Do you think Weston could have done it?'

'What makes you think that?'

Jake sat back in his seat, closed the door, and turned around to make certain no one else could hear him. Steph turned the car engine off. She knew cars were ideal places for sharing confidences while looking ahead through the windscreen. Silence. The wispy grasses swayed through the wire cage of the shopping trolley. The dull brown paint on the neighbour's front door was peeling, allowing glimpses of postbox red from a previous life to show through. The rain made wobbly streams on the windscreen. Jake needed space.

So much had been going on, she hadn't thought of Carter all day. Now he loomed over her and she felt sick. She couldn't do what he wanted, but did she have a choice? Suddenly, Jake spoke and dragged her back to the present. 'She was always emailing Justine, you know.'

'Really?'

'It started about a year ago when Justine was her pet. After a coaching session at college or at Weston's house, she would email Justine to tell her how brilliant she was and what to improve.'

'What did Justine think?'

'She thought it was great. Weston's a fantastic teacher. Justine said she's the best teacher ever. Gave her confidence and made her believe in herself – 'til the big bust up.'

'Oh?'

'Yes, last Friday – before the concert. You wouldn't have noticed, being new, but Justine should have been on last and Weston demoted her. Justine got in a right state. She was already upset about her granny, and for fucking Weston to do that to her – it was the end. Anyway, on Saturday she got an email from that bitch woman.'

'What did it say?'

'Don't know. She wouldn't let me read it. Got really upset. She cried for a bit, then said that she'd show Weston how fucking good she was and that she didn't need her help. Then she worked on her audition piece all day, like I told you.'

'Right.'

'She played one bit so loud, over and over again, but couldn't get it right. She kept stopping and crying. She was furious with Weston or herself. She wouldn't let me help. She said she had to sort it. So I left.'

His head down, tears dripped onto his jeans. 'If only I'd stayed...'

'Don't blame yourself, Jake. We don't know what happened.'

'Will the police find out if Weston had anything to do with it?'

'They'll find out what happened. I know it's grim...'

'Thanks for the lift.'

Jake blew his nose, climbed out of the car and shut the door. Stooped and turned in on himself, he looked so fragile. His jeans were fashionably torn across his thighs, his grey hoodie screaming 'FRACK OFF!' Exhausted with grief, all hope gone, he slowly lifted his arm, put his key in the lock, paused and then opened the door.

Raindrops running down the windscreen distorted the pile of rubbish. Had Jake convinced her? Was convinced too

75

strong? Persuaded, then – that he wasn't involved in Justine's death? He loved Justine – or said he did. But he hadn't told the whole truth in their earlier conversations, had he? No, if she was working the case, she wouldn't take Jake off the list of suspects yet.

CHAPTER FIFTEEN

EDMUND

Rowe SUGGESTS that lists can provide the basis of a chapter or bits can be used in sections of memoirs. Here is a list of the positives and negatives of being home schooled.

Confidence – Both positive and negative. I have absolute confidence in my ability and knowledge. I know more and have read more books than the other students. In English today, a student whispered that I was 'cocky'. After the lesson, I asked Grace what it meant. She looked confused, then said, 'confident' and that I wasn't to worry.

Swear words – This is a problem. I don't know many. I listen hard at college to work out their meaning. Is being a 'douche bag' a good or bad thing? The F-word is used as a common adjective – not for sex. They say 'Fuck off' to friends all the time, but they don't get upset.

Perfectionism – This is a definite positive. Mother insists all work I do with her must be perfect. College tutors accept mistakes and don't worry if students don't get an A or 100%. I find it frustrating when tutors say you can't be perfect, when I know you can.

Parents – This is a positive. Mother is everything to me. I owe her everything. Other students don't respect their parents and don't tell them important things. They avoid their parents as much as possible. They lie to them about what they're doing. I tell Mother everything.

Food – Here I do feel deprived. I've never eaten pizza or burgers. Mother calls it 'junk food'. I wish we had a freezer full of pizza and burgers like other students. We eat off plates with knives and forks and sit at a table. They eat in front of the TV with their fingers, which sounds fun. If Justine was here, I know she'd take me to the canteen to try pizza or a burger.

Technology – I am minus a technical life. No phone, no internet, no Facebook or something called Instant-gram. They send gaffs, which are small pictures or videos, and they laugh at cats that look like Hitler. We have a television, but we rarely watch it. Mother has a computer used for writing performance programmes and essays, but it doesn't get the internet. The students all live in a virtual world called a cloud. I live for my cello in the real world. Positive or a negative? Not sure.

Different – I look different, sound different, am different. I find it difficult to make friends. Do I mind? They talk rubbish and trivia. I need to work, to achieve. I think I must stay different. I can't be like them, so I will be like me.

Clothes – Now this is where I would like to change. I look so different from everybody else. They wear jeans and tops. I have to wear chinos and shirts and a blazer with smart shoes (business wear, a tutor called it). I really want to wear what they do and to feel like them. Maybe before I leave college Mother may let me.

Happiness – I had a happy childhood. Mother was always there. All her attention, all the time. I was never bored and always worked hard to achieve. In English and Theatre Studies they talk a lot about unhappy childhoods. They sound bruised. Angry. Resentful. Useful for their creative writing, they say. I feel safe here at home, not safe in the canteen.

Friends – Positive and negative. I spent time with children my age. Six home-schooled children met at HomEdSoc (snappy title!) arranged by Noah's bossy mother. We went to Norwich Castle for a Medieval day, Minsmere Nature Reserve to watch birds (how dull was that?). Summer afternoons we'd go to play on a farm – in a barn, on swings, a slide and a climbing frame. (Waste of time.) Several of them had escaped school bullying. They pushed me off the slide and didn't allow me on the zip wire. Mother sat frowning on the hay bale – a world away from the other mothers.

People came to talk to us – an archaeologist, then a van with cages of small animals to stroke. A weasel bit my hand. Mother panicked – was my finger damaged? It was fine. Mother decided my peers bored me. She was right. I'd rather be with my cello or her. We stopped going.

At college they 'hang out' a lot – which means wasting time, not doing anything. I go to my lessons, then go to the library or to the practice rooms or go home.

CHAPTER SIXTEEN

STEPH

As STEPH WALKED TOWARDS HIM, Derek thrust his head through the bottom bars of the oak gate. Felicity, the dog lady, opened it to let him out. He dashed up to Steph, his tail wagging. His unconditional, enthusiastic greeting always flattered her each time she appeared after work, but she suspected that it also had something to do with the likelihood of an evening walk then supper. Rolling in the same way as the English bulldogs she bred, Felicity shuffled towards her. When she laughed, the folds of her face wobbled – just like her dogs.

'He's had a decent run round today. That whippet was in again, and Derek spent the entire day trying to catch him. Failed, I'm afraid – never gives up, I'll give him that! He's had a grand time and he'll be wanting his bed when you get him home.'

'Thanks, Felicity. See you tomorrow.'

Lost in a pack of dogs, Felicity waddled back to her thatched cottage through the canine war zone of humps and holes in the rough grass. Stowed in the back of her car, Derek panted, then collapsed and slept as they drove home. As soon as she pulled up outside her flat, he bounced up, wagging his tail, full of energy and staring expectantly.

'Right. We'll go to the common. I could do with some fresh air. You've had the whippet – I've had Hale. Rather good to see him again – still fancy-able too.'

Her pulse quickened, and she laughed out loud as she imagined chasing Hale around a field like Derek and the whippet!

'Just listen to me – pathetic! Didn't think I'd ever have a dog as my best friend!'

Opening the tailgate, she snatched Derek's lead as he jumped out. He stood taut and alert, then tugged, desperate for a walk. She paused. Felicity had said he should be exhausted. Derek pulled again, this time harder. She gave in and turned towards the common.

After Derek had watered next-door's gatepost, they strolled along Wellesley Road past the rows of Victorian terraces with tiny walled gardens. A skip full of hardboard door panels, woodchip wallpaper and stained turquoise carpet stood outside a terraced house. She smiled as she recognised that Oakwood was becoming 'Chelsea-fied', as they had called it in London in the nineties.

Halfway down Wellington Road, she waited while Derek had another pee stop and appreciated a particularly fragrant lamppost by a neat semi-detached house. She looked up, and there, lit in the bay window like a film shot, was Edmund practising his cello. This was the first time she'd come this way, and she was surprised to see that this was his house. She'd assumed he lived in one of the posh Edwardian houses on the road to the pond.

He sat at an angle facing into the room, his music lit by a standard lamp to his right. His mother hovered behind him, her back to the window with her hand resting on his left shoulder. She leaned forward and circled him with her arms to point out a phrase on the score with her right hand. He gestured to the notes with the end of his bow and then slid it along the line of music to show her another section. Both of them examined the black dots intently. Then Edmund sat back and laughed. She ruffled his hair. Playfully, he pushed her aside. She laughed and then flicked her hand towards the music. Edmund pulled his bow across the strings. They obviously got on well.

The sound of the cello reached her through the open window. Faure or Brahms? Whatever it was, it was thrilling! Sublime. Wanting to listen but not to be seen, she stepped to the left side of the gatepost. She closed her eyes to catch every note. Derek lay down on the pavement and sighed.

'What is it about that boy that fascinates everyone?'

The voice made her jump and move further along the fence. She swung around to see Marlene humping Derek's head. Caroline, out for her evening walk.

'Marlene – do leave Derek alone, darling. That lad produces a magnificent sound, don't you agree? What a talent! Off to the common?'

'Yes – where else?'

'How wonderful to see you. I could do with some company tonight. Margaret's been moaning on and on about Harriet ever since we left college. Oh, what a relief to get some sensible conversation!' Caroline had a theatrical way of saying the dullest of words – elongating their vowels to make them sound intriguing or mysterious. No wonder she hypnotised her Art A Level students, who all adored her.

They walked together towards the common. The smell of damp leaves got stronger. The sinking sun lit up the trees, turning them black. Soon, as the evenings drew in, this walk would be in the dark and she'd have to stick to the roads in the winter.

Caroline was wearing another floaty, ankle length dress – this time pale blue with dramatic ivory peonies splashed across it. Once again it was a bizarre choice for dog walking, but exquisite. Its bold design worked so well with Caroline's long grey curls. So few women could get away with it. Since her recent foray into Miranda Modes, Steph had become fascinated by other women's clothes. Maybe she was becoming a proper woman at last.

'Sooo, who do you think did it? The college is squirming with speculation.'

Steph gasped. She was horrified. How could Caroline use this throwaway tone? Surely she was affected by the tragedy of this young girl's death? It sounded as if she was chatting about an intriguing whodunit on the TV rather than a student whose life had stopped. She'd seen this distancing before from those who were safe, on the edge, not intimately involved in a violent death. But Caroline's flippant comment still took her aback.

Without waiting for a reply, Caroline continued, 'Margaret suspects Harriet did it.'

'How do you know anyone "did it"? The police are still investigating.'

'Come on. Of course they think it's suspicious – they wouldn't be trampling around college so long if they didn't.'

Steph turned to check that no other dog walkers were around. She was concerned where this was heading, especially if Caroline knew something that Margaret hadn't told the police.

'What makes Margaret think Harriet is involved?'

'Now, my dear. Margaret has a fascinating theory, and

although I haven't told her, I actually think there could be something in it.'

'Really?'

'Last year Justine was happy working with Margaret. Then Harriet wooed her away so – you know...'

'No?'

'So she could seduce her.'

'What? Justine was a student!'

Steph hadn't expected this. Such a relationship couldn't, or at least shouldn't, happen. Yet Jake had told her that Justine spent time in Harriet's house and was her 'pet', and that it was Harriet's email that had upset her.

Caroline repeated her claim. 'Margaret is sure that Harriet wooed Justine away from her last year so she could seduce her. Then, and this is the point, then Justine must have threatened to expose Harriet or perhaps blackmail her. So Harriet had to—'

'What? This is a crazy idea!'

'No, think about it. It's obvious. Edmund took Justine's place in Harriet's affections, and I dare to hazard her bed. So Harriet – er – removed Justine.'

Steph was gob smacked. She'd experienced extreme rumours following a suspicious death before, and they had even followed some of them up, but this – this was unbelievable. Wasn't it? Caroline was now warming up and embroidering Margaret's theory.

'My dear, Harriet has the most awful reputation. She covers it up well. She's married, if you can call that a marriage. He's never here – too busy earning shed loads of money. Harriet has a reputation for frolicking when he's not here and occasionally even when he is! I don't know where she gets her energy! Affairs are so exhausting, don't you agree? Over the last year rumour has it that she's worked her way through most of the new male members of the common room.'

Derek stopped to concentrate on sniffing a moist patch just below a sculptured willow fence. Caroline was painting Harriet as a total bitch, and Steph suspected that Margaret would contaminate her with further stories each evening. Could any of it be true? Surely it was just envious gossip?

With a touch of impatience, Caroline tapped her crimson fingernails along the top of the fence. She glanced at Derek snuffling in the wet patch. Marlene sat still, her back to Derek – a superior white fluffy cushion.

'Boy dogs are strange creatures, aren't they?' said Caroline. 'Constantly sticking their noses into vile wet patches. Some-times I think they don't go on a walk for exercise. It's a more olfactory experience – don't you agree?'

Steph snatched at his lead and pulled him away. She felt she needed to defend Derek, her new best friend. 'I suppose it's males protecting their territory from invasion, you know; getting familiar with who's on their patch.'

'Typical of men, don't you think, to enjoy grubbing around in the baser elements of life?'

'I've never thought of it like that. You were telling me about Harriet's affairs?'

'Was I?'

'Her – what did you call it – frolicking?'

'Oh yes. She has the most fearful reputation – racy, one might say. She picks them up with little effort, gets bored, drops them, then moves on to the next one.'

'Does Margaret have any evidence about all this or is it just common room gossip? It's a serious allegation to suggest that a teacher is having a sexual relationship with a student.'

Caroline bent down and released Marlene's lead. 'Off you

go, my darling! I think we can let them off here. No one else seems to have dared to venture into the dark, dark wood this autumnal evening.' She pointed at an oak tree, silhouetted against the glow of the setting sun. 'That would make a sensational picture – so filigree, so moody.'

Caroline swept the debris off a fallen tree trunk and sat down; Steph joined her. They watched as their dogs trotted around the clearing. Derek, black-and-white splodges, an unkempt but honest working dog, racing his unlikely partner, a delicate white fluffy cloud, her legs moving in a blur. A total contrast, just like their owners – one in work clothes, the other on the look-out for a cocktail party.

'My dear, Harriet may be a splendid teacher and a big name in the music world locally, and I believe nationally, but the rumours arrived before she did.'

'Really?'

'Yes. Margaret picked them up. A small world, the music world.'

'And?'

'And let's just say... she's a woman with a past and, it would now appear, a present.'

'But not with students, surely? That's appalling. And a female student?'

Caroline stared at a magpie as it swooped above Marlene's head across the clearing.

'Vicious birds, don't you agree? Now where was I? Harriet is... shall we say, flexible? In our relationships, some of us place ourselves on a – what shall I say? Yes – on a ruler: firmly on one end, say heterosexual, or at the other end, homosexual. Some of us have fixed relationships, which may last a lifetime, but others hover on a space for a while then – well, they change position. Harriet is one of those. But of course, my dear, ambition drives all Harriet's moves on her ruler.'

'What do you mean?'

'You must have met people like Harriet in your previous job? Those people who use their bodies to get what they want out of life – money, promotion, fame?'

'That's rather cynical, Caroline.'

'Realistic, my dear, realistic.'

'But a student?'

'Students? Oh, that doesn't bother Harriet. When she first arrived, she favoured Jeremy, a Year 13 tuba player. I mean – a tuba? How unromantic is that! Of course, she got bored, so she stole Justine from Margaret and bestowed all her attention on the poor girl. Harriet showered her with additional coaching, in college and at her beach house in Southwold – constant emails and texts. So unprofessional, but Harriet has her sights set on higher things.'

'Like what?'

'That, my dear, is the question. Precisely the right question to ask. A new job in a conservatoire, perhaps? Now Edmund stands in Harriet's spotlight and that is a rather dangerous place to be, it would appear. Well, lovely to see you, Steph, must dash. Supper calls. Marlene, say night-night to Derek. Come!' And with that, Caroline and the white fluff dissolved into the twilight.

CHAPTER SEVENTEEN

EDMUND

TONIGHT, I saw Steph, the lady from college. She stood at my gate in the gloom and listened to me practising. She has a black-and-white, funny-looking dog, which stopped to pee on our gatepost. She thought I couldn't see her. She moved further along the fence. I could still see her. She listened, so I played louder. Mother had her back to the window so wasn't able to see her. At the concert, Steph was in the front row with the Principal. I've spoken to her several times in reception. She said she liked music and enjoyed going to Snape concerts with her husband. She knows a lot about music for a receptionist.

I will look out for her each evening and play for her and her dog. I've always wanted a puppy, since I can remember. It would have been good to have the Timmy dog on the front of Mother's book *The Famous Five*. Brown, hairy, sticky-up ears, waggy tail, expressive eyebrows would be the perfect dog. My dog. My best friend.

When I was younger, I used to kneel on the armchair in the bay window, watching the dog procession to the common. I would have loved any of them – terriers, sheepdogs, mongrels. As long as it was a dog. And mine.

Rowe says it's important to have 'pin head memories. The tiny, detailed memories from your childhood that mean something special to you. Times that you can capture and pin down, like the butterflies in Victorian glass cases'. I wanted a dog. I ached for a dog. Whenever I raised the idea, she always squashed it. She said she had enough to do looking after me and her piano pupils.

Piano pupils? They've always been so important. They give us money. Mother said we don't have much. We moved to Oakwood when I was two. Father inherited our house from his great aunt, and he gave it to us when he left. He also gave Mother enough money (she won't tell me how much) to look after me until I'm twenty-one.

I sometimes look at her and wonder if she's happy. She doesn't laugh or smile, and she loses her temper a lot. She says that she has all she needs, yet when she gets angry she hits me. She cuddles me afterwards in case I'm hurt. She says she has me and my music. I am the centre of her life. If, or rather when, I leave, I'm not sure how she'll cope. For years she has structured her days around me. I can't remember her doing anything else but me. When I think of the future I worry. I am her life.

It's stressful and an enormous responsibility thinking about that. What if I fail? What if I don't get to play in those concert halls? She wanted to play on those stages herself as a concert pianist. Her dreams depend on me. I can't fail.

A cat would have been easier. A ginger striped cat. Mother is right. I suppose it would be a distraction. I do – I did so want a dog. Now it's too late.

———

EACH NIGHT when I practise at home with Mother I pretend that she is Harriet. When she puts her hand over mine to show me the fingering, it becomes Harriet's touch and makes me tingle. When she brushes against me to show me how to bow a phrase, it's Harriet's body I feel close to mine.

Harriet and I spend a large chunk of each day working together. She knew how sad I was to lose Justine and said we must work our way out of it. She is there for me before college, at lunchtime, after college and in my free periods. She swapped some of her lessons with Margaret so we would have more time together. The other students often look in through the glass panel, then walk off. They know how hard we are working together.

Sometimes when she shows me how to play a phrase, she stands behind me, her breasts moving against my shoulder blades, and her hands stoke mine as she demonstrates the fingering and bowing. I love being in her embrace, as I've begun to think of it. If anyone opens the door, she sometimes moves towards the piano. But we aren't doing anything wrong. She's showing me how to improve.

In music lessons she asks a question and looks directly at me. I always know the answer, but occasionally I lower my head and she asks someone else. Most of the time they have no idea and she asks me anyway. Sometimes it feels as if there are just the two of us discussing the set pieces.

Yesterday we were working on our compositions. Every-one's head was down in silent concentration. I breathed in her perfume before I saw her. Lime and basil enveloped me. Then her hand, elegant crimson nails, eased the pencil from my fingers. She touched where my fingers had been, then changed a minim to a crotchet and added a rest. She was right. She gestured to her desk. I followed her. Chosen, I sat beside her.

Her elegant hands flattened the manuscript page, brushed the specks of rubber from my corrections and checked my composition. She added a crescendo hair pin on one stave, a slur in another bar. I was so close, I could taste her break time coffee on her breath. Under the desk, her thigh pressed against mine. She murmured her thoughts. The class was on one railway track, Harriet and I on another. They faded into a blur, while we were entranced by composing our music. She moved closer and pointed to a bar. I remember her words – 'Umm, that passage, so evocative.' The others left for break. Neither of us noticed. We continued creating together.

The other students don't talk to me much. But then, I don't have much time for them. They live on their phones. They jostle and push and joke while I walk apart. My head is full of music and Harriet. I am with Harriet all the time. Even in class we are alone, together. I am so happy.

CHAPTER EIGHTEEN

STEPH

THE QUIET START to the morning shattered as Peter strode into reception and demanded, 'Steph, please tell Jane to cover the phones, then come into my room.'

Wondering what was so urgent, Steph walked into Peter's office. He was distressed and could hardly keep still as he handed her a phone.

'Look at this. Tell me what you think.'

She had seen a great deal of pornography in her previous job, but she was shocked, not by the image she held, which was tame compared to what she was used to, but by those in the photo. She knew them. The female was Harriet and the male, Edmund.

A naked Harriet was lying on her side on top of a grand piano, parallel to the keyboard. Her left hand supported her head and her right held something over the keys. She was looking down at Edmund, sitting on the piano stool, also naked, his hands on the keyboard. It was difficult to make out what Harriet had in her hand. Steph tried to expand it on the phone. She lost the picture altogether.

'It'll be easier to see it on here.' Peter typed something, made a mistake, started again, then swivelled the computer screen. An exploded view of the couple screamed out. It felt like watching TV with her parents when people did stuff. She blushed. In this college and in front of Peter the image was so extreme. But the picture was now clear. Harriet held a puppeteer's control rods with strings attached to Edmund's fingers.

'You'll have seen worse in your former role no doubt, but here? It's appalling! It's out there for everyone to see. I've tried to get it removed, but the IT technicians can't find the address. I don't know if Harriet and Edmund have seen it yet. I must go over and find them.'

'How did you find it? This isn't your phone.' The phone's white plastic case was covered in a complex pattern of sparkly pink stars and rhinestones.

'It belongs to Grace, one of the College Reps. You know, long dark hair, played the piano at the concert?'

Steph nodded, picturing this girl who always seemed to be at the centre of what was going on. Peter continued, 'I was walking around the campus when I noticed groups of students gathering around their phones – fascinated at something. Whenever I got close, they turned them off or shoved them in their bags. Then I spotted Grace and asked her if I could have a look. It took a little gentle persuasion, but she handed it over and – you see.'

'Lucky you found it so soon.'

'I've called your lot in. This is cyber bullying.' Peter paced towards the door, then appeared to change his mind and returned to his computer.

'Just look at this.' Peter pointed to the neck and shoulder of Edmund. 'The skin tone is different. His face is paler than his shoulder. And it's the same here.' He touched the screen, and another enlarged shot flew into view, this time of Harriet.

'And then there's this...' Peter gestured towards the large breasts thrust out at the viewer. She was puzzled, not sure what he'd seen.

'Well, perhaps you haven't noticed, but Harriet – Mrs Weston – isn't that... size. Nowhere near.'

'You're right. They've superimposed the heads on those bodies.'

Peter moved closer to the screen. 'They look like the College ID photos – easy to copy if you hack into the system. Whoever did this is highly skilled. The heads look natural – well, until you enlarge it.'

'On a phone it's really convincing,' agreed Steph.

'Malicious, isn't it? Vile. Nasty. How could one of our students do that to a member of his peer group and one of our teachers? We've had bullying on social media, some sexting, but never pornographic images like this between a teacher and student.'

'Have you any idea who did it?'

'I can think of a few students who might have the skills. Normally I'd deal with it in college, but as it's linked to the music department and possibly Justine's death, I've called your lot in.'

She was disappointed that she'd become 'your lot', and it was the second time he'd said it. She'd been working so hard over the last few weeks to belong to 'his lot'.

'The police may be able to trace the origin of the post, but that could take some time,' she said. 'A series of servers in Russia and the Far East are often used to hide the trail, which makes it difficult. We'd be better off starting with the students you suspect, then examining their computers. They must have downloaded the photos of Mrs Weston and Edmund to create the image. I assume whoever did it thought it was a prank, not a criminal offence. "Denigration", it's called. Whoever did it could get a maximum of two years in prison.'

The phone rang. Peter lifted the receiver and listened.

'Right, Jane. Send him in, please.'

He turned to Steph and smiled. 'Well, at least they're taking it pretty seriously. They've sent in the cavalry. Your Chief Inspector Hale's not available so someone else is here – a Detective Sergeant Carter. You must know him, Steph.'

The door opened. She held on to the back of the chair to steady herself as Carter slithered in.

CHAPTER NINETEEN

EDMUND

TODAY I LOOKED different when I arrived at college. Despite asking, I'm not allowed jeans or a 'hoodie', as I've discovered they're called. Mother reluctantly agreed that a polo shirt under my jacket was acceptable. She insists I have to be different from the rest.

Every day on my way to the music centre I walk through Main Quad, where students hang out, as they call it. They share pictures on their phones, laugh, push each other around. Today they were strange. As I approached, they fell silent and held their phones close to their bodies. They looked ashamed, embarrassed, as if they'd been caught doing something they shouldn't.

As I got close to the door Grace came out to meet me, took my arm, steered me into the first practice room on the right and shut the door. She told me to sit down, so I perched on the piano stool. She pressed buttons on her phone, then handed it to me. She said something about the Principal taking her spare phone but this was the main one so it was all right. I couldn't see anything at first, so she took it from me and made a picture bigger by moving her fingers.

On it was a photograph of me playing a grand piano with my back to the camera. I was naked. Harriet, also naked, reclined on top, her breasts thrust out at me. She was holding a wooden cross, a puppet controller with strings attached to my fingers.

Grace looked at me as if she expected me to speak. I tested how I felt. Flattered that we were naked together, but annoyed that Harriet was pulling my strings. Grace continued to look at me. Her face had become a question mark. I was not sure how to react. Was I meant to be angry? Embarrassed? Laugh it off as a joke? I didn't know what she expected. I scanned her face for a signal. She looked sad, regretful – as if it was her fault.

I decided. I smiled, shrugged my shoulders, opened my cello case and pretended nothing had happened. She looked puzzled. I realised it must have been the wrong reaction. I turned and slammed the lid of the piano over the keyboard. The angry crack made her jump. Then I turned towards her and dropped my head, as if I had been hit and was in pain. She moved towards me, her arms open. I had got it right. I lowered my head further. I sniffed. She handed me a tissue, wrapped her arms around me and hugged me. She smelt of hair spray. She told me not to worry and that she'd get me a coffee.

Mother would find out somehow and I knew I had to tell her first. Grace gave me her phone and showed me how to dial the number, then left. I made it sound as if the photo was nothing and explained that it was a joke, a fake. I told her it happened all the time in colleges, but I didn't know if it did. She shouted. I was pleased that Grace had gone and not heard her screaming anger. She threatened to come to college – again. I knew she would.

I looked out of the window and wondered how many of them had seen it. Probably all of them. Grace carried the coffee in her left hand. She was kind, tall and got good marks – on theory. Her practical was getting better. She could lose weight. She's not as beautiful as Justine and doesn't smell of rosemary.

CHAPTER TWENTY

STEPH

CARTER SOUNDED like a corny TV show cop, complete with hackneyed script. He nodded at Steph, presenting himself as a cheery old colleague rather than the vile bastard who had terrorised her. She was nauseated by his cheesy, bland clichés and concerned that Peter might assume all of her ex-colleagues were like this cocky little man. Thank goodness he had met Hale first.

From his comments and his bored expression, Carter obviously thought it was a fuss over nothing. His promises were toe curling. He would find out who had committed this criminal act, and a disgusting one at that. He would put a stop to this disgraceful behaviour in a college with such an excellent reputation. He would track down the perpetrator and bring him to justice in a matter of hours... So it went on. If it hadn't been for the fear that flooded through her the moment he walked in, she would have found it funny.

Steph wondered how much of Carter's guff Peter was swallowing. He caught her eye then said, 'Sergeant Carter, you will have Steph Grant's help in getting this dreadful mess sorted out as soon as possible.'

Her pulse quickened. She looked down at the red Persian rug, suddenly fascinated by a threadbare patch. She tried to get control and slow her breathing, hoping neither of them noticed.

'Thank you, but I don't think that will be necessary.' At least the feeling was mutual.

'No, this must have priority.' Steph was becoming familiar with Peter's calm but firm tone of voice when he rose to a challenge. 'Steph will help you while you are in my college. Most of our students are under eighteen, and if their parents or carers can't attend for your interviews, then Steph can be the appropriate adult. We need to get this sorted as soon as possible.'

For once, Carter looked unsure of himself. He glanced down at the scribbled bullet points on the top page of his notebook, flipped it shut and put it in his pocket in an attempt to look as if he meant business. 'I'll need a private room while I'm here please, Principal.'

'Yes, we'd anticipated that. I've set the meeting room aside for you. There's a computer in there linked to the college system. Our technical team will ensure you have all the access you need. Perhaps you will give me an update on your progress at the end of the day?'

Dismissed, Steph led Carter out to reception, where he stood for a moment taking it all in. She watched as he inspected the two black leather sofas and the glass coffee table, scattered with prospectuses and albums of press cuttings recording students' achievements.

'Strange idea sticking this glass box on that old building. This is where you work, eh?'

Steph took a deep breath and tried to remain calm. The knot in her stomach tightened. She said nothing and watched him step over to the light oak desk and pick up the Toblerone-shaped metal nameplate. He read it out loud, as if discovering her name for the first time.

'Mrs Stephanie Grant – very posh. You've landed all right here. Now enough of all this pissing about, let's get down to work. Where's this meetings place? Ah, I see – opposite. It'd better be private. This investigation needs delicate handling.'

Carter, delicate? An oxymoron, surely? She looked across at him, now picking something out of his front teeth. She shuddered as if she'd seen a snake.

Dan Stokes, Chief IT Technician, arrived at the meeting room door.

'Steph.' He nodded at her then indicated Carter. 'This the policeman?'

'Detective Sergeant Carter.' Dan took no notice of Carter's correction but walked into the room, sat at the computer, turned it on, typed in a password, then rolled the chair back so they could see the screen. Pleased to be involved in something other than Carter, Steph felt her panic subsiding.

'The Principal said that you're to have full access to our system. You got it. Just switch it on. Password is CYBER-B. Capitals. I am on extension 547. OK, Steph?'

'Yes, thanks so much, Dan,' said Steph.

He left. He had not looked at Carter once.

'Flaming weirdo, eh?'

'He's a lovely man and good at his job.'

She hurried towards the door, finding it difficult to be anywhere near him.

'Er, how do I get to this porn again?'

Typical of Carter. Detail was not his forte – neither, come

to that, was the big picture. How he kept his job was a miracle, with his sexist and racist comments. She knew that underneath he longed for the old days when the police could get away with using a little gentle persuasion on their suspects, like, for example, bull whips. His tales of the wild frontier in the north had been difficult to swallow, but other colleagues had assured her it was true of life there in the nineties. Now she'd seen the other side of him, she believed it all.

'Right. Get me a list of all the IT and computing students. Whoever did this knew what they were doing.'

'No shit, Sherlock,' muttered Steph as she opened the door. She was about to shut it when Carter grabbed her arm and yanked her back, so his lips were close to her ear.

'And I'll soon be popping round to leave the first parcel for collection. I'll phone to confirm.' He let go of her arm and patted her bottom as she moved away.

Feeling faint, legs wobbly, she reached the reception desk and held on to it. She took a deep breath, relieved to be away from Carter at last. The door opened and his voice followed her 'And a cuppa would be good – milk, two sugars!'

CHAPTER TWENTY-ONE

STEPH

STEPH DISCOVERED that organising an interview timetable for computing students, while ensuring that they didn't miss any lessons, was a time-consuming, complicated puzzle. Move one student into a space and another one had to find a different slot. Absorbed, she welcomed the distraction that pushed Carter out of her brain for a while.

Carter had been working in the meeting room on his phone for about an hour. He emerged to tell her that the police IT experts claimed they could not remove the image and he would have to find the culprit in the college and get him to take it down. Everyone assumed it was a 'him'. Indeed, when Steph drew up the list of interviews, most students in the group were male.

She was writing the last name on the list when the sliding doors swooshed open and Mrs Fitzgerald invaded reception.

'Mrs Grant, I insist on seeing the Principal now!'

'Good morning. I'll phone through to see if he's free.'

'His door's just behind you, isn't it? You must know if he's in there.'

'Please take a seat and I'll tell the Principal you're here.'

Before Steph could pick up the phone, Mrs Fitzgerald glanced at the police car parked in the disabled space by the front door. 'I see you have the police involved. This horror needs to be resolved as soon as possible. I'm amazed the Principal hasn't had that disgusting image removed. Last Friday, we had the appalling behaviour at the concert and now this – this outrage!'

Mrs Fitzgerald's piercing voice attracted the interest of a group of passing students, who stopped to see the drama unfolding. Clearly they were transfixed by her appearance. 'Even my gran wouldn't wear that!' Another: 'Looks like the fucking charity shop didn't want it and gave it back!' Steph shooed them away and, wanting to stop this disturbance, moved towards Peter's door, which opened magically.

'What is going on here? Ah – I see. Do come in.'

Just as Mrs Fitzgerald dashed towards his door, Peter raised his hand and stopped her. Steph followed his gaze. A female police officer walked into reception followed by an exhausted looking couple. Justine's parents. The police officer walked towards Steph.

'Good morning. I'm Joyce Sims, the police liaison officer working with Hale.' She paused, apparently trying to take in the tableau before her. 'I phoned earlier to make an appointment for Mr and Mrs Dixon to talk with the Principal. Sorry, we're early.'

Justine's parents looked hollowed out. Wearing their holiday clothes – light coloured trousers and bright shirts – they were out of synch with the scudding grey clouds outside the glass walls that promised rain. They must have come straight from Norwich airport. They needed to be in the college the same way the students needed to be there. The last place Justine had breathed.

Moving towards Justine's parents, Peter placed his hand on Mrs Dixon's forearm and said softly, 'I am so very, very sorry. We all are. This must be a dreadful time for you both – I can't begin to imagine how you are feeling. Please come through. Mrs Fitzgerald, sorry, but I'm sure you understand.'

Mrs Fitzgerald stopped bristling and stood aside to let the Dixons pass. She stood at the desk, reading the notice about visitors being polite as if it was important news. From her body language, it seemed that her anger had dissolved. She had become another parent needing help.

'May I get you a coffee?' Steph gestured to the sofas.

'No, thank you.' Mrs Fitzgerald replied as she sat upright on the left-hand sofa, facing Peter's office door.

'I'm sorry you were interrupted, but I'm sure you understand the need for Justine's parents to talk with Mr Bryant.'

'Those poor parents! They look as if they've just got back,' said Mrs Fitzgerald. 'Someone told me they'd been away... You know what this town's like. A pity they didn't take Justine with them. I suppose we're always wise after the event... I mean, a few days' away wouldn't have hurt her, and now she wouldn't be... would she?'

'Yes, it's a tragedy.' Steph rearranged the prospectuses and local papers into neat piles on the coffee table.

'Edmund said the students have created a shrine to Justine. Could I see it, do you think?'

'Yes, it's through here.'

Steph gestured to the left and held the door open. Mrs Fitzgerald went before her along the corridor to the old building. The wall of perfume hit them first, then the ever growing heap of the tributes forced them to walk in single file.

In the old entrance hall Mrs Fitzgerald paused and stared at the enormous pile of bouquets and toys, now two, or even three layers deep in places. She lowered her head as if in church. The same movement Edmund had made. She picked up a card from a bunch of bright pink carnations and read it. Then she bent down to replace it in precisely the same spot. It was difficult to tell if she was sneering or she was touched. She read another card and shifted a spray so that the yellow roses beneath were no longer crushed, then nodded to Steph and muttered, 'Thank you. It's had an enormous impact on these young people.'

'Yes. They're devastated.'

They returned slowly to reception. On an interrogation course some years ago, Steph had seen that if silences were created, the person being interviewed often gave something away. She waited. Silence. No spectacular gifts here then.

When they reached the sofas Mrs Fitzgerald remained standing, watching the students drive out of college. Steph stood beside her, her back to anyone who might walk through reception. She was sure no one could hear them. It was worth a try. 'I'm sorry about that awful picture. It must have been so upsetting when you found it.'

'I didn't. Edmund phoned me on one of the student's mobile phones. I've not seen it – we don't have the internet.' She made it sound like a disease. Then she turned to Steph. 'He described it. It sounded vile. It must be all over the town by now. He's only seventeen – he would never – they invent these things all the time, don't they?'

'The police will try to find out who was responsible.'

'I do hope so. Edmund knows so little of the internet and mobile phones and such like. He's never had any of them – too busy playing his cello. I thought this was a good college, but now, I wonder if coming here was the most awful mistake.'

Steph stopped herself blurting out that Edmund belonged to the world, not to her. Perhaps this was not the time for some honest parenting advice. Anyway, would this obsessed woman listen? Probably not.

'It was apparent when he was four, you know, that he had a rare talent.' Mrs Fitzgerald cut through the silence this time. So it did work sometimes!

'Really?'

'Yes, his father made cellos and double basses. One day Edmund played in the workshop with an old cello and started to make sounds – ghastly, they were. He begged us to teach him to play properly. He was always desperate to practise – it was like an addiction. By the age of seven, he'd got Grade Eight Distinction. That's when I decided I should educate him at home. It would allow him to practise up to five hours a day.'

'That sounds a lot.'

'Oh no, quite usual in children who are musical prodigies. Edmund has the talent and the determination to achieve. He'll do anything to get to the top—'

Peter's office door opened and Justine's parents and the police liaison officer emerged. They waited while Peter went to speak to Mrs Fitzgerald. 'I won't be long. Justine's parents would like to see the student tributes before they leave. Please go through and wait in my office.'

'Thank you, Mr Bryant.' Mrs Fitzgerald swept through his open office door. Peter closed it behind her. Steph returned to her desk as Peter took Justine's parents to see her shrine.

A little while later Peter returned to his office, visibly downcast. Opening his door, he pulled himself up to his full height, ready for the next challenge. Steph peeped through the glass porthole on the meeting room door. Harriet was sitting across the table from Carter. She was red faced, clearly trying to remain as calm as possible. How could she have anything to do with this or know who'd done it? Harriet was a victim and the talk of the college. She must be having a dreadful time.

Carter wore that creepy, sympathetic look she knew so well from the past. It made her feel queasy. He must have thought it made him look sensitive to women. He leaned towards Harriet over the table. Surely he wasn't going to hold her hand? No – he sat back as Harriet regained her dignity and appeared to be taking control. Steph could hear her outraged tone, but not her words. Good for her.

After Harriet, he planned to see Edmund. Poor lad, he'd be mortified. At least his mother was in college and could be with him. As she was finishing some photocopying, Edmund arrived in reception. As usual, he was immaculately dressed in beige chinos and a white polo shirt. At least the business shirt had gone and he was dressing down a bit.

'Thank you for coming down. I'm sorry, this must be so upsetting for you.'

'Yes, it has been.'

His eyes were a little red but he held his head up high. She felt sorry for him having to cope with this cruel cyber-bullying. He appeared to be such a sensitive boy with a prodigious talent.

'Sergeant Carter from the Suffolk Police is helping us to find out who's behind all this, and I know he'd like to speak to you. Your mother's in with Mr Bryant at the moment, but she'll be in the interview with you.'

'Thank you, Mrs Grant. She said she was coming into college.'

'Call me Steph – all the other students do. Do you have any idea who may be behind it?'

'No. It must have something to do with poor Justine's suicide.'

'Really, how?'

'I've heard them saying she did it because of me and Harriet.'

'Oh?' Steph prompted him.

'Yes, they say that Justine was upset about the concert and that was the reason. The police think it's suicide, don't they?'

Peter's door opened and Mrs Fitzgerald burst on the scene.

'Edmund, my darling!' She rushed towards him. 'What an awful day you've had. An absolute nightmare! I'll take action against the college and whoever perpetrated this vile thing.'

She stopped talking as she noticed Justine's parents returning from visiting her shrine and approached them. 'I am very sorry for your loss. Such a promising young musician – outstanding musicality for her age. Really mature interpretation and intonation. What a dreadful waste!'

Justine's parents stared at her, then thanked her. They looked numb. Perhaps they'd only heard her tone of voice, not her words. Peter saw them to their car before returning to his office. As soon as his door closed, Mrs Fitzgerald patted Edmund's arm.

'Right Edmund, it's almost lunchtime – you've no lessons this afternoon. I'll drive you home. Come along now!' She stepped towards the door, expecting Edmund to follow. He stood still.

She turned and stopped. 'Well, come on! Hurry along!' Her patronising tone made Steph recall Mary Poppins.

Edmund, embarrassed by this public torment, cleared his

throat. 'No, Mother. I – we need to have a word with the policeman in there about the photo.'

'But that's absurd – you're the victim, darling, not the perpetrator.'

'I know, Mother, but he needs to talk to us. Steph, may we wait over there until he wants us, please?'

'Yes. I'm sure he won't be long.'

Edmund and his mother sat side by side, looking at nothing, their stiff figures reflected back at them in the glass wall. Edmund's composure and maturity had been impressive in the recent performance Steph had just witnessed. Performance? She replayed the exchange with Edmund as she collected the dirty cups. She glanced at the odd mother-and-son combo on the sofa. They were so different. But then, if he'd never spent time with his own age group but only practised his cello most of the day, he wouldn't be like the other students, would he?

She picked up the tray of dirty cups and left reception, through the double doors that joined the glass box to the old building, along the corridor towards the tiny kitchen. Just before Justine's shrine a shadow leaped out at her. Two cups clattered to the floor as the tray tilted.

'Jake – what the hell do you think you're doing, jumping out at me like that?'

'Sorry, Miss – Steph. I didn't mean to scare you but...' Jake replaced the cups on her tray then, hood up, stared at her intently through his tiny porthole. His breath floated towards her. He'd been drinking.

'Please, I need to tell you something. But not here, not in college. In your car,' he whispered, breathing beer over her face.

'Oh Jake! What have you been doing?' Did he know something? He looked desperate and walked on the spot, like Derek frantic to go out. She could feel his electric tension.

'Look – I'll pick you up at the corner of Telford Lane in ten minutes when my lunch break starts and we can talk then.'

He jogged down the corridor past Justine's shrine. His movement pushed a wave of the overpowering smell of flowers towards her. How and when would they be able to clear it up and not upset the students? That question was trivial compared to the one she asked herself – what the hell was she doing agreeing to drive this boy around in her car?

'Shitting Henry!' she sighed. 'Now what have I got myself into?'

CHAPTER TWENTY-TWO

EDMUND

MOTHER WAS in college again today. I knew she'd come. There was no way of keeping her away. She was so angry when I told her about that picture. Anyone could see it was false. The heads were at the wrong angle for a start and the skin colour was different. Harriet's skin is much paler, almost transparent, or is it translucent? Whatever the right word is, it is so soft and wonderful to touch. So much younger than Mother's.

Why can't she realise that college is my world, not hers? Why does she have to keep appearing? Keep interfering? I can manage by myself if only she'd let me. I need her to let me go. I'm so embarrassed when she comes in. She looks so different from the other parents.

Going to college and meeting Harriet has given me a new taste – a taste for independence. I no longer want to depend on Mother for everything I need, like a toddler, for that's what she thinks I am. I want to be an adult – an equal partner, and that's how Harriet treats me. She has shown me a new way of playing, of expressing myself. She has given me a voice. It's as if I've been mute, then she's touched me and I've been able to speak. Not even in her language, but in my own. She has given me my own voice.

Rowe suggests including examples of what he calls 'praxis' when 'theory becomes action or, when reflecting on a life, an action makes significant change'. Going to college and meeting Harriet has made a significant change and taken me to a turning point – a fulcrum – in my life and my relationship with Mother. The moment has come when I need to change. To take, not to be taken.

Last night, when Mother needed a cuddle, I stepped into that moment. The moment when I stopped being her child.

Afterwards, I watched as the amber light outside the bedroom window rippled across the faded yellow wallpaper. The curtains shivered. The window was closed, but a draught forced its way through the warped frame. It felt sordid after Harriet.

I pulled up the sheet – covered her exposed breasts. Her nipples, tiny bumps beneath the thin lemon fabric. I knelt astride her. The material became taut under the weight of my thighs – a tight shroud.

She laughed – nervous, not sure. She sensed a difference. I felt so powerful – I could have done anything. She sat up, smiled and reached towards me in the old way. I pushed her back and swung my legs over the side of the bed. I wrapped her kimono around me and went to the bathroom. The ripples transformed to waves on the wallpaper as I left. There had been a change.

CHAPTER TWENTY-THREE

STEPH

JAKE HUNCHED up against the dark fence, hidden by a hedge of fading blue hydrangeas. Steph almost drove past him. She slammed on her brakes. He trotted to the passenger door, opened it and sat beside her.

'Seat belt? We'll go to the car park in Scott's Wood. We'll talk there.' Steph opened her window to get rid of Jake's beer smell. They drove through streets of Victorian terraces and soulless sixties slabs, and out to the large Edwardian houses on the very edge of town. According to Caroline, Harriet and her husband lived in one of these mini mansions.

At last, they reached Scott's Wood. An old Audi was parked in the east car park, so she continued driving to the more secluded west side. Was it better to be seen talking to a seventeen-year-old boy in public, which suggested she had nothing to hide, or try to hide it? This time she hadn't asked Peter's permission. No going back now. They parked in the flickering light under the silver birches.

'Right, Jake, what do you want to tell me?'

He took out a tissue, blew his nose and stuffed it back in his jeans pocket. He checked to see if anyone else was around. The car park and the edge of the wood were deserted. Some papery leaves fluttered down in the wind, which pushed the picture-book white clouds across the blue sky and blew the promised rain away. He looked at Steph, then his chin went down on his chest. He sighed. The beer smell got stronger and Steph lowered her window further.

'Well?' she said.

His eyes searched hers as if he was looking for an answer. 'If I tell you something, will you promise not to tell anyone?'

'I can't promise that. It depends what you tell me.'

He took in a deep breath. 'I did it.'

'What?' Her stomach lurched. Jake, a murderer? And she was alone, no witnesses, no recording of his confession. He frowned and looked puzzled.

'The posting – the porn...'

'Oh – the photo!'

Her relief must have been obvious as Jake looked at her as if she was barking mad. 'It's a criminal offence! We did it in computing.'

'Yes, I know. Now tell me, what have you done and how did you do it?'

Jake described how he'd hacked into the college database, copied and pasted the ID photos of Harriet and Edmund onto the porn image, then uploaded the fake photo.

'I didn't think the police would be called in.'

'But you just told me it's a criminal offence. What did you imagine would happen?'

Steph sneaked a glance at Jake, who wiped away a tear. He pulled out his tissue and blew his nose again. She broke the silence. 'What on earth made you do it?'

'I was so angry with them.' He paused. His eyes misted over. Steph passed him a fresh tissue.

'Them?'

'They've taken my Justine away. She did it because of them.' He wiped his face, caught his breath. 'She felt betrayed. She couldn't get to music college without Harriet's help, and now she's always with him and she ignored Justine. She was so miserable. She thought it was the end of her life, so she...' He started sobbing. 'I only did it as a joke.'

'A joke? Edmund and Harriet don't think it's funny. How do you think they feel?'

'Not great.' He said it so quietly she could hardly hear him. 'I saw Edmund and he looked pretty upset.'

'Not great? Pretty upset? The whole college has seen that photo and laughed at them. They feel humiliated, hurt and very angry. Some people think it's real.'

'No! Surely not?'

She raised her eyebrow and stared at him, not wanting to let him off the hook. She said nothing.

'I'm sorry,' he mumbled into his chest.

'It's not me you should apologise to, Jake. Now, I suggest we go back to college and tell Mr Bryant what you've done. Then see if we can get it taken down.'

Steph saw him wince, obviously terrified at the suggestion.

'What if I took it down myself and we didn't tell anyone?'

'What do you mean? Wouldn't they be able to trace it back to you?'

Why was she even asking the question? She should drive him back to college immediately and turn him over to Peter.

'No, I created a trail that can't be traced.'

'Then why didn't you just take it down? Why tell me?'

'I needed to talk to someone and you – well, you listen to me. Shall I do it?'

Steph felt dizzy and slightly nauseous. She was an accessory, at least. Now what was she to do? She should tell Peter, Hale and even Carter – he'd love that, knowing she'd known. Jake had been stupid – really, really stupid, but did this pathetic lad deserve a criminal record?

She looked at Jake, now a panicky, desperately worried child. She knew what she should do but he'd lost everything that mattered to him, and if this came out, it would ruin his future too. He deserved one more chance.

She sighed. 'Look – I'll drop you close to home. And Jake, I will not lie. I will not tell the police or Mr Bryant, but if they ask me if you had anything to do with it, I shall tell them the truth. Do you hear me?'

She didn't know what else to say. He would get rid of the cyber porn and save his future. This lad who was really a victim and who had lost his Justine and who was now – well – just lost. Once again, she'd crossed the line.

CHAPTER TWENTY-FOUR

EDMUND

I HELD Harriet's hand and helped her down the steep cliff path. The pebbles slid on the loose grey soil on the dusty track. She squeaked as she slipped, grabbed the branch of a bush, steadied herself, then stopped and looked down at me, annoyed. She was not in control.

I laughed at her reluctance to give herself to the slope and run down it. At last she gave up and we slid down the last few feet. She landed on top of me on the sand and we rolled over and laughed, pleased to have reached the bottom of the crumbly cliff. She looked around. The sandy bay was deserted. We were alone.

The sun was at its highest point. The sand burnt our feet as we walked naked to the edge of the sea. The waves gently folded over, a slapping sound that did not disturb the calm or the sand. Silence. Time stopped. We were the only people in the world.

We stepped into the water, so warm we could barely feel it. We swam to the sandbar, about 250 metres out to sea. Slow, sinuous breaststroke. The water became shallow and we walked out onto a beach in the middle of the sea.

She lay on her back, her pale body glowing against the rippled sand. The sea had forced the sand into dried sand waves. They disappeared as soon as we moved on them, leaving sand angels.

We made love, in the rhythm of the waves that surrounded us. We became at one with our world. As our music-making fused into one sound so our bodies created one moment of bliss.

Exhausted, we lay side by side, drying on the sand. The sun disappeared behind a cloud. The afternoon became early evening. We swam back to our clothes and turned our faces to our lives once again.

This is one of Rowe's 'special' moments, and I've written it to help you share and chart my growing love for Harriet. Twelve years older than me, but our love made us equals. I know how special that magical moment was in our life together. We spoke to each other through our music and, in that defining moment, through our bodies.

Harriet never talks about her husband. I'm sure she no longer loves him. I'm falling in love with her – at least I think I am. I can't stop thinking about her. Her perfume, her touch, the tingle I get inside when she's in the room.

She was wearing a maroon flowing scarf in the lesson yesterday, which got in the way when she bent over me. She took it off and left it on the back of my chair. I hid it in my cello case and hold it now and sense her. I breathe her in. Her unique beauty. I am falling in love with her. I know she feels the same way about me.

It will be difficult in Oakwood. We could be possible in London. The age difference would not be so great there. I know I must never tell her my hopes for our future together, just live in these 'special' moments. But one day we'll go to London and she'll teach at a music college. We'll live in Bloomsbury, play music together and wake up together. She'll be my muse. After music college, she'll come on tours with me as my accompanist. I feel so happy when I picture our future together. Harriet Fitzgerald, I love you, I adore you.

CHAPTER TWENTY-FIVE

STEPH

STEPH OPENED the front door just enough to check out her flat. She was terrified in case Carter was waiting, sitting on her sofa. She held her breath – all clear. Carter had invaded her home and smashed the joy in her new life. She couldn't stop thinking about his threat and what he wanted her to do. Now, in the gloom, her sitting room felt unwelcoming. And on top of it all, she was haunted by what she'd agreed with Jake. What had she done? Luckily, she hadn't met Caroline on her dog walk. No way could she face her gossip or hearing about Margaret's delight at the porn photo.

She re-played the day. The right thing was to take Jake back to college and turn him in. Turn him in. So final. So simple. So right. Yes, that would have been the right thing to do. Peter would have been sympathetic but forced to report him to the police, and Carter... Carter would have loved it – revelled in it. He'd claim the credit. A complex case solved by him in one day, when all he'd done was sit in a room and drink tea.

Jake had been stupid, naïve and so wrong, but – there

always was a but – if he'd been caught, his life would have been ruined. Like Sam Odawale. Too late now. As she watched Derek hoover up his dinner, Steph realised she had no choice. She trusted that Jake was right, and they wouldn't be able to trace the origin of the photo, or, now it had disappeared, they wouldn't bother.

The doorbell rang. Her heart rate rocketed. Carter's threatened return? Derek gave a short, dutiful attempt at a bark, then returned to his supper. Through the peephole she was relieved to see it was Hale who stood on the doorstep with his laptop. Opening the door, Steph smiled. 'Hello. What brings you here?'

At that moment Derek galloped to the front door and jumped up, knocking Hale's computer from his hands. Steph bent down to pick it up. Luckily, it had a shell case fixed to it. 'I'm so sorry—'

'I didn't know you had a dog. When did that happen?'

'When I moved here. I've a garden out there. It leads onto the field.'

'What do you do during the day?'

'Doggy day care. You love going to see Felicity, don't you, Derek?'

'Derek! What sort of name is that?' Hale snorted.

'His name – it suits him.'

'You going to ask me in?'

She moved aside, smiled and gestured to the green armchair by the fireplace. 'Welcome to my new abode. Like a drink?' She shut the door.

'That'd be good. No, on second thoughts, some water, please. It's so heavy out there. If only we could have a storm and breathe again.'

Steph grabbed two glasses out of the top cupboard. Hale

looked around the room. 'Nice flat. Better than the one I've had since Sheila threw me out.'

'The flat upstairs is still for sale. You could share my garden.'

'A little far from the station, perhaps?'

And too close to her, no doubt? Steph filled two glasses with tap water and added some ice cubes. A slice of lemon – or even cucumber? No, perhaps not. Too much.

They sat either side of the mottled grey-and-white marble fireplace. He fitted into this space perfectly, but Hale could fit into any space. Why had he come? Perhaps he knew that she'd helped Jake. It felt as if it was stamped on her forehead. She wiped the thought away. Jake would never admit it, and she was the only one who knew.

Hale put his glass down on the table beside him. 'An exciting day you've had up at the college. Carter came back to the station as I was leaving. The air was blue when he'd finished. I wonder if he can ever get a complete sentence out without using the F-word. He said the porn site's been taken down.'

'Oh? What does that mean?' asked Steph, turning away to pick up her glass, hoping her anxiety for Jake didn't show.

'Now there's no chance of tracing where it came from – not that we'd have much luck doing that, anyway. I suspect it was one of the brighter students thinking it was funny. Very bloody funny! After all, it's not revenge porn or sexploitation, so I think we let it go. What a waste of time when we should be investigating Justine's death.'

The phone rang. Both stared at it. She froze. Hale nodded towards it, 'Take it – might be important.'

She picked it up, knowing that only one person had this phone number and hoping it was someone offering double-glazing or insisting she should claim for a car crash she'd never had. 'Hello.'

'It's me, Carter.' She nearly dropped the handset and had to concentrate on keeping her face fixed in neutral and her hand from shaking. 'Just to let you know that, following my request, the porn has been taken down. As I've decided it was a student prank, I will take no further action.'

'Right. Thanks for letting me know.'

'And I'll be in touch later this week about the help you'll give me.' The line went dead. She looked at the receiver as if it was about to bite her.

'Everything OK?' asked Hale.

'Fine.' She sat down again. 'That was Carter telling me he'd removed the porn site and closed the case.'

'I'm amazed you gave him your private number.'

'I didn't.'

She hoped she wasn't blushing, and that Hale hadn't got the wrong idea. Carter and her? Hell would freeze over... not in a month of Sundays... pigs would fly over Suffolk first. A full set of clichés rushed into her brain. She shuddered, brushed the thought of Carter out. She'd worry about his threat later.

Hale took out his notebook. 'Now down to business.'

'Sorry?'

'Your alibi checks out.'

'I didn't know I needed one. Was I a suspect?'

'Come on Steph, you know we can't count anyone out at this stage.'

'But I've only been in the college five minutes. What motive could I have?'

'Last month, I investigated the murder of a man, stabbed by his neighbour with a garden fork after an argument about which one had leased an allotment. You never know what pushes someone to murder. We had to check.'

'Yes, but—'

'Anyway, we know from the ANPR cameras in Oakwood and the college CCTV footage that you're in the clear. You arrived in college after Justine died.'

'You checked the ANPR for my car from here to college?'

'Of course, we did. Your alibi stacks up. Now, I've come to ask you something.'

'What's that?'

'Would you be willing to work on this case as a civilian detective?'

'A what?'

'Civilian detective. The Met started it and Suffolk has followed. Retired detectives work on single cases. You'll have a contract and get paid. Helps with the manpower crisis.'

She noticed that his eyes were focussed intently on her face, as if he was assessing her reaction. He continued, 'You understand us, we know you and you're there, in the middle of the crime scene. Perfect fit. What do you think?'

'I'm flattered, but I must talk to Peter Bryant first.'

'Oh, that's sorted.' Hale smiled. 'Your new boss thinks it's a great idea. Saw the advantage at once of having you working with the police. He wants us out as soon as possible.'

Shitting Henry! What a cheek! For a moment she was furious. These two men had been sorting out her life for her before they'd asked her. Typical!

'I must think it over, Hale,' she said, trying to gain dignified control.

'Come on, Steph, you know you want to say yes. You'd be back with the old crowd. We need to make some headway – your help could be crucial—'

'Is Carter still on your team?'

'Carter? Why? No, he isn't. He moved to Vice, or was it Drugs, just after – while you were ill. Why do you ask?'

'Nothing. He's just not my blood group. We never got on. OK, I'll do it.'

'Great! Let's get you up to speed. We're now treating Justine's death as murder, not suicide.'

'I know you thought it suspicious, but now you're convinced it's murder?'

'Yes. We've found no sign of a suicide note at home or college. She doesn't appear to have visited any suicide websites or chat rooms. There's nothing to suggest she killed herself, and we've got evidence that someone else did it.'

'Really?'

'Yes, the PM confirmed it this morning. Justine died from exsanguination – from the slit arteries on her wrists. But the pathologist thinks she couldn't have cut herself with the enormous dose of drugs – morphine or barbiturate – they found in her system. She'd have been out cold.'

Hale looked down at his notebook. 'The tox report will take about four days. But from the initial examination of her stomach contents, the pathologist thinks Justine ate a Chinese meal,' he turned over a page in his notebook, 'probably late on Sunday night.'

He flipped over a few pages. 'Here it is. They found partially digested fragments of water chestnuts and what they suspect is duck skin. They think she ate pastry, similar to a croissant, just before she died, and drank grapefruit juice. Oh, yes... she also drank red wine at some point, probably the night before. She died around five thirty to seven o'clock on Monday morning. Now, tell me, what have you found out from your end?'

'How do you know I've found anything out?'

'Oh, come on, of course you have. You can't help yourself.'

Steph told him about her conversations with Jake, omitting the one about the porn photo. After all, she comforted herself, when she let Jake off she had no idea that she'd be back working for the police again, even as this strange creature called a civilian detective. She told Hale about the rumours going around college and Margaret's weird accusations. She was surprised, yet pleased, that she could summarise all the gossip succinctly and she'd not lost her touch.

Hale, as ever, was encouraging and positive. It was as if she'd given him golden nuggets in his search for the truth. But then he frowned and ran his fingers through his dark hair – still no sign of baldness – a movement she associated with his frustration when he was getting nowhere fast. She grinned as he unfolded one of his A3 trademark mind-maps, full of spidery writing with complex arrows between the boxes.

'Now your Jake—'

'He's not my Jake—'

'I assumed he's another of your needy young men – you do seem to collect them! Anyway, from what you say, Jake claims he didn't see Justine again after eleven o'clock on Sunday morning, when he left her to go home to look after his sister. Right?'

'Yes.'

'So, either he's lying, and they shared the red wine and the Chinese – incidentally we're checking CCTV footage outside the two local Chinese takeaways – or someone else was there. Now who could that be? Looking at my map of her relationships, it could be...' Hale smoothed the mind map on his knees and traced his finger along the lines from the central box. 'Who could have known that Justine was alone? Margaret? She could have visited to comfort Justine after the concert, but why would she kill her?'

'She wouldn't – Margaret had got what she wanted. After the row at the concert, Justine was back with her until she left for music college. Justine was a weapon she could use against Harriet. She wouldn't kill her; she was too valuable.'

'That makes sense. Harriet? She was furious with Justine for the sabotage at the concert – do we know who was responsible, by the way?'

'Peter had arranged to see all those involved, but then we found Justine.'

'Perhaps it's something you could find out from your end?' He paused and looked across at her, sipping her glass of water. Silence. 'Would you like some paper and a pen, or do you have a notebook handy?'

'Sorry. Yes, I have one over here.'

Embarrassed, she leaped up and dashed to her desk by the French windows. She knew she didn't have a notebook but didn't want to admit it. But then, she hadn't known that she'd be needing one.

Sifting through the piles of paper she planned to 'sort', she grabbed an address book with a William Morris design on the cover. Turning the spine towards Hale, she hoped he wouldn't notice the graduated edge with letters on each step. She opened it at the letter 'i', knowing it was a blank page, and hoping they wouldn't need to get to 'j'.

'Sorry.' She resumed her seat. 'Let me re-cap. I'll explore who caused the disruption at the concert.'

Steph jotted notes. She was aware that her tone had changed to that of the briefing room. Sharp, factual, business-like. She was sad at the loss of the lighter, chattier side with

Hale; it had become a professional conversation and most definitely nothing more.

'Moving on then.' His finger re-traced the path on his map. 'Where were we? Harriet? Justine had humiliated her. She's a proud woman and, from what you say, holds grudges. She could have visited, ostensibly to effect a reconciliation, but in fact intending to remove this annoying barrier to her future with Edmund, her new protégé. Then there's the fanciful version that Margaret's given you via Caroline. Justine was threatening Harriet, so she might have had a motive.'

'So, Harriet's the prime suspect? Unless there's someone outside college we don't know about yet?'

'Someone we don't know about,' Hale repeated. 'Hang on! Didn't you say earlier that Harriet was having an affair with someone in college?'

'David Stoppard – the new Head of English.'

'Perhaps Margaret's right.' Hale wrote a note in the top corner. 'Maybe Justine, to get revenge, threatened to tell Mr Harriet about Harriet's affair, so Stoppard gets rid of her before she opens her mouth?'

'You're right. Sorry. Just remembered, I overheard Justine hinting at that in her row with Harriet before the concert.'

'Harriet and Stoppard then?' said Hale.

'What about Edmund?' Steph got up to get another glass of water. Hale held out his empty glass to her. 'We know he visited on Saturday with a bottle of wine, which Jake and Justine drank. He could have returned on Sunday night with another.'

'Why would he want to kill her?'

'Perhaps he couldn't cope with being rejected by her?' She handed the glass to Hale.

'You're right. We mustn't overlook Edmund.' Hale added a

box for Edmund on his mind map. 'But he's only been in the college a few days.'

'So had I, but you checked up on me.'

Hale laughed 'Fair point! Both Edmund and his mother – Imogen Fitzgerald, isn't it? – are ambitious, but they've already got what they want – star billing. You're right, we should add them.' Hale drew a second box on his map.

Hale looked down at his diagram. 'Yes. I'll see all of them. In the meantime, will you go through the college emails to check Justine's, Jake's and Harriet's accounts – in fact any of the teachers involved? I have Justine's phone and I'll get the tech guys to apply for a production order so we'll have access to her texts and messaging.'

'Fine.' Steph jotted down a list of actions.

'Here's Justine's diary – see if you can find anything.' Hale handed Steph a maroon leather journal, with a leather clasp secured by a little gilt lock and key. Steph placed it gently on the table beside her, aware of the potential secrets hidden in its pages.

'Was the key in it?' she asked.

'Yes. You'd expect her to have hidden it somewhere?'

'Perhaps she trusted her parents so didn't need to lock it away from them.'

'Look at the time! Same time tomorrow if that's OK?' He got up, put the papers in his bag and opened the door.

'Perfect. See you tomorrow.' She shut the door and stood with her back against it. She felt so alone. So very alone. It had been good to have male company, even if it was about business. How life had moved on. Now both she and Hale were single. A widow and a divorcé.

Mike, her husband, had been Hale's boss. They'd got on well and enjoyed Friday night curries. She felt a flash of anger that Mike could no longer share such moments with her. Why did it have to happen? She knew why. She should stop asking. Too many fourteen-hour days, too much booze, too much junk food, too much stress – a heart attack waiting to happen. He didn't have to wait long. It was Hale who'd found Mike, folded over his desk. He'd died working.

She'd tried to go on alone – filled her diary, pretended she was fine, and then she'd hit the wall. Now she was, as they say, 'getting there'.

Yes. It was good to see Hale again. Very good. She opened the fridge to find a 'Gourmet Meal for One'. They all tasted the same but filled a gap and were quick. Derek stood by the dog cupboard looking up; hope glinted in his eyes.

'No chance, sunshine. You've already had your supper. Now I've got work to do.'

CHAPTER TWENTY-SIX

STEPH

Dear Justine,

*I am so furious with you I can hardly write this email. How dare
you ruin my concert? After all I've done for you. You should be
ashamed of yourself, behaving like a spoilt child having a
tantrum. You ruined a precious moment for me, sabotaging my
concert, all because of your childish jealousy.*

*After tonight, there is no way I can help you or even support
your application to the Royal College. Musicians need thick
skins, resilience, the ability to take knocks and to get on with it.
Tonight, you showed me you have none of those qualities. I am
no longer prepared to coach you or to spend my free time
helping you to improve.*

*Please don't bother coming to apologise – I will not accept it.
Margaret Durrant will take over your performance coaching
from now onwards. You will continue to attend my A Level*

classes but as one of the music group. You will get no additional
help. I want nothing further to do with you.

Harriet Weston

SHAKEN by this vindictive and unprofessional email, Steph closed her eyes to concentrate on the implications of what she'd just read. She was interrupted by the phone. 'Good morning, Oakwood College.'

The silence was shifted by some heavy breathing, then his voice. 'OK Steph? Keep an eye out for me. I'll be round to see you soon.' The phone went dead. She held onto the desk to keep her balance; she felt sick and faint. She tried breathing in slowly, but her panic blocked her throat and she caught little gulps of air.

'Are you all right, Steph?' A gaggle of students peered at her as she forced herself to relax enough to slow her breathing to almost normal.

'I'm fine. Must be hot in here this morning.'

Re-assured, Zoe, a music student, was the spokesperson for the group. 'Please Steph, could you make us an appointment with Mr Bryant? We want to ask him about singing at Justine's funeral.'

'What a lovely idea. He's free at one fifteen. That's Zoe, Denise and...?'

'Saffron Blake. I'm in Justine's music class with the others.'

'I remember you now – I saw you playing the saxophone at the concert.'

'Thank you. See you later.' The girls trooped off towards Justine's shrine. Steph hoped they were going to lessons too. The atmosphere in the college had remained subdued – the volume still turned down, the brightly coloured hoodies and tee shirts at the start of the term replaced by uniform greys and blacks.

Steph stared at the clouds scudding across the pale blue sky. Placing her hands firmly on the desk she counted to seven as she did her breathe in, hold it, then breathe out routine for a few minutes until she felt her pulse slow and her brain return. Carter was invading every corner of her life. How was she going to get rid of him?

At last she felt calm enough to return to the appalling email. It was outrageous that a tutor should write to a student in this way – unprofessional and really nasty. No wonder the poor girl was distraught when she'd received it.

She continued her search through Justine's home email. Her college account had been unremarkable – appointments for tutorials, rehearsals and deadlines for essays – but her home email was crammed with messages from Harriet. They commented on Justine's looks, advised her on clothes to wear for concerts and gave her technical tips on violin playing.

It felt as if Harriet had been running Justine's life for the last year. From the emails, Steph pieced together her life. She had regular coaching at Harriet's Southwold beach house at weekends and occasionally even stayed the night there. Steph wondered what Justine's parents thought about this relationship. But then, Harriet was promising she could get Justine to the top. Many parents pay for additional tutoring, while this had come free.

Could Harriet have been having an affair with Justine, as Margaret suspected? It was a close relationship, with Harriet the dominant, controlling figure, but Steph found little evidence of a more intimate partnership. Justine must have been flattered to have a woman who was a tutor and twelve years older taking such an intimate interest in her life.

There was a crash as the corridor door was flung open and its handle smashed into the wall. Steph's head jerked up to see what the emergency was. A student dashed towards her.

'There's been an accident!' Grace, breathless and panting, threw herself at the reception desk. 'Please, we need help!'

'Where? Do we need an ambulance?'

'In the drama studio. No – I don't think so – no, I don't know – you'd better come and see!'

Steph called out to Jane to cover reception, grabbed the first aid kit from beneath her desk and ran off with Grace to the drama studio. Steph was the 'designated first aider' and she'd taken the training course in August to prepare for the role.

The drama studio was at the far end of the campus, beyond the music centre. They ran across Main Quad, through the foyer, then into the studio. It had no windows, there was retractable seating on four sides, and spotlights threw three pools of light onto the dull black floor. A scaffold tower stood beside a body to the left of the central pool of light.

Steph dashed towards the heap on the floor. 'You haven't moved him?'

She knelt beside the boy, who was lying on his side. It was Edmund. His eyes were open. He gave her a faint smile.

'I fell. I'm fine – I think. A little dizzy and my leg hurts. They told me to lie here until you came.'

The drama teacher, Sam Griffiths, hovered around Edmund like a buzzy fly. It was his first teaching post and he looked terrified. Whatever had happened here, he would be held responsible. Three girls, who had been standing over Edmund, stepped back to re-assure Sam. A group of tall male students, who looked more like rugby players than sensitive actors, hung around behind the scaffold tower.

'Did you lose consciousness?'

'No.'

'Do you feel any pain anywhere?'

'Not now. My knee's badly grazed – it's bleeding, you can see through that big rip in my trousers. No broken bones.'

'Let's make sure first, eh?'

Happy that Edmund was in one piece, she moved him so he could sit up and lean against the tower. Sam jumped forward and applied the brakes so it was secure.

'You're right, Edmund, it's just your knee. You've been lucky. We'll go to the medical room to get it cleaned up. You can walk all right?'

'I think so.'

Alone with Edmund in the medical room, Steph cleaned the wound on his knee, applied butterfly plasters, then taped a dressing over it. His knee poked through the enormous hole in his trousers. No way could he go back to his mother like that.

'Your knee will stiffen up later and I expect you'll have a massive bruise there. How did you do it?'

'We were acting. I was on top of the tower then, somehow, I fell off. It was an accident. They were a violent mob trying to de-throne a tyrant.'

'Yes, but you're supposed to pretend – that's what acting is. You're lucky you didn't do yourself some real damage. Now, if you like, I'll mend that tear in your trousers.' She handed him a pair of tracksuit bottoms. 'Put these on while I fetch the sewing kit.'

Steph frowned as she walked back to reception and reflected that Edmund appeared to be having a grim time. Kids could be so cruel. They'd decided that Edmund was different – not in their tribe – and he didn't help himself by dressing like their dads.

By the time she returned with the sewing box, Edmund

was sitting on the bed in his newly acquired tracksuit bottoms. They really didn't suit him!

'Right – now drink this. Give me your trousers and I'll sew up that hole.'

'Thank you so much.'

Steph sat on the red plastic chair beside the bed and started sewing. First aid was fine, but sewing was not one of her greatest skills.

'You've been having a tough time of it. First that photo, now this. You must wonder why you ever joined us.'

'I came because of Harriet Weston. She's an exceptional teacher. Whenever her students appear at competitions, they're always way ahead in style and technique. Her students have – I don't know – a sparkle the others don't.'

Edmund had recovered quickly, and the putty shade on his face was being replaced by a more human colour. He no longer looked as if he might faint.

'Do you find it difficult being here after being home schooled?'

'No. Not really. I've read more, so it's fine in lessons. They're better at using computers and smart phones. I'm no good at that; we don't have them. But that's about all.'

'Really?'

'Yes. I realise now that Mother was an excellent teacher. I'm not behind at all. In fact, in some things, I'm way ahead.'

'But didn't you miss spending time with children your own age?'

'I met them at music competitions. Actually,' he lowered his voice as if afraid of being overheard, 'I sometimes think they can be a little silly. They waste a lot of time when they could do something more constructive.'

Steph thought of the students she'd met. Bright, lively kids most of them, bursting with curiosity. They experimented with life as they should at that age, but most of them had fun and emerged unscathed.

'Really?'

'Yes, they spend hours playing computer games, sending each other prurient messages on their phones and watching videos of cats that look like Hitler. I'd rather be working for my next music exam or concert – so much more worthwhile.'

'I see.'

No wonder he was being bullied. He was so different and appeared to be proud to be so.

'Sometimes though, I think I'd like to go to a party, just to see what it's like.'

At last, a hint of rebellion, of wanting to have fun. The final stitch in place, Steph cut the thread and handed the trousers back to Edmund. 'Now, are you able to go back to lessons or shall I phone your mother and ask her to come and collect you?'

'No, please don't phone Mother. I'll go back to the music centre for my practice session. Thank you for helping me.'

With that he pulled down his tracksuit bottoms and stood in front of her in his boxers. Taken aback, she held up her hand. 'Hang on, Edmund! Just leave them on the bed. I'll pick them up later.'

How did that happen? It was as if she wasn't there. She plodded back to reception, suddenly feeling exhausted. Every time she had a conversation with Edmund, his intensity over-came her. He might be polite, confident and driven, but she wasn't convinced that home schooling was the right way to prepare a boy for the world, even for someone with his talent.

CHAPTER TWENTY-SEVEN

EDMUND

MOTHER WOULD SAY it was a 'curate's egg day' – good in parts. In Theatre Studies we were exploring political satire, corruption and power in the play *Ubu Roi*. I was Ubu as, apart from Grace, I was the only one to have read the whole play.

Sam (the drama teacher who's performed *Ubu* at the Edinburgh Festival) and I enjoyed a fantastically stimulating discussion about Ubu's greedy self-gratification. Grace and I made some good points. The others listened. They chose me to be Ubu, and I was pleased to get the main part. Really pleased. In most of the lessons, they've behaved as if I'm not there. The fact that they gave me this part showed me they thought I could do other things as well as my music. Even the music students have now forgotten Harriet's mistake putting me in the top spot at the concert.

The lighting tower is a high scaffold construction on wheels, used to angle the lights over the performance area, and it made a convincing palace balcony. We pushed it to the middle of the acting space, put the brakes on to fix the wheels, and I climbed up to the wooden platform at the top.

I felt so powerful – at the top of the world. It was easy to imagine how Ubu felt as he looked over his kingdom with his subjects below in the gutter. I stirred up the mob into a wild frenzy and really got into the part. The words rushed into my mouth. I declaimed my plan for ruling their world. They cheered, waved at me, acknowledged me as their leader. 'Ubu Roi! Ubu Roi!' they shouted in deference to their king.

Then Dave flipped the brakes and pushed the lighting tower slowly around the acting area. It was a great idea – a dictator's procession through the mob, his subjects. Without warning, the tower juddered as the other boys grabbed it. They ran madly around the acting area and pushed the scaffold faster and faster. I became dizzy. I gripped the rail at the top, but as they shoved it too fast around a corner, it wobbled, leaned over dangerously and threw me off.

They stared at me with shocked faces. They're much bigger than me. They have sculpted gym muscles and aren't very bright. I lay there. Still. I didn't move. I felt dizzy and thought I would pass out. I didn't. Sam was in a real panic. As the teacher, he'd be in real trouble if I'd been hurt. Luckily for him and the boys, I wasn't. I decided it was best not to make a fuss.

Steph mended me and my trousers. On the way home I smeared the sewn-up rip with mud. I told Mother I'd been playing football and fell over. She immediately went into panic mode – checked my hands for injuries, then told me not to play football, never, ever again.

I protect Mother from the truth. She's finding the change difficult. I'm no longer with her all day. She has her adult piano pupils, but they don't fill the gap I've left. I need to stop her coming to college to talk to Mr Bryant and Harriet so often –

almost every day. Mother worries I'm not accepted by the other students and they might bully me. I don't think they were bullying me – they just got carried away, they were playing their parts.

CHAPTER TWENTY-EIGHT

STEPH

DEREK BARKED at a wave sploshing on the pebbles. He pulled on the lead, desperate to splash around in the sea, chasing his ball. He looked up at Steph expectantly, his head on one side. She decided not to throw his ball for him until Caroline and Margaret arrived. Marlene, the perfectly behaved dog, would probably not approve of swimming, and if they were to go for an early supper at the Harbour Inn, she didn't want to risk having a soggy Derek under the table.

'What a glorious evening, my dear. You've met my partner, Margaret, haven't you?'

As ever, Caroline looked as if she was starring in a 1930s romantic film – this time as a female coastguard. She floated up the beach towards Steph and Derek in bright blue wellington boots, decorated with yellow daisies, and a long yellow shiny raincoat with sou'wester. Margaret was shorter, stouter – wearing jeans, walking boots and a navy Barbour. She looked more like the traditional dog walker found on Suffolk beaches.

Margaret moved forward and spoke loudly in what Steph considered a posh accent. 'Yes, we met at the concert. You were with the Principal, I recall. I've heard so much about you from Caroline. So instead of staying at home, like Martha cooking supper, I decided we'd be truants and eat out. So glad you could join us.' She giggled like a schoolgirl out for a jolly treat.

'I suggest we go this way, along the dunes rather than the beach, so that Derek doesn't get tempted into the sea. We can always come back by the beach if he insists on a swim, don't you agree?' Caroline stalked off, back up the beach, then turned left onto the dunes.

Derek looked up mournfully at Steph. How could she explain that he could crash through the foamy waves later? She unhooked his lead and catapulted his ball down the green scrubland that stretched between the dunes and the road. He dashed off after the ball while Marlene, off the lead, trotted elegantly alongside Caroline.

Steph's mobile rang. She pulled it out of her pocket to see the display show 'unknown'. Carter again. Caroline stopped, 'Do take it. We can wait.'

'Oh no, it's nothing.' Steph switched her phone off and pushed it deep into her pocket, pretending all was fine. She turned away from the sea, her back to the wind and Caroline, to adjust her zip while concentrating on a gull pecking at a gobbet of grey fish, waiting for the knot in her stomach to loosen. A deep breath in and she was able to turn and nod to Caroline; they continued walking.

They passed some beach houses on the right-hand side, small weather-boarded bungalows built beside the road, with enclosed gardens that opened onto the green.

'What a superb view they have,' said Steph, struggling to keep her voice steady.

'I'm sure they must flood in the winter. A short-sighted

purchase if ever there was one,' grunted Margaret, trying to keep pace with Caroline.

'Good heavens, Steph, déjà vu! Just look at that – spooky, don't you agree? He's even playing the same tune we heard the other evening. Same tune – different woman!' Caroline pointed to the last of the beach houses in the line, which was a weather-boarded house with a large glass sunroom, facing the beach. Through the window they could see Edmund playing his cello, with Harriet standing behind him. She leaned in and put her arms around him. Even from a distance it looked like an embrace, as she held his bow with her right hand while her left covered his fingers on the stave. They appeared to be one cellist with two heads.

'That's most unprofessional. No, it's disgusting. Look what she's doing now!' Margaret moved closer to get a better look. Harriet took off her over-blouse, threw it on the chair behind her, then returned to her position behind Edmund wearing a flimsy chemise.

'She's probably hot. All they're doing is practising.' Caroline put Marlene on her lead as they were getting close to the harbour car park.

'Music teachers see pupils all the time in their houses, don't they?' asked Steph.

Margaret started searching for something in the deep pockets of her jacket. 'Yes, of course they do, but they don't push their breasts into their pupils' backs or wear so few clothes. Looks like she's seducing him. She'll be dragging him off to bed next.'

Margaret continued to dig into her pockets until she found her phone.

'What on earth are you doing? You can't just take photographs like that.' Caroline tried to grab Margaret's phone, but she resisted, stepped sideways and continued pressing the button.

'I think these photographs might interest the Principal, and I'm sure that boy's mother should see them. Even if she knows he comes here for lessons, she'd be disgusted at that level of intimacy.'

'Margaret, stop interfering. Harriet's already threatened to tell Peter Bryant you can't cope with teaching with your condition.'

Margaret pushed Caroline to the side so she could get a different angle for her photo. 'But she's abusing that lad – it's immoral and illegal. She's using her powerful position to groom him. She'll bring the college into disrepute. If this gets out, we'll be on the front page of the *Daily Mail*!'

'Stop exaggerating! He looks fine. Harriet Weston can never please you whatever she does, can she?'

'I can see the headline now – *Every Good Boy Deserves Favour – and look how he got it!*'

'Too long, and most normal people wouldn't understand your musical in-joke. Do you, Steph?'

'Yes, it's the mnemonic for teaching children the right-hand notes on piano music. The notes on the lines are EGBDF.' She threw the ball for Derek and walked ahead, pleased with herself that she hadn't appeared a total moron.

Margaret put her phone away and the tussle between her and Caroline ceased. They enjoyed their walk to the Harbour Inn for fish and chips by the river. Derek's patience was rewarded at last and he ran in and out of the crashing waves, chasing his ball most of the way back to the car. Harriet didn't feature again until they were about to leave, when Margaret moved towards Steph and said, 'I've really enjoyed our walk and supper. Thank you. Now don't forget what we saw. I may need you to be a witness later when I tell Edmund's mother and the Principal about that sexual assault.'

'For heaven's sake, stop it! She won't say anything. It's been lovely to see you and Derek – Ciao!' Caroline put her arm on Margaret's shoulder and guided her to the car. Steph could hear them bickering as they changed their shoes and stowed Marlene in the car boot. She was convinced that Margaret would carry out her threat. More trouble for Edmund, then.

CHAPTER TWENTY-NINE

STEPH

THE DOORBELL RANG. Steph shoved her walking socks under a sofa cushion on her way to open the front door. She checked through the peephole. Hale was early.

'Good to see you. All right if I plug this in over there? We can sit at that table, look at some excerpts and catch up.'

'Over there's fine. Drink?'

'Water, please. How was your day?' Hale settled himself at the table and booted up his computer.

'Mad! Didn't think I'd play so many roles. Today it was counsellor, nurse, seamstress, catering service. I went through Justine's emails on her college and home accounts and discovered a collection of messages to her from Harriet. They're in the blue file on the table.'

Hale looked at her, puzzled. The table was bare.

'Where did I put it?' She looked around to see where she'd dumped it when she'd rushed in from college. 'There it is.' She picked up a blue file from her desk and pulled out a pile of printouts.

The landline phone rang. Steph was going to ignore it but

Hale stared at it. She grabbed at the receiver. 'Hello.' She kept her voice as neutral as possible.

The silence buzzed in her ear, then a whispered, 'I see you have company. Don't worry, I'll call another time.' She replaced the receiver; she could almost smell his rank breath down the phone. 'Wrong number,' she said before Hale could comment. She placed the printouts on her desk and re-ordered the pages as if looking for a particular email. She couldn't face Hale until she felt calm again and she was no longer gasping for breath. He noticed everything. At last she could speak.

'Harriet appears to have run Justine's life for at least a year, and this last email is vicious, so vitriolic.' She handed him the email on the top of the pile, then put the rest in front of him. 'I've printed off a sample for you to get the feel of them, and that email dated last Saturday is the one that really upset her, according to Jake.'

'Jake's becoming an excellent source of information.' Hale was a man who could talk and read print-offs at the same time.

She picked up the glasses, abandoned in the search for the folder, and carried the water over to him. Now with the melted ice cubes it didn't seem so glamorous – glamorous? What on earth was glamorous about water?

'Thanks. You're right, those emails are full on – that last one is dreadful. I bet your Peter wouldn't approve. Has he seen them?'

'He's not *my* Peter and no, he hasn't seen them yet. I thought you should first.'

'I think we'll hang onto them for a while longer before we let him see them – OK?'

'Yes, but he knows I've been going through the college email accounts. He gave me the passwords.' She felt uncomfortable, as she'd suspected she might. She wasn't sure how she could be loyal to both men at the same time and wondered what she would say if Peter asked her about the emails. She'd better prepare a vague comment until Hale gave the go ahead to show him.

'If he sees them now, he might react – reprimand Harriet for unprofessional behaviour, then she might get rid of other evidence. No, while she's a suspect, we stay quiet. You OK with that?'

'Absolutely.' She sat down beside him to look at the recorded interviews. Leaning towards him to look at the screen, she breathed in. He smelt good – some cologne she couldn't identify. She breathed in again – stimulating but restrained – very expensive – sexy. She pulled herself away – a little too close.

'As agreed, I saw Margaret, Harriet and Stoppard. I have downloaded some of the more interesting excerpts for you.'

They watched the first interview. Margaret confirmed all that she'd told Steph about finding Justine's body, but she didn't try out her lesbian-grooming-blackmail theory on Hale. Nothing there then. She looked older on the screen and her hands shook constantly, despite her attempts at holding them still.

Harriet in her interview appeared calm, but she picked at the skin on the right side of her thumb with her forefinger and kept crossing and re-crossing her legs. She also looked rather flirty with Hale. Perhaps Caroline was right about her reputation.

'Stop! Could you re-play that part again?' Steph pointed at the screen.

'Sure,' said Hale, zooming the pictures backwards. 'Here?'

'Yes, that bit about Justine.'

Hale: Did you notice anything unusual about Justine last Friday at the concert?
Harriet: No, she was on great form – played 'Schindler's List' beautifully.

Steph noticed that Harriet pulled herself up in her chair and blinked, then her eyes moved up to the left. She couldn't recall if people look to the left or the right when they lie. She thought it must be the right for remembering and left for lying. She'd look it up after Hale had gone. No doubt Harriet was lying here.

Hale: Wasn't there an argument about when she played her piece in the concert programme?
Harriet: Oh that... that was nothing. (Her eyes turned to the left again.) *I explained that Edmund, a new student, was a little nervous and it would be helpful if Justine went first to give him confidence – to show him how we do things at the college. She agreed that he should go after her. She said it didn't matter to her one little bit.* (Harriet took a sip out of the plastic beaker of water beside her on the table. She turned away a little from the camera fixed in a bubble in the top right corner of the room.)
Hale: So, you didn't have a row with Justine about her not getting top billing?
Harriet: No doubt Miss Durrant has been bending your ear, Chief Inspector. Oh yes, Margaret and I had words – she is a very difficult, embittered old lady. She was interfering with a judgement call that I'd made in my role as Director of Music. Justine was happy, so why wasn't Margaret? She's never been, shall we say, comfortable with me taking over from her. Margaret's got a terminal illness, you know. Why the Principal keeps her on is beyond me. No, Justine was fine about it.

*Hale: Did you contact Justine over the weekend about the
students disrupting the concert?*

Harriet: No. (Again she glanced to her left.) *Some of her
childish friends made a little noise – a slight disturbance at the
end. Justine felt embarrassed and left very quickly with her
parents. I was planning to see her on Monday morning then—*
(A long pause, she opened her handbag, took out a tissue and
dabbed at her eyes, again turning away from the camera lens.)
Will you excuse me? It really has been quite a shock. (She
sniffed delicately.) *Justine was my star pupil. I had such high
hopes for her and* (She paused.) *now...* (She sniffed, paused,
blotted her eyes again before looking across at Hale.) *now... you
must have some idea of how upset I am by her death. Do we
have to go on much longer, Chief Inspector? I've nothing more
to add and I'm finding this all... rather... distressing.*

'That's it. What do you think?' asked Hale.

'We both know she's lying, and that Oscar-winning performance was out of Disney. Did she really expect you to believe
all that melodramatic distress?'

'It would appear so. She thinks the only witness to her row
with Justine was Margaret and not you.'

'I only do her photocopying – I don't exist! And I notice
she didn't mention the scene after the concert where Peter and
I saw her bullying Justine. Harriet was vicious. Peter dealt with
it so well.'

'Masterful, was he?'

'Stop it! What about Stoppard?'

'You're welcome to watch it, but there's nothing there. He
confirmed that they spent the weekend together at her Southwold Beach House, then he left late on Sunday evening and
drove back to Oakwood, alone.'

'Oh, the Southwold Beach house? I came across that earlier. A rather beautiful bolt hole. I saw Harriet coaching Edmund there. Margaret kept saying Harriet was abusing or seducing him. Actually, I think at one point she called it grooming.'

'And was she?'

'It looked a little hands on, but then, Margaret's out to get Harriet whenever she can. They were close, but I don't think it was abuse. A little unwise with a well-endowed seventeen-year-old boy, perhaps?'

'Well-endowed? How would you know that?'

'You wouldn't believe it if I told you. Trust me, he may a prodigy, but he's a normal boy all right! Going back to Stoppard. Do you think Stoppard could be lying to protect Harriet?'

'He could,' said Hale.

'And Harriet or Stoppard could have come into college early to meet Justine to silence her, if she was posing some kind of threat.' Steph held out the empty glass to Hale, offering a re-fill. He shook his head and unplugged his computer.

'You're right. Harriet hasn't got an alibi for the early morning. Come to that, neither has Stoppard. Joyce is looking at the ANPR footage between Southwold and Oakwood and the college CCTV to check. Have you got anywhere with Justine's diary?'

'I had a quick look, but not in detail. I'll spend longer on it tomorrow.'

'And our techies should have pulled off all her texts and WhatsApp messages from her phone by tomorrow evening when we'll meet again. OK?'

'Absolutely. See you tomorrow.'

CHAPTER THIRTY

STEPH

'Please Miss, do you have a hole punch I can borrow? My course work's due in and I lost my one at home.' The voice belonged to one of the gang of lads who spent much of the day in the smoking area. At least he'd also done some work. He grinned and took the hole punch with *RECEPTION* stuck across it under Sellotape. He continued to beam at her.

'Isn't that the right size?'

'It's perfect but... I'm not much good at presentation and it matters. I can never get the holes in the same place – any chance you could help me, please?' He smiled at her, looking lost, pathetic, like a three-year-old wanting attention.

'Give it here and show me what you need to put in the folder. It's in the right order, isn't it?'

As he handed over the red folder, a pile of typed sheets fanned across the desk. They both grabbed air as all the pages slid onto the floor. Crawling around together, she learned that his name was Theo, that he loved Media Studies and that he supported Norwich City. He was a charmer and would go far.

They'd almost collected the full set when a pair of black

patent court shoes and tan tights appeared at eye level. The legs belonged to Mrs Fitzgerald. She frowned down at Steph.

'Good morning, Mrs Fitzgerald. As you can see, we have a minor incident here.' Steph handed her pile of papers to the boy kneeling beside her. 'Theo, why don't you go over there to get them sorted out on that table? Then I'll help you put them in the folder.' She grasped the edge of the reception desk and hauled herself up from the floor.

'Sorry to bother you when you are so busy. I've come in to see Margaret Durrant.'

'Is she expecting you?'

'She phoned me earlier and suggested I come in at break to meet her in the music centre. It is about break time now, isn't it?'

Margaret must have carried out her threat to reveal her suspicions that Harriet was grooming Edmund. Steph stepped behind the desk and pushed the visitors' book towards Mrs Fitzgerald. 'Please sign in and I'll take you over.' As Mrs Fitzgerald bent closer to sign the book, the nauseating smell of moth balls wafted over the desk. Steph took a step back.

She led Mrs Fitzgerald from reception, walked down the corridor and out of the old building into the sunshine. Steph took a deep breath in the fresh air, which diluted the moth-balls. She led the way as they weaved through groups of chattering students enjoying their break outside. Mrs Fitzgerald approached these lively young people as if they were about to attack her, and she grasped her bag in front of her, shielding her chest.

In her head, Steph tested several opening questions to find out why Mrs Fitzgerald was visiting Margaret before deciding on, 'Edmund seems to be doing really well in music. I didn't realize Miss Durrant taught him, too?'

'She doesn't – well, not the practical side and that's what matters. I think she teaches some theory. He's doing so well with Harriet Weston. She gives up her own time to coach him. She said he might get to the BBC Young Musician of the Year.'

'Really?'

'She's an excellent teacher. When I picked him up the other evening after a coaching session in Southwold, she said he stands a chance of winning it.'

How easy it was in the police force. Just flash the badge and 'open-sesame', they gave answers to her questions. Many of them were lies, but at least she could ask straightforward, full frontal questions instead of this pussyfooting around. She tried again. 'How kind of her to give up her own time. Is Miss Durrant planning to give him extra coaching too?'

'No, I don't think so.'

Steph saw Margaret approaching. 'Ah! Here she is.'

'Thank you for bringing me over, and also thank you for mending Edmund's trousers. Silly boy – he knows he shouldn't play football in case he injures his hands.'

So that was what he'd told her about his fall. Margaret picked her way towards them with care. 'Thank you, Steph. I'll bring Mrs Fitzgerald over to sign out when we've finished.'

If Edmund's mother already knew about his visits to Harriet's beach house then what was Margaret up to? She watched the two women walk into the music centre making polite conversation and noticed that Margaret's limp had become more pronounced.

When Steph arrived back in reception she found Theo still sorting the sheets of paper into piles. She sat down beside him and started punching holes. It took about fifteen minutes to organise his folder. There were occasional interruptions – several phone calls requesting prospectuses and the date of the open evening. Steph checked the caller ID before answering. She had decided to ignore those identified as 'unknown'. No need to worry; Carter must be busy too this morning. Grace, owner of the sparkly phone, arrived and enquired if Peter had finished with it yet – she said it was only her reserve, but she'd like it back.

Just as Steph and Theo were finishing, Mrs Fitzgerald swept into reception looking rather flushed. After she'd signed out, she looked at Steph. 'You were right. Miss Durrant has offered to give Edmund some additional lessons to make sure that his theory is up to scratch.' She replaced the pen then marched out, her handbag held at waist height once again.

For the first time since Steph had met her, it appeared that Mrs Fitzgerald had found something good to say about the college, but it was a shame she couldn't smile and be pleasant about it. Theo went away with a grin on his face, grasping a perfectly organised folder, and Steph returned to her desk to have another look at Justine's diary.

It was so different from her own teenage diary, which was full of angst and rants. Justine got on well with her parents and she described days out with them, holidays in National Trust cottages and gîtes in France. Jake often went with them and enjoyed spending time with her parents, according to the anecdotes Justine recorded. Her family sounded fun.

Page after page in her diary recorded happy family times and her solid, loving relationship with Jake. He came across as a nice lad, and Steph felt she had been right in letting him off. A few scattered entries were closer to those expected of a normal teenager – worries about her lack of 'likes' on social media, her unflattering photos, her clothes, her angst about having red hair and being called a 'ginge'. The diary sharpened the tragedy that this girl, who had so much going for her in her life, could have been taken out of it so soon. There was no evidence in the entries that Justine was a likely candidate for suicide. From her diary, apart from the wrinkle over the concert programming, Justine appeared to be happy and hard-working, and was looking forward to a bright future.

The phone rang, cutting through Steph's thoughts, and as she answered it, she thrust the diary in her bag under the desk. 'There's been an accident over here!' cried Harriet in panic. 'I've phoned for an ambulance. Please tell the Principal to come over at once!'

CHAPTER THIRTY-ONE

STEPH

THE AMBULANCE THREW blue pulsing light on the concrete walls of the music centre. It pulled round to the back doors of the recital room, hidden from the students leaving their lessons for lunch and attracted by the possibility of a drama. In Peter's absence his deputy, Paul Field, had summoned the senior tutors to keep the students away from the music centre. As he bossed people around, his voice rose a panicky octave. It was obvious why he was only Deputy Principal. Steph missed Peter's calm control.

Surrounded by a cluster of music students, Margaret lay in a heap at the bottom of the stairs. She didn't move. She lay on her stomach, her head turned to one side, her left arm stretched out as if she'd tried to cushion her fall. Her legs were splayed up the first few stairs at an awkward angle. The paramedics eased her off the stairs onto her side and, after removing a hoodie placed over her by a thoughtful student, pulled her skirt down below her knees. She was breathing, but unconscious. The paramedics took her pulse, checked for broken bones, put her in a neck brace, then strapped her onto a stretcher, taking care to avoid exacerbating any injuries they couldn't see.

An agitated Harriet paced around them as they worked. She darted over to Steph and the Deputy Principal. 'I came out of my lesson before lunch to see her on the floor – there – at the bottom of those stairs. She must have lost her step. She was breathing, I'm sure, but she hasn't opened her eyes. Is she badly hurt?'

'Calm down, Mrs Weston.' Paul Field looked up from the activity around Margaret and noticed the stunned students for the first time, then erupted. His squeaking voice created panic in what had been a calm foyer. 'Now students,' he clapped his hands loudly, 'off you go! Go back into the music room! Off you go! Stay there. I'll tell you when to leave. We need space here!' He flapped his arms like a panicky goose while he herded them back into the music room and shut the door. The paramedics exchanged glances at this sudden and unwelcome disturbance. At that moment, the main door crashed open and Caroline dashed in.

'Margaret! What's happened? Is she badly hurt? Oh my God – look at her! Is she alive?' Caroline threw herself against the stretcher, now on a trolley. Steph took her arm and steered her away so the paramedics could wheel Margaret into the ambulance. 'You can go with her to the hospital.'

'Thank you, Mrs Grant. I'm in charge here. I think I can manage very well, thank you.' Paul Field dismissed Steph with another flap of his hands, stepped in front of her and turned to Caroline. 'We don't know what happened here. We'll find out, don't you worry. You go to the hospital and I'll get cover for your lessons. Don't you worry.'

He helped Caroline up the steps into the ambulance.

'Now, let us know as soon as there is any news? I'll cover your classes, so don't worry about them. Your place is with Miss Durrant. Don't give college another thought. Your students will be—' The tall paramedic cut him off by closing the door. 'Right, you can go now.' The Deputy Principal took a step back and slapped the side of the ambulance as he gave it permission to leave. The paramedic climbed into the cab and the ambulance drove off, blue light flashing.

Paul Field scurried back into the music centre and opened the classroom door. He squeaked over the student chatter. 'Now, if any of you—' He stopped as he realised they hadn't noticed him. He clapped his hands. The students listened. 'Now if any of you, anyone at all, has any information, or knows what happened here, please stay behind. Otherwise, I suggest you go to lunch. Off you go! Go to lunch!'

The students, who were in Year 13 and had all performed in the concert, must have known Margaret well. They trooped out of the classroom, heads down. One girl, who had been crying, stopped in front of the Deputy Principal. 'Do you think Miss Durrant will die?'

'There's no need for all this hysteria. The doctors will look after her. Now run along to lunch.' The classroom was empty. It appeared no one had any information for him.

Harriet moved towards Steph, desperate to talk about what had happened. 'I've no idea how long Margaret was there. She wasn't there when I came in for period three. She must've slipped. It's dreadful – I hope she's OK.'

Once again Paul Field barged in front of Steph, this time to talk to Harriet. 'We must go over to my office at once. Immediately. We need to get your statement recorded formally in the accident book ASAP. No time to waste. We cannot afford to have any health and safety issues in this college. We did a thorough risk assessment when Miss Durrant moved up to that office. This is most unfortunate. Come along.' They left the music centre and headed towards the old building.

The foyer was empty. Steph looked at the spot where Margaret had been found. No blood on the grey cord carpet, no sign that anything had happened there. She climbed the stairs and checked each tread for marks. Nothing. At the top of the stairs again, nothing. She walked along the corridor to Margaret's office.

It was surprising that a woman suffering from Parkinson's should have a first-floor office. Harriet must have taken the larger room on the ground floor when she became Director of Music. Margaret's base resembled a large walk-in cupboard, with just enough space for a desk, a filing cabinet and three chairs – one behind the desk, the other two in front. Record company posters hung on the walls showing classical performers – Katherine Jenkins, Yo-Yo Ma and Nicola Benedetti. A tray with coffee-making kit and mugs sat on the top of the filing cabinet. Two of the mugs were dirty with the dregs still warm.

Steph explored to see if there was a kitchen or loo on this floor so Margaret could fill the kettle without going up and down stairs and found there was a galley kitchen next door to her office. She had created her mini empire a floor away from Harriet.

Unable to find any evidence of a struggle or a fall while carrying a tray, Steph grasped the well-designed handrail as she descended the stairs, which were low rise with wide treads. There were no apparent trip hazards here. She opened the main door to go back to reception.

Edmund appeared from the first practice room on her right and joined her as she returned to the old building. 'I'm so sorry about Miss Durrant's accident.'

'Yes. It's dreadful, isn't it?'

'She must have slipped on those stairs because of her illness.'

'Really?'

'The Year 13 students, who had her last year, have been saying her Parkinson's is getting worse. Will she be all right, do you think?'

'We'll know when the doctors have examined her.'

'The orthopaedic department there has an excellent reputation, you know.'

Once again, the maturity of this lad shook her. 'How do you know that?'

'I had RSI – repetitive strain injury – when I was younger, from overdoing my practice. They sorted it out.'

'Is that what you were doing in the music centre – practice?'

'Whenever I have free time I go there to work on my repertoire. I've a concert on Saturday at the Snape Maltings.'

'That sounds impressive.'

'I'm a member of the Aldeburgh Young Musicians there.'

'Wow! That sounds important. I used to go to lots of concerts there with my husband.'

He glanced across at her. 'Perhaps you'd like a ticket for mine? I can get you two comps if you like.'

'That's very kind of you. Yes, I'd love that, Edmund. Thank you.'

They reached reception, and Steph moved behind her desk. She straightened the visitors' book. Edmund watched her, then he looked down at the entries. 'Oh, I see Mother's been in again. I think she finds it difficult now I'm not at home all day. Anyway – back to work. I'll drop the tickets in for you later.'

So, she had somewhere to go on Saturday. Could it become a date? Who would she ask to join her?

CHAPTER THIRTY-TWO

EDMUND

TODAY THERE WAS the most awful accident. Margaret fell downstairs and went to hospital. She's in a coma and the other students said if she ever woke, she'd be a vegetable. That sounds grim. It really has been a depressing day.

Rowe says to make the characters live in your memoirs you should include 'subtle details about them, not a slab of Dickensian description'. I will start with the 'slab' and scatter it through my writing later.

Margaret Durrant is an excellent theory teacher and knows so much about music. She plays really complicated, long piano pieces from memory. She is older than Mother and looks like a rosy-cheeked granny in a children's book who would bake lots of cakes. She is not well and each time I see her she appears frailer and frailer. Her hands shake – she holds them. Her foot taps – she holds her leg still. Her voice wobbles – she clears her throat. She is an excellent teacher. Her illness will soon get in the way of her playing the piano. Now she may never play the piano again. It is so sad. She may live, but her musical life will die.

She lives with Caroline, Head of Art. They look unusual together. Caroline is tall and wears colourful, dramatic clothes. She looks like a walking painting or the 1920s people in my encyclopaedia. Margaret is shorter, rather large (not fat) with short grey hair and in sensible older clothes that I imagine Mother will wear soon. Tweed skirts and cardigans and flat shoes. I suppose she needs the flat shoes to help her keep her balance.

Yesterday, the day before she fell, she phoned home. She asked for Mother. I heard Mother on the phone – her voice was whispery and she shut the hall door. Through the door I heard her say she would come into college. I felt sick. Another visit to college. How many more? How can I stop her?

When she came back from the hall, I asked Mother what Miss Durrant wanted. Mother said she wanted to talk about my theory work. She was lying. There is nothing wrong with my theory. I always get full marks – 100%. Why does she have to visit college so often? It's my place. Why does she have to interfere? I want her to stop.

Mother came into college today, a little while before Margaret fell down the stairs. I was in the practice room and I saw her cross Main Quad with Steph at the start of break. Margaret was limping a lot as she went out to meet Mother. Such a shame.

When I got home, Mother told me that Margaret would give me extra theory lessons, which was so kind of her, and it was such a pity she had fallen. But afterwards, when I thought about it, she'd said it in a strange way. It made me wonder if she's telling me the truth.

Now Margaret lies in a hospital bed – sleeping. No one can wake her. I imagine Caroline sitting beside her playing her favourite pieces – Schubert and Chopin – trying to wake her with music. She's in a deep coma. I wonder if she would like her students to play for her?

CHAPTER THIRTY-THREE

STEPH

'You're now convinced it's murder?' asked Steph.

'Absolutely sure. A massive dose of drugs sedated her. There were no hesitation marks on her wrists, just clean slits. They found her fingerprints on the knife handle but in the wrong place. Clever set up, but not clever enough. She's good, that pathologist. Not much gets past her.'

Hale, who was driving Steph's car, turned onto the A12 on their way to Snape Maltings for Edmund's concert. When she'd phoned to ask him, Hale had hesitated, said he was sorry and would have to phone back. Steph had spent most of that evening plucking up sufficient courage to make the call, and as she ended it, she immediately regretted making it. She felt surprised but thrilled when he rang back a few minutes later to apologise for the abrupt end to the call and explain that he had to swap his stint on the duty rota first. Having done that, he'd love to join her and thanked her for asking him.

Steph's research supported his comments. 'Justine's diary suggests that she was perfectly happy, in love with Jake and working hard for her future – not suicidal. Far from it.'

'And her mobile phone showed nothing. The usual stuff you'd expect, but nothing that hints of suicide.'

He concentrated on overtaking a tractor that refused to pull over, despite the slow procession it was leading. Steph's mobile rang. She looked at the screen and turned it off. Carter was not going to ruin her evening. She turned to watch the trees whizzing past though the passenger window, hoping her panic didn't show. Her clenched stomach relaxed and she faced forward.

'We could do with a lucky break. There's a lot going on in your music department. Did you say there's been an accident?'

'Yes, Margaret Durrant fell down the stairs. She's in a coma. Everyone's saying it was her Parkinson's that made her fall.'

'And was it?'

'No evidence otherwise – and yes, I looked.'

Hale glanced across at her. 'You'd better watch your step there.'

'Don't worry. I'm fine.'

'And I've interviewed your Jake—'

'He's not my Jake—'

Hale continued. 'Nothing there. He came across as devastated – a lad in shock. You got all there was to get out of him.'

Except the photo. Except the photo. Should she tell him? No. 'I don't think he's involved.'

'Then I met Mrs Fitzgerald and Edmund. What a weird couple they are! She wouldn't let him get a word in.' Hale stopped to let a shire horse pulling a dray, loaded with beer barrels to cross in front of them into a pub car park. 'Now where was I? The only surprise was that Mrs Fitzgerald didn't know he'd taken a bottle of her wine to Justine's house to say sorry. Horrified by that, she was. I bet they had words after. He took it from her wine rack.'

The trees on the A12 were just starting to turn from washed out, dusty green to the vibrant reds of autumn. Steph glanced at Hale and relished sitting beside a man once again. To chat and to share a companionable silence was awesome. Should she tell him about Carter to see if he could help? No, it might spoil the evening. He became aware of her looking, turned and grinned.

'Good idea of yours. I need a break. We're getting nowhere fast.' Hale turned off the A12 onto the Snape Road. 'Anyway, we're out to enjoy ourselves this evening. Where are we eating?'

'I booked a table at The Plough & Sail for six thirty. It's at the entrance to Snape Maltings. Easy to walk to the concert from there.'

'All these years in Suffolk and I've never been to a concert there. Sheila wasn't interested in music, but she appreciated the retail opportunity.'

'Really?'

'I got dragged once to that vast kitchen shop, full of things you didn't know you needed until you saw them. Then, of course, you had to buy them and that was before we found the boutique!'

Steph didn't want to get involved in criticising Hale's ex-wife. She'd always wondered what he saw in Sheila – apart from the obvious. They'd married far too young, and Steph always saw her as a trophy wife. Happy to pose, perfectly groomed in her cabinet. Sheila had never been happy, married to a police officer, and eventually left him for some wealthy businessman. Hale had been very different when he was with her. Quiet, unchallenging – a passive foil to her beauty. It wasn't a surprise when they split.

Hale seemed to be uncomfortable for a few miles, then he sighed and broke the silence. 'I wonder what your Mike would say if he could see us now?'

'He'd think it was a good plan that we were heading to The Plough first. He always enjoyed eating there before a concert. Here we are – just park over there on the left, by the river. Then we can beat the rush at the end.'

After two large glasses of Merlot and rare Red Poll fillet steaks and chips beside the log fire, they strolled past the old brick maltings to the Peter Pears Recital Room. They bumped into Mrs Fitzgerald.

'How lovely to see you. Edmund will be pleased that you came.'

'It was kind of him to give us tickets. Mrs Fitzgerald—'

'Do call me Imogen.'

'Imogen, this is a friend of mine, Philip Hale.'

'Oh, it's you! I didn't know you knew each other – what a surprise!'

'We used to work together in the Suffolk police,' said Steph.

'I didn't realise you were a police officer. Please excuse me – there's Harriet Weston.'

They watched as Imogen swept across the foyer to greet Harriet. The two women made such a contrast. About a decade separated them, but it looked like an era. Harriet, elegant in a designer navy trouser suit, and Imogen in her pleated skirt, brogues and cardigan – a study in beige. Hale and Steph moved back to join the crowd in the queue at the bar and observed the two women chatting at the door.

'She's out of the ark, isn't she? I think we should go in before Harriet notices us.' Hale took Steph's arm and steered her towards the recital room doors. It felt good being in such close contact with him. She leaned against him, and he pressed his fingers into her arm and grinned at her.

The performance area was on the floor just inside the doors. The audience sat above on raked seating, and their seats were near the back, which gave them an excellent view of the musicians. About eight rows in front of them, a man squeezed in front of Imogen to sit beside Harriet.

'Is that Mr W?' asked Hale.

'No – that's the Head of English, David Stoppard.'

As he sat down, David leaned across and kissed Harriet on her cheek. She then turned to face him and kissed him on the lips. As he settled, he put his arm around her shoulders.

'A bold move in public! Ever seen Mr Weston?'

'No. He's a rare sighting, according to Caroline. Too busy earning shed loads of money in London. He needs it to keep her in shoes.'

'Now, now! Must say I admire her brass neck for bringing him here.'

'Shameless – that's Caroline's view.'

'Ah – the all-knowing Caroline.'

'Shh! Here comes Edmund.'

The auditorium lights lowered. Edmund walked into the performance area and sat on the stool in the spotlight. Cello in hand, he looked older, confident, as if he owned that stage. As he had in the college concert, he had removed the spike and gripped his cello between his thighs. Once again, his fluid, confident movement conveyed the essence of the music. Steph had never seen the Bach Sonatas played so emotionally and with such physicality. He played as if he was composing the music himself.

A standing ovation rewarded him at the end of his recital. Edmund accepted the applause graciously and walked off stage. Steph and Hale remained in their seats until they saw Imogen and Harriet leave, engrossed in conversation, while David Stoppard trailed behind them.

It took some time for the predominantly elderly audience in the rows below them to totter down the stairs. It was sad there weren't more young people in the audience to hear this prodigious talent.

'Hope there's never a fire here,' said Hale, as they queued on the stairs.

'You're supposed to be off duty. Look, there's the fire escape.' She turned and pointed to the very back of the hall above the last row.

By the time they reached the foyer about five minutes later, they could see that something was going on. In a corner towards the exit, Imogen and Harriet were having what looked like a quiet row. With outstretched necks and sharp arm gestures they spoke in low voices as they tried not to attract attention, but from their body language it was obvious that they were having a fierce argument.

A space had opened up around them. The two women ignored the fascinated audience, who tried to pretend they weren't listening but clearly wanted to know what was going on. Steph and Hale moved under the stairs so they could hear the exchange without being seen. Suddenly the quiet voices became rather loud, and Steph could hear every word.

'No, I disagree! That rapid pace was not Bach's intention. You've destroyed Edmund's sensitive interpretation,' said Imogen.

'On the contrary. The audience thought his playing was magnificent. I've helped him move up to the next level.' Harriet stepped closer to Imogen, who stood her ground.

'What! How can you say that? This evening's performance was verging on a pop concert. You're turning Edmund into a – a performing seal.' Emphasising her final words, Imogen retaliated, moving towards Harriet.

'He's finding his own voice at last.'

'What does that mean?' Imogen's loud challenge attracted even more attention from an increasing audience.

'You've hot-housed his talent so well. But now he needs a professional to help him develop his own style.'

'That's you, is it?' Imogen spat back.

'You've done a great job, but you've taken him as far as you can.' Again, Harriet appeared to be calm and reasonable in contrast to the red faced, furious Imogen.

'We'll see about that! He's my son – I'll decide his future.'

'He needs space to grow up and find out who he is as a musician and a person.'

'You think you can take him over, don't you? Well, you can think again. Your meddling has already killed one of your students.'

'What?' Harriet stepped back as if she'd been hit.

'You caused her death and you will not hurt my Edmund.'

'How could you? How dare you?'

At that moment Edmund appeared beside them, flushed and adrenaline-fuelled after his performance.

'Mother! Harriet! What's going on?'

Before either of them could answer, David Stoppard put his arm around Harriet and nudged her towards the exit. He turned to Edmund.

'Well done, Edmund – a sterling performance. We must be

'going.' With that, David propelled Harriet outside. Through the glass doors, Steph watched Harriet gesticulating at David, presumably berating him for interfering.

Steph moved between Edmund and Imogen. The tension between them was electric. But Imogen, her face crimson, did her best to resume her polite persona. 'Thank you for coming. Edmund?'

Prompted to speak, Edmund turned to them. 'It was so kind of you to give up your evening.'

'It was my pleasure. I love those Bach Sonatas and you played them beautifully,' said Steph.

'Hear! Hear!' said Hale.

'Thank you.'

'Now, Edmund. You've got your coat? Good. We should get home. Good night.' With that, Imogen marched Edmund out of the double doors, towards the stream of headlights leaving the car park.

Hale edged towards the doors, following them with his eyes. 'She doesn't mince her words, does she?'

'Who? Harriet or Imogen?'

'Imogen – but come to think of it, I wouldn't like to take Harriet on either.' He held out Steph's coat.

Steph turned to face him. 'Imogen's comment about Harriet causing Justine's death. Was it a throwaway comment or do you think she knows something?'

'Whatever she meant, there's a hell of a lot of tension between them. Poor Edmund's stuck in the middle.'

She slipped her arms into the coat sleeves and he lifted it up around her shoulders. His hand lingered on her back as they walked towards the door. 'It'll be fascinating to see what happens next week in your music department after that little spat. That poor boy. He may well be a genius, but he's suffering for it. Look at the time! I fancy a drink!'

'Shall we try the pub again?'

'No, let's go back to yours.'

CHAPTER THIRTY-FOUR

EDMUND

I WAS BUZZING when I came off the Snape stage. Lots of people in the audience stood and held their hands in the air as they clapped. I was so surprised and excited. All my hard work was at last paying off. I love performing and I love the applause at the end.

Harriet had told me two of her contacts from the Royal College would be in the audience. She brought them to the dressing room before I played and they said I was lucky having Harriet as my teacher and they looked forward to meeting me later in the year at my audition. Then they left. I was so happy I felt I could erupt. Harriet hugged me. As I held her, my cheek touched her gold earring. I moved so I could touch her hair with my lips. I kissed her hair, but I don't think she noticed. As we moved apart, she said how proud she was of me, wished me luck and said she'd see me afterwards.

After the recital, when I got back to the green room, the older chap of the pair was there waiting for me. He said he was sorry they couldn't stay longer but their taxi was waiting and how thrilled he was to hear my original and creative interpretation and he'd send me an email via Harriet and very well done.

I got changed, packed up my cello and walked out to the foyer. I felt so excited by the way I'd played and the applause and the comments of the Royal College man. Several people standing around drinking and chatting or putting on their coats looked across as I walked past and said, 'Well done!' and 'Bravo!' or just smiled at me. I felt so important. Such a success. I felt it was possible that at last my dream could be real.

I couldn't see Harriet and Mother at first, then I saw them by the stairs. They weren't talking, they were shouting. Everyone was watching. They were so angry with each other but trying hard to appear they weren't. Just after I arrived, David Stoppard grabbed Harriet and took her away. Steph, who I'd invited, talked to me and Mother. I don't know if she saw the argument.

Mother was silent most of the way home from Snape. She ignored me. I said nothing. It's best to leave her when she's in one of her moods, so she doesn't get angrier. I kept checking the speedometer – she drove faster than the speed limit most of the way home. I watched for blue lights in my wing mirror.

On the drive home, I was so unhappy, really wretched. I thought she'd love the reaction of the audience – instead she behaved as if I'd played terribly. I tried to tell her about the Royal College people, but she told me to be quiet while she was driving. I wanted to share it with her so much, but she wouldn't listen.

I suspected she was angry Harriet had coached me in a different direction. I enjoyed playing the Bach in the new way. It wasn't the way Mother wanted me to play it. The Royal College man said it was original and creative, so Harriet must be right. Harriet is good. Mother is good too. She has got me to such a high level of technical skill, but Harriet is brilliant at creating an amazing performance. She must be part of my future. Surely Mother must see that?

As we turned into Oakwood, at last Mother spoke. 'I have decided you will leave college and get away from that woman's influence. We will return to our original plan. I will discuss it with the Principal on Monday morning.'

When she got out, she slammed the car door so hard that the window fell down into the gap, way down inside the door. She didn't notice. It's an old mini and things fall off it. Luckily, it wasn't raining.

She opened the house door, shoved me into the hall, pinched my arm hard and glared into my eyes. 'I mean it, Edmund. You will leave college. Do you understand?' She pushed me and my head hit the wall, hard. I wiped the spit off my face. She jerked my head against the wall, again and again. It hurt. It went on and on until I said I understood and agreed. Then she put her hands either side of my head, pulled me towards her and stroked my head where it hurt. She kissed it better and hugged me close to her. She smelt of sweat and moth balls, not perfume like Harriet.

In that moment I decided I would leave Mother. She would have to let me go. She couldn't own me for ever. Harriet was right, I'm finding my voice and I don't want Mother to shut me up.

CHAPTER THIRTY-FIVE

STEPH

STEPH WOKE to the sound of the shower. She moved across to the space that Hale had left and breathed in. His sharp cologne lingered on the pillow. It had been the first time since Mike died. She grinned. She felt so – so alive! It was a good thing that she'd lost that weight over the summer – she hadn't had to breathe in too much. In bed, Hale was as he was in life. Thoughtful, gentle and rather good. What a shame he'd left for a shower. Still, there would be other times, wouldn't there?

Wouldn't there? What if she was wrong? What if...? What if...? She caught her breath as the familiar feeling flooded over her. Not now. Go back. Get control. She closed her eyes and breathed in. Held her breath. Counted to seven. Then out to seven. After several cycles, she felt calm. Her panic subsided.

The door to the ensuite slid open. Hale stood in the doorway, one towel wrapped around him; with another he dried his hair and beamed at her. 'Is there anything you would like to do? I'm all yours – well until eleven, when I'm due at the station.'

'Wow! What an offer!'

Hale climbed on the bed, opened the covers and gently stroked her breast. Aroused, she reached for him, pulled him closer, thrilled at feeling his taut weight on her. She hadn't realised how much she'd missed this human, animal contact. Once again, they made love. Slowly, very slowly. Making love, not just sex. So tender. So right.

Over breakfast she sat opposite him, watching while he read the paper. It had been years since she'd enjoyed sitting far too long over coffee and toast. Just being together. Breakfast spread before them, listening to the news on the radio and commenting on the duplicity of politicians and the absurdity of what was going on in the world.

'What are you doing at eleven?'

'I got an email from DC Taylor, known as Tigger by the team. He's good news – the others could learn from him. He's been through the ANPR and seen that Mr Weston's car left Oakwood at about seven on the morning we found Justine's body. He told us he wasn't here and was away on business, so we've called him in.'

'So, he's lied?'

'Not only to us but to Harriet, it would seem. He set off from Salisbury Road, not his home. I wonder what he was doing there...'

'This town is rampant!' Steph got up to make more toast and, as she passed, draped her arms around him. His head sank back against her. He looked up, and she bent down and kissed the tip of his nose. He grasped her hands and held them close to him.

'Anyway, despite his apparent playing away he could still have something to do with it and he lied. We'll be seeing him later.'

Talking to his upside-down face, Steph said, 'I need to take Derek out for a walk before it rains. You can come if you like.'

Responding to the 'W' word, Derek sprinted across the room and sat up beside her, ears erect, hopeful eyes fixed on her.

'Good idea. Forget the toast. Come on, boy!' Hale stood up, pulled his coat off the back of a chair and patted Derek's head.

Derek leaped up, delighted to see his lead in Steph's hand. He sat blocking the door, so they had to take him out or walk through him. They pulled on their coats, left the house, locked up and headed towards the common.

Passing Edmund's house, they both sneaked a look up at the bay window. As expected, he was practising. His mother stood over him like a guardian angel. Or was it a guard? Hale raised his eyebrow and Steph nodded, relishing their unspoken communication.

As they neared the common, engrossed in criticising the latest government cuts on police funding, Derek forced them to halt. He crouched down in attack mode, and although they paused and looked around, they couldn't see what threatened him. A white fluffy dog bounced up; Derek stood up, helicopter-wagging his tail, and licked Marlene's nose in greeting.

'Strange, she never moves far from Caroline's heels and here she is by herself.' Steph picked her up, much to Derek's disgust, and looked around for her owner. Slowly Caroline walked around the corner towards them. Head down, exhausted, lost in her own thoughts. No floaty dress today, just a pair of jeans and a blue cable pullover, topped by a rather well-worn red jacket. Steph didn't know what was more shocking, Caroline's careworn appearance or her complete disregard for Marlene's whereabouts.

'Caroline! Are you all right? What a stupid question – of

course you're not.' Putting Marlene down, Steph rushed towards her and gave her a hug. 'How's Margaret – any news?'

'Still in a coma. They've given her drugs to keep her under and hope that when they stop them, she'll come back. I've been sitting by her most of the night but had to leave to take Marlene out.'

'You should have phoned. I'd have taken her out for you.'

Caroline noticed Hale for the first time and gave him a puzzled look. 'Aren't you the policeman who's investigating Justine's death?'

'This is Philip Hale, my old boss and a – a friend. He's in charge of the case.'

'You're the one who interrogated Margaret the other day. She said you were very thorough.'

Hale leaned across Steph and shook Caroline's hand. 'I'm so sorry to hear about your partner's accident.'

Caroline held onto Hale's hand and stared into his eyes. 'That's just it – I don't believe it was an accident. I think someone pushed her.'

'What makes you think that?'

'If you've got a few minutes, come with me and I'll show you why. I only live ten minutes away and there's something I want you to see.'

They walked beside Caroline back the way they had come, then turned left to a row of Victorian cottages close to the railway station. At first sight they resembled friends out for a Sunday morning stroll, but there was an urgency in Caroline's steps as she led them up to the house and opened the front door.

The house could have come off the cover of a magazine. The elegant window box contained tiny pink-leafed pelargoniums, and the antique brass knocker on the gleaming navy-blue door epitomised Caroline's artistic flair. Inside, a narrow black-and-white diamond tiled entrance hall led to a steep oak staircase.

'You see?' Caroline gestured to the stairs.

They looked up the stairs.

Caroline waved her arm towards the steps once again. 'When we moved in, that cheap hardboard was everywhere. All the original bannisters, newel post, handrail – all gone. It was disgusting. I shuddered every time I went near it, so we demolished it. The plan was to source a Victorian handrail with bannisters from an architectural junkyard and to restore it, but we've not found the right one.'

Hale and Steph looked up at the stairs while Caroline stared at them as if they were dim. 'Well, can't you see? Margaret can manage these open stairs with nothing to hold on to, and they are much steeper than those in the music centre. Why should she fall down there when she's perfectly safe here? She carries trays, bags – all sorts of things here and she's never slipped or lost her balance. Not once. They said she was carrying nothing when she fell at college, and they were shallower steps with a handrail. Yet she falls down. I'm convinced someone pushed her. Now she's in a coma and I might never speak to her again...' Caroline burst into tears.

Steph put her arm around Caroline's shoulders and hugged her. 'I know you're exhausted. Why don't we make you a hot drink? I bet you've had nothing to eat, have you?'

'No, thank you. I've got to get back to the hospital. But I'd be so grateful if you'd walk Marlene this evening. She must wonder what on earth is going on.' She grabbed a bunch of keys from a turquoise art pottery bowl on the oak table. 'Here, take the spare keys. Thank you so much. And thank you both for listening. Believe me, I know she didn't fall. Her Parkinson's isn't that bad and she has excellent balance.'

Hale reached out and held her hand. 'We'll look into it and I promise we'll keep an open mind.'

Caroline snatched her long red coat off a hook. 'Thank you. I know I'm right.' She opened the door to let them out, shut and double locked it, then dashed towards her car, jumped in and drove off, her tyres squealing.

'Well, that was a surprise! I saw nothing in the college, and I looked.'

'I'm sure you did, but Caroline has a point. You need to watch your step in that college. Something's going on there. But who would want to harm Margaret, and why?'

CHAPTER THIRTY-SIX

STEPH

THEY WATCHED as Derek sniffed the backside of a white poodle. Not attracted by its perfume, he ran off, snuffling under the gorse bushes.

'Is he always that crazy?' asked Hale.

'He's not crazy! That's normal for a dog. We're a little more subtle about it, that's all.' Steph surprised herself by the strength with which she defended Derek. She moved towards a bench on the edge of the clearing in a patch of sunlight. Hale followed. They sat basking in the sun, their eyes closed.

At last Steph spoke. 'This is what I find most difficult about being alone.'

'What? Ignoring someone?'

'No! Not being able to do this. Just sitting and enjoying being together and not having to talk.'

'It's good to be out of the office and to breathe. It's been mad.'

Derek bounced up to check they were still there and lick Steph's hand, then he smashed off again under some bushes on the other side of the clearing. Her phone pinged as a text arrived. Carter had started sending texts promising a visit, telling her it wouldn't be long now, that he was looking forward to seeing her. She sneaked a look at the message and shoved the time bomb in her pocket. She was exhausted by his phone stalking and wanted it to stop. As for what might happen at his next visit, she was petrified to think of it. Now or never!

Steph sneaked a sideways look at Hale. 'There's something I want – I need to talk to you about.'

'A moment ago you said you enjoyed sitting and not talking – that didn't last long, did it?'

'It's about Carter.'

Hale turned and stared at her. 'What is it between you two? I didn't think he was your type.'

'He isn't. It's that he's – well – he's blackmailing me.' Steph blurted it out. She exhaled slowly, relieved that she'd said it to someone at last.

'Carter? Blackmailing you? What have you done to be blackmailed about?' Once again Hale studied Steph's profile. She could feel his eyes on her but continued to stare ahead, finding it easier not to look at him but to talk to the trees at the far edge of the clearing.

'Derek – leave that poodle alone. Here! Bone!' She held out some treats. Derek inhaled them and scampered off, tracking smells once again.

'Come on. You can't make a pronouncement like that then stop. What have you done? What makes him think he can blackmail you?'

'You remember the county lines case in Ipswich on the Rayleigh Estate?'

'I think so.'

'One of those kids forced to become a runner was a sixteen-year-old called Sam Odawale. I'd come across him on a shop-lifting case and supported him when I was in the Youth Offending Team. Got to know him well and became a sort of mentor for him. He was a good kid when you got underneath all the usual crap. He had no one else. School had more or less given up on him. His mother had died from an overdose. No dad on the scene and he lived with his granddad, who was in a wheelchair and had dementia. That snake Rispoli moved into their house—'

'Oh him! Looked like a weasel – nasty piece of work. Enjoyed using a machete, didn't he?'

'That's him. Well, he planted a knife in Sam's bag and he got suspended from school and that was the end – he had no choice. Rispoli threatened to kill his grandad, who was away with the fairies. Anyway, Carter was the one who arrested Rispoli in a drugs' raid, traced him back to Sam's house. Rispoli claimed he was Sam's runner and it was Sam who was in charge of the deal line.'

'How did you get involved?'

'By sheer chance. They sent me to the house with Johnson to bring in Sam and any drugs I could find. I found the entire stash in Sam's bag. He told me what was going on, so I trans-ferred all the drugs to Rispoli's sports bag. I called Johnson into the bedroom to witness the huge stash I'd found in Rispoli's bag, then took Sam to the station with a tiny amount of it in his jeans pocket. They charged Rispoli and Sam got off as it wasn't worth charging him.'

'How did Carter find out what you'd done?'

'Rispoli was more of a rat than a weasel. He turned over the guys above him.'

'Yes, I remember. We impressed the Met by closing down a major line into Suffolk. I don't see...'

'Listen! In their heart to heart, Rispoli told Carter that no way would he be stupid enough to keep the stuff in his own bag.'

'So, he worked out you moved the drugs and saved Odawale?'

'He claims he has hard evidence. He now wants to use my flat to drop off drugs he's creamed off the top in raids. He said someone will collect them and leave cash in exchange. If I don't do it, he'll turn me in for perverting the course of justice, hiding evidence and – well, you name it. Farewell pension. Hello prison.'

Hale paused, fascinated by a crow nibbling at the remains of what could have been a rabbit carcass. 'He's right. You stepped over the line. Odawale may have been innocent, but it was not up to you to fabricate the evidence. Why did you do it?'

'It wasn't fair that Odawale should go down for being a vulnerable victim.'

'You've dealt with loads of vulnerable victims – why him?'

'Oh, it wasn't just him, was it? I came back to work too soon after Mike's death and thought everything was fine when it wasn't. I was all over the place.'

'I thought you coped so well.'

'I made sure it looked like I did. But I was numb, muddled and made so many mistakes. I wasn't thinking; part of me had gone with him. Work was bad enough, but going home was worse.'

They sat in silence, entranced by the vicious bobbing of the crow picking at the bones. Steph sighed, wiped her eyes with her sleeve.

'I didn't know what I was doing. I came back to work and pretended I was fine. I squashed it down. I didn't even cry that much. Then it all – everything was so exhausting.

Getting up, getting through the day, even getting to sleep was so hard.'

Hale put his hand over hers and gently squeezed it.

'Everyone was so kind, but you can't keep going on about it, can you? When I saw Odawale in a mess, which wasn't his fault, poor kid, I just did it. I thought – no, I didn't think – it was a way of doing something good, of lifting the grey for a moment.'

They sat still. Derek chased an oak leaf as it flittered around in the wind. He gave up and came to Steph. She stroked him behind his ears and he sat down beside her.

'I knew it was wrong, it was stupid, but it felt right. All those years of sticking to the rules, then I did that. It got worse after that. I was petrified you'd work it out or someone would call me in. The guilt on top of everything – well, one day I couldn't get out of bed and over a year later here we are. It's come back to bite me.'

This could be the end. The end of her work on the case. The end of her relationship with Hale. It had only just started and already it was over. No way would he want to spend his time with her now. She felt conflicted. Grubby and ashamed of what she'd done, but also proud. Sam was a victim who had a plumbing apprenticeship and the possibility of a life, a future.

Hale spoke first. 'Well, we are where we are. I can see why you did it, but I can't condone it. I sympathise with the poor kids who get dragged into these county lines. But what you did was wrong. Now, let me think of a way out of this mess. Leave it with me.'

'Really? Do you think you can do anything? I want it to stop. I feel I'm walking through a swamp.'

There was an electronic beep, and Hale pulled his phone out of his pocket to read a text. 'Must go. There's Taylor in the car. Must see Mr Harriet and find out why he's been telling us stories.'

Hale strode off, his hands in his pockets, head down, kicking at a few crunchy oak leaves as he went along the path. He hadn't kissed her or made any physical contact. No 'see you later' or 'I'll phone'. That was that, then. She had no choice. She had to tell him. She'd crossed the line all right.

Derek sat to her right, at the end of the bench, head on one side, looking up at her as if he sensed her misery, or was that a ridiculous idea? Rage flooded over her. All her life she'd been independent and solved her own problems; now she felt like a pathetic damsel in distress. She should have been able to stand up to Carter and sort it out herself. Angry, she grabbed her phone out of her pocket, pressed the text message app then typed: *Piss off Carter. Tell whoever you like. I'm not going to help you.* Before she could change her mind, she pushed the 'send' button. Action taken, she felt freed at last. She'd tell Hale later what she'd done, thank him for listening, but assure him she'd got rid of Carter herself. Why had it taken her so long to act? Simple, wasn't it? If only she'd done it before confessing it all.

The sun had disappeared. She pulled her duvet coat around her to combat the wind, stood up and walked. Derek, tail between his legs, followed, looking puzzled.

'Come on, boy. Let's go home.'

CHAPTER THIRTY-SEVEN

EDMUND

Rowe says that memoirs are more vivid, more authentic if you write as if the reader is there – right beside you at an important event. So, come with me to a beach party. At last – invited to a party! It was about one hundred metres from Harriet's house, but the others didn't know that. I could see it above the dunes. The lights were on and I knew she was there. If only I could have taken her to the party.

We were close to the opening of the harbour where the sea smashes up the narrow gulley, then crashes out again. The tides there are vicious. If dogs fall in, they get swept out to sea. Thirty-eight fell in last year, but most got saved by the lifeboat.

Mother was angry, again. She shouted at me and told me not to go. She said I could do without the distraction. That I would get drunk or drugged or drowned. Perhaps all three. She was annoyed they'd invited me. I told her it meant they accepted me and I had to go to see what it was like.

It was Grace's eighteenth birthday party. Actually, it felt like my party too, as I was eighteen the day before but Mother would never dream of letting me have a party. I walked on the sandy path to the flat bit in the shelter of the dunes, before the pebbles slide down to the sea. The fading light made the flames from the barbecue sparkle bright red. I was so excited – my first party. Mother had reluctantly agreed that a white shirt with my trousers was appropriate. If only I could have some jeans. I carried my anorak, in case it became cold when it got dark.

I slid down the steep sand bank and onto the pebbles without falling over. I was worried in case I did and they saw me. I crunched across the pebbles towards the group of about twenty. My whole music set stood around in a circle, drinking and laughing together. Would they let me in? By the edge of the sea, I spotted the rugby boys from Theatre Studies. They jumped about by the foam, skimmed stones and shouted and tried to push each other in. Enormous children playing together. They looked drunk.

Grace smiled at me and waved, and I went over to her. She said she was pleased I'd come, then poked the fire, built in a square brick barbecue. The bricks had been stacked up, not cemented. An old, blackened metal grid sat above the glowing coals with burgers and sausages strung across the bars. Could this count as junk food? The fat fell, sizzled and made the flames jump up. Cool boxes, like families have when they picnic on the beach, spilled over with spikes of bottles of beer and white wine. This was my very first barbecue, but I didn't tell them that. It smelt like a bonfire.

A picnic table held slabs of raw meat, bags of bread rolls with white seeds on top, plastic cups, red wine and a mass of bottles and cans. As people arrived, they added to the collection. They brought a bottle of wine or four cans of beer held together in plastic rings. I didn't know to do that. Why didn't Grace tell me? I'd got her a birthday present and a card. The pale pink wrapping paper dotted with silver stars looked wrong on a beach beside the bottles. I bought her a perfume called 'Happy' as I thought the name suited her smile. Mother gave me the money. I gave Grace the present, and she looked surprised but very pleased.

She handed me a white corrugated plastic beaker and asked if I'd like beer or wine? I said wine. Red wine splashed over the top of the cup and plopped on my shoes. I tasted it. It was bitter, cold, sharp. Like vinegar. They were all drinking so I did too. I didn't like it much, but I drank and kept up with them. I stood outside the music group, which felt safer than being with the rugby lot. They were getting very noisy and didn't notice me. I gulped more wine and coughed as it went down the wrong way. I finished the wine and Grace poured me another. I drank that. Then another. It was warm by the flames. The sausages burst open and their insides spat fat and bits of meat and the burgers got black burnt edges.

I slithered my feet until I got inside the music circle. They stopped talking and looked at me. John, quite a good pianist, moved to let me in properly and said, 'Good to see you outside music lessons.'

Mike, the trombone player, looked across and said, 'Didn't Harriet want to come with you tonight?'

They all looked down into their drinks.

'No, of course not. This is Grace's birthday. None of the other tutors are here, are they?'

Mike, who never spoke in class, continued, 'Justine used to be Harriet's pet before you came.'

'What do you mean?'

Before he could answer, Dave, one of the rugby boys, smashed through our circle and snatched the large plastic bottles of tomato sauce and mustard off the table. He chased

John towards the sea, squirting at him. I stepped back out of the way towards Grace.

John screamed and jumped around to miss being hit, then Dave herded him towards the sea. He held the sauce bottle weapons and squirted the mustard and tomato sauce. John tripped and fell into the edge of a wave as it dashed in. Not deep water, but his shirt and trousers were soaking wet when he got up from the foam. He staggered and fell to his knees as his feet got pulled down by the moving stones beneath the water. He was angry, not calm like he is in class. John scrambled up between waves, rushed at Dave and headed him in the stomach. Dave fell back and crashed on the pebble shelf. John stamped on his legs and fell on top of him. They rolled around on the pebbles at the edge of the surf. Were they playing? Were they trying to hurt each other? I wasn't sure.

Grace saw the scuffle. She screamed. Jake pistolled down to them and pulled John off Dave, who couldn't be that good at rugby if he let John, a pianist, sit on him. They stopped. Jake pulled Dave up too. They stood, laughing and dripping. It must have been a joke all the time as no one seemed angry now.

They bounced up the beach to stand by the fire. Dave had his arm around John's shoulders, and they laughed as John called Dave a 'dickhead'. Steam rose off their wet shirts, and they looked as if they would burst into flames. They saw me staring. 'Fancy a swim?' Dave shouted at me. 'No, thank you.' I was worried they'd throw me in the sea. It was rough. I've heard there's a rip tide that pulls you out and I saw the tide had turned. The sand was soggy mud, left behind as the water ran back out to sea.

The boys wobbled and swayed a bit as they gulped beer straight from bottles. Foam ran down Dave's chin and splashed on his shirt in a dry patch not soaked by the sea. Jake flicked beer at him from his bottle. Dave ran backwards to escape, but his feet sank in the shingle and he fell on his back. He was drunk and needed help from two others to get up. He went to the edge of the dunes and sat on a pile of sand and stared at us.

At last the food was ready. I needed to take the vinegar taste away. I felt dizzy. I wasn't sure what I was eating. Something in a roll – a sausage or burger? It was black, crunchy, burnt. Is this what eating junk food is like? I tried to swallow as I didn't want to upset Grace.

Without warning, Jake rushed at me and rammed me in my stomach with his shoulder. My breath exploded through my mouth and I fell. Fell on my back with my right hand under me. Jake trapped me and sat on top of me and he slapped my head and face – it stung. I couldn't speak or cry out. The mouthful of bread roll grew in my spit. It filled my mouth. I couldn't get rid of it. I started choking. I coughed. Sick spurted out on the sand.

He screamed at me, 'You fucking killed her! You did! You killed Justine! You fucker! I'll kill you!'

The punches got heavier, stronger, and they really hurt. I swallowed at last. I tasted blood. My lip was bleeding, and my front tooth hurt. I managed to pull out my right hand and tried to push him off with it, but it wouldn't work. It felt numb – not fixed to my arm. Had he stamped my hand off?

I couldn't move. I couldn't get up. He wouldn't let me. The stones bit into my head and neck. Jake's punches got harder. My face throbbed. My lip hurt. I closed my eyes and sand scraped under my eyelids. His foot raked across my hand and I screamed. I felt his weight go. Somebody must have dragged him off me.

I pushed on the pebbles to get up. Electric pain zipped up

my arm. I fell back down. Jake jumped back and stamped on my hand shouting, 'You fucking killed Justine!' I tried to move my hand, but I couldn't feel it.

'Don't hurt his hand!' I could hear Mother shouting. No – it was Grace. She threw water over my hand. I screamed. It felt boiling hot on my hand. It was cold water. The pain was hot. Blood dripped from it with the water. I struggled to stand up. I felt faint but kept my balance on the moving stones. I held my injured hand to my chest and covered it with my other hand to look after it.

They all stared at me. At the blood soaking into my shirt, at my mashed hand. Grace reached out to me, but I pushed her away with my shoulder and stumbled up onto the pebble shelf. Someone grabbed at my shirt, but I ran. Ran away. My feet sank deep into the sand and the pebbles. Each step was painful and slow. I didn't want to fall as they might come after me. The pebbles sucked at my feet.

In the distance, over the dunes, I saw Harriet's beach house. The sunroom was lit up. I knew that I had to get there, to get help for my hand. I ran over the dunes, across the grass to the window, and fell against it. I slumped by the wall. The pain stopped.

CHAPTER THIRTY-EIGHT

STEPH

HALE HAD NOT PHONED. He just arrived. Rang the bell and walked in as if the earlier conversation hadn't happened. He ruffled Derek's ears, like they were old pals, and was just about to speak when his phone rang. He went towards the kitchen to take it.

If he didn't mention it, then she wouldn't either. She had confessed, and he'd said he would help. After all, he was on her team, wasn't he? She breathed in slowly. Counted. This dating thing was exhausting – already. That's if it was dating? She was obsessed with working out what was going on, searching for meaning in the slightest word or gesture, the lurching stomach when the phone rang – or worse, if it didn't.

Hale listened intently to his phone while putting his coat back on. The call finished and he grabbed his car keys. 'Quick, Steph. That was Taylor. Thought I'd like to know there's just been a fight called in at a party involving your students. Someone's hurt and they're sending for an ambulance. We need to go. Will Derek be all right?'

'He'll be fine. Let's go.'

They rushed to Hale's grubby old black BMW Series 3, an unmarked police car in need of a wash, with blue lights in the front grill and on the edge of the side mirrors and the front lights. It was like the old days rushing off to the scene of an incident, but now it appeared all the students and their misdemeanours were hers.

The traffic parted to let them pass, and they made it to the harbour in ten minutes. The ambulance had beaten them and stood at the kerb with its doors wide open, its blue light flashing across the dunes.

Steph pointed. 'That's Harriet Weston's beach house. What's the ambulance doing there when the party is over there, near the harbour? I can see the kids.'

'I think we're about to find out.' Hale pulled his car up behind the ambulance and Steph leaped out. Hale jogged behind her across the rough grass, towards the frosted glass door, which swung open in the breeze.

Steph led the way into the beach house towards the group around a dining table attending to a boy slumped in a chair. It was Edmund, who was pale and shocked and dazed, as if this was happening to someone else. Could he be drunk? She sat down in the chair beside him and he looked up at her and smiled weakly. Two female paramedics were removing blood-soaked kitchen roll from his hand and were dressing it with bandages. The bright light made the blood florescent red, and the familiar metallic smell hit her and reminded her of Justine. Harriet was on the phone, with David Stoppard standing beside her, looking concerned.

'No, Imogen – listen! Edmund is fine. He says he tripped over and a brick from the barbecue hit his hand and then he squashed it and damaged it further as he fell on it... No, I don't think it's badly damaged, but the paramedics think he should go to A&E to make sure he has no broken bones... What's that? No, I wasn't at the party. Edmund came here to get help. I called the ambulance... No, don't come here. Go to the hospital. I'll go in the ambulance with him and meet you there.'

Steph looked at Edmund's hand. 'That's rather a lot of damage from a fall.'

'I'm so sorry to have caused all this fuss. It's nothing much. It was an accident. What are you doing here?' He spoke slowly and enunciated precisely; his consonants got particular attention.

'They phoned Chief Inspector Hale when Harriet Weston called the ambulance and said it was college students involved in a fight. Is that what happened?'

'No. No fight. I'm not used to drinking. I fell over and hurt my hand. It was the bricks – the bricks from the barbecue. They fell on my hand. I came here to get help from Harriet. I tried to stop her calling the ambulance.'

'Rubbish! You need to get that seen to as soon as possible,' Steph urged. 'And it looks to me as if it's more than a fall, Edmund. Whoever did this should be charged with assault. This is serious for anyone, but particularly for you.'

Harriet moved around the table and rested her hands on Edmund's shoulders. She stood over him, watching as the paramedics worked on his hand. 'She's right. Your hands are so important – they're your future. You should talk to the police.' She turned to David Stoppard, who was putting on his coat. 'Thanks for your help. I'll go with him now. No need for you to come. Imogen Fitzgerald will give me a lift back.' The paramedics finished the bandaging while Harriet saw David to the front door.

'Thank you so much for all that you've done. It feels fine now.' Edmund nodded at the paramedics.

'It may feel fine, but you need to get an x-ray to make sure you've no broken bones. You seem to have a lot of accidents,' said Steph. 'A few days ago in the drama studio and now this?'

Before Edmund could answer Harriet bustled in, grabbed her jacket and tapped Edmund on his shoulder. 'Right. Come on. Let's get going.'

Edmund and the paramedics walked towards the back of the ambulance. Harriet made way for Steph and Hale to leave the beach house, then pulled the door shut behind her, leaning on it to make sure she had locked it.

'Thank you so much for coming, Chief Inspector. I'll try and get him to talk to you. Hang on – I'm coming!' Harriet clambered into the back of the ambulance. The doors were closed and it drove off up Ferry Road, its red lights disappearing into the dark.

Steph walked alongside Hale towards his car. 'That looked nasty. Hope he hasn't got any broken bones.'

'What happened in Drama?'

'I'll tell you in the car.'

Hale seized her hand and pulled her towards the sea. 'Why don't you tell me as we take a little walk by the sea? We could have a chat with a few of those lads at the party over there. At least it might put them off bullying him again if they think we're involved.'

CHAPTER THIRTY-NINE

EDMUND

THE SMALL BEACH house was full of people, all asking questions. Who did it? Where exactly did it hurt? Could I move my fingers? I just wanted the pain to stop and for them to stop talking at me. When Harriet stroked my shoulder, I felt better.

She heard me bash against the window when I fell and picked me up with that Stoppard man. They helped me into the house and called an ambulance who called the police. Steph said it was 'an assault' and I should report it. I told them we were all drunk, and I tripped and the bricks from the barbecue fell on my hand. It was no one's fault but mine.

I sat on the bench seat in the ambulance. Harriet put her arm around my shoulders, stroked the top of my arm, and I felt warm and safe with her. I love her touching me but even she couldn't take the hurt away, and the bumps in the road made my hand throb and the pain got worse.

We sat waiting to see the doctor when Mother slammed through the double doors and made everyone look up to see what was wrong. She grabbed me, pulled me to her, which made my hand hurt more. She shouted at Harriet and told her I should never have gone to the college, that this was all her fault and she'd ruined my career.

I tried to stand up to her, but Harriet pushed me back onto the seat. She was magnificent and stood still and calm and dignified. She refused to shout back at Mother, which made her even more furious and lose her temper more. Spit flew from her mouth onto Harriet's coat, but Mother didn't notice. All the people sitting waiting to see the doctor were looking at her shouting and I was so embarrassed. Why did she have to come? The drunk man slumped at the end of the row woke up and shouted at Mother to 'shut the fuck up'.

Mother 'shut the fuck up'. She collapsed into the chair beside me with exploding breath, a shrinking balloon. She stroked my arm and it jogged my hand, which hurt it more, so I asked her to stop. She did. We sat staring at the wall and the drunk man snoring.

Hours later we saw the doctor. She held the x-ray up to the light box and, in a soft voice, told me there were no broken bones. She injected my hand around the large cuts and sewed them up. She looked tired, like I felt. She said I could go home, that I would have enormous bruises and be sore and must keep the plasters on and not to get into fights again. I could see Mother taking in a big breath to tell her I didn't fight. I didn't want her to shout at the doctor, so I pulled Mother away with my good hand and thanked the doctor for her help. We walked out to Harriet, who looked gentle and sleepy. Even in the harsh white lights of the waiting room, she looked beautiful.

CHAPTER FORTY

STEPH

'Don't you wish you were their age again?' Steph paddled along the edge of the smooth waves as they lapped into the shore, up to her ankles in the cool water. Hale walked beside her, but further up the beach, beyond the reach of the surf. She hadn't persuaded him to remove his shoes and socks.

He looked up towards the dunes, to the group of students standing around the dying embers of the barbecue. Another group had lit a fire closer to the sea and sat around it smoking and drinking and chatting; segments of their faces flickered in the light of the flames.

'No. I'm not sure I would. It was easier for us. No social media; there were drugs – but nothing as serious or scary as they are now. A good night out for me was three pints of cider in a pub pretending to be eighteen.' Hale stepped further up the beach to keep his leather shoes away from the saltwater.

Wiping her feet on a tissue, Steph slipped her feet into her sandals and joined him as he walked towards the bonfire. Two students recognised them, quickly buried something in the sand and stopped talking as they approached. An unmistakable sweet odour wafted their way, and it was strong stuff from the smell of it. Steph glanced at Hale, who shook his head and rolled his eyes. This was not what they were after.

'Hi, do you mind if we join you for a few minutes?' Hale indicated for Steph to sit on the edge of a piece of driftwood, an enormous tree trunk, now grey-white and smooth. The fire was hot and two boys, wearing rugby shirts, were toasting or burning sausages on sticks.

The chat and laughter had disappeared as they arrived. It felt as if they'd thrown a bucket of water over the fun.

'I wonder if any of you saw anything earlier when a boy had an accident near the barbecue?' Hale started off hopefully. Silence.

'Why don't you ask Grace? It's her party and she was by the barbecue when it happened,' said Josh, one of the rugby boys. 'I know there was something going on, but you can't see much from this far away.'

'Grace, you say. That sounds like a good idea—'

'Hi, Theo.' Steph smiled across the group. 'Hand your media coursework in?'

Theo squinted through the flames, then suddenly grinned. 'Hi Steph, didn't see you in the dark. Yeah, it's in. Fingers crossed it's OK.'

'Hope so. Good party?'

Hale moved back away from the firelight into the dark.

'Would you like a sausage?' Theo held out a burnt lump on a stick. It looked disgusting.

'That's really kind, but no thanks. Have you been in? You look wet.'

'Had a dip earlier, helped by my friends. It was freezing! What're you doing here?'

'I'm with an old friend and we thought we'd wander along.

This is a great place for parties – must've been brilliant in the summer. It was so hot. Like Ibiza, without the foam discos.'

'Or the dickheads.'

'You're right. I'll go up and see Grace.' Steph pushed herself up from the sea-smoothed tree trunk.

'You may be lucky and find some wine's left.'

'Umm – can always hope.'

'Wait – I'll show you where it is.' Theo handed his burnt offering to his mate, left the circle and crunched up the pebbles with Steph. Hale kept well back, out of the conversation but within hearing distance.

'Did he have to go to hospital then? We saw blue lights near that beach house.' He looked concerned.

'Yes. They thought it was best.'

'Will he be able to play his cello again?'

'Don't know yet.'

'He's been asking for it, you know.'

'Has he?' Steph slowed down and pretended to shake some grit out of her sandal, as she didn't want to arrive at the barbecue too soon. They stood in a dark spot on the beach where she thought the students wouldn't be able to see them.

'Those first weeks, especially the week before Justine died, he lived in that music room with Harriet. Justine was always in tears. Worried she wouldn't get through the audition. She was the best until he came. Jake was so angry with him for fucking up Justine's chances.'

'Oh?'

'He thinks if Edmund hadn't come to college, Justine would still be here. Now that little shit gets Harriet all to himself.'

Steph took off her other shoe – or was it the same one – and shook it. 'Really?'

'He's always hanging around her. We think they're – you know... it's all over college. Justine said Harriet changed the whole timetable to spend more time teaching him cello. All the Year 13s are working with Margaret now.'

'Don't they like that?'

'She's good – not as good as Harriet. They all blame him. And he doesn't help himself, dressing like a dickhead. He's totally up himself – doesn't come to the canteen. Surprised he came tonight, especially after that row with Jake.'

Theo staggered slightly, regained his balance, then peered at Steph, assessing her reaction. She could make out his face in the gloom and saw he was upset, also that he'd had a very good party.

'I got on with Justine – not like that, but as a friend. We'd known each other from primary school. I was gutted. But...'

'Yes?' Steph prompted him.

'Look, Jake was so upset about Justine – he only did what he did tonight because he thought he might have caused it. It's guilt. He needs to blame Edmund.'

'Sorry, Theo – I'm confused.'

'Justine said she was busy all Sunday – wouldn't see him, but Jake worried about some email she'd had or something, so he went round there – round the back Sunday night and found them sharing a Chinese.'

'Justine and Edmund?'

'Yeah. He went ape shit – told Edmund to piss off. Jake had a fucking awful row with Justine and he finished it.'

'How do you know all this?'

'Justine phoned me that night – asked me to talk sense to Jake. She was alone, her mum and dad were away, she was hysterical. I nearly went round there, but she said she had to go to bed – she was going to college early next day. She said she'd be fine – didn't sound it. Told her I'd talk to Jake first thing and see her in the canteen at break. But then – well – she – you know.'

'Did you talk to Jake?'

'No. He was so upset. He blamed himself. I thought if he knew Justine had told me about their row, it'd make it even worse.'

He wobbled again, lost his footing as he sank into the loose pebble bank and fell against Steph. She held him up until he found a firm footing, amazed that he was so coherent with the amount that he must have put away over the evening.

'Sorry, lost my balance then.'

'So, no one knows what Justine told you then?'

'You do now, but that's all. That's why he was so angry with Edmund tonight, because he blames him but himself more. He's worried it was their row made her do it.'

'I see, do—'

A scream near the barbecue cut in. Two boys were fighting, with a girl trying to pull them apart and screaming. Hale rushed up the beach, grabbed the larger boy by the collar of his jacket and pulled him off with such force that he fell on his back on the shingle. Hale put out his hand and helped him up. It was Jake. He was out of it. He could hardly stand.

'Now lads, what was that about?'

'Fuck off!' Jake swayed and was about to fall over again. He was wasted.

Steph stepped in and held Jake's arm to steady him.

'Jake, it's Steph. Let's take you home. Look at that blood – it'll stain your shirt.'

Steph grabbed a handful of paper serviettes, held them under his nose then pushed his hand up to hold them in place. She poured some mineral water from a bottle onto a few more and dabbed at his shirt, then she handed him the soggy paper, 'Here, wipe under your nose with this. I think it's stopped.'

In the firelight, she could see that his nose was no longer dripping. He tried to clean up the smears under his nose and on his chin. She grabbed a pile of serviettes, held onto his arm and helped him up the beach to the dunes. She glanced at Hale, who understood and jogged off towards the car, parked outside Harriet's beach house.

It took a while to get Jake to the car park, as his knees kept collapsing under him and his feet didn't always go in the same direction. All the time he was mumbling or shouting about Edmund, but Steph could make nothing sensible out of his slurred words. She hoped he wouldn't throw up in Hale's car – that smell took forever to get out.

At last she balanced him on the rail at the side of the car park, and Hale drew up beside them. They lifted Jake into the back seat and immediately he fell asleep, making mumbling noises. On the drive back to Oakwood they were silent, apart from Steph's directions to Jake's house.

'How do you know where he lives?'

'I took him home from college one day, as he was upset.' Steph wasn't actually lying – well, by omission perhaps – but now was not the best time to tell Hale all about her involvement in the porn photo. She checked her phone. No missed calls, no texts. What a relief to be rid of Carter at last.

Luckily Jake wasn't sick, and they handed him over to his mother, who was angry and embarrassed about the state he was in but relieved he was safe. Would he remember this tomorrow? Probably not.

On the short drive back to her flat, Steph told Hale about the conversation with Theo and how Jake had lied about not seeing Justine on Sunday. 'I really liked that lad. He must be riddled with guilt.'

'It does explain a lot about what happened tonight. I'll see him tomorrow, when he's sobered up, to find out what happened that night. He's in for a monumental hangover.'

He parked outside Steph's flat and she noticed a light shining out through the sitting-room window.

'Did we leave that light on when we left?'

'Can't remember – must have done.'

The key needed a bit of fiddling to work. It felt stiff, as if the tumblers had shifted, probably by the damp, and she'd have to squirt WD40 into it. The door opened and – nothing. No barking, no jumping up, only silence. Where was Derek?

'Derek! Derek?' She heard a whimper from behind the armchair. Derek was lying on his side, shaking, in a pool of vomit. He lifted his head and wagged his tail slightly when he saw her. It took all the energy out of him and he collapsed back into the mess.

'Poor Derek. Let's get you cleaned up.' She grabbed the kitchen roll, rushed back to him and wiped up the mess under his head. He lolled back onto the wet patch, then started retching again. He threw up where he lay, apparently unable to stand. As she folded the paper around the second pile, she noticed something and held it towards Hale.

'Ugh! I don't want to see it!' He moved a few steps back.

'Look! What does that look like to you?' She held the paper towards him.

'Chunks of steak? Some red meat? Ugh, throw it away.'

'I've never given him red meat like this, and there's no way he picked it up anywhere today. Look, there's masses of the stuff.'

'So?'

'Someone's given it to him and it must be bad or... no... he wouldn't!'

'Who wouldn't what?'

'Carter. After we talked this morning, I sent him a text telling him to piss off. He must have got in here again and poisoned Derek. Look at him, he can hardly move.'

Derek lay like a sack on the floor. She was right. He hadn't moved, apart from lifting his head slightly to throw up once again. He made a soft whimpering. She leaned down and picked him up in her arms; his head flopped down. He was in a bad way.

'Quick, we need to get him to the all-night vet. That bastard Carter!'

CHAPTER FORTY-ONE

STEPH

'Any news from the vet?' Hale leaned over reception and signed himself in, checking his watch, one o'clock.

'He's recovered quickly. They think he'd only just eaten the poisoned meat and he'd vomited most of it up.'

'That's good.'

'He has to stay on the drip, having his kidneys flushed, but then he'll be fine. I'm so relieved. They even asked me which radio station he liked while he's in there.'

Hale laughed. 'On a more serious note, I've asked our locksmith to put a new five-lever lock on your front door and another on the porch door. I'll bring the keys when I pick you up later.'

'Thanks.'

'I borrowed a pool car while mine's being cleaned. Dreadful smell.'

'Sorry about that.'

'No, I wasn't having a go at you. Don't know why I said it. Just pleased Derek will be OK.'

'Don't know what I'd do without him. Did you check on Carter?'

'You're right.' Hale made sure no one could hear them. 'Carter was off duty last night.'

'It had to be him. The little shit. I should never have sent that text. It's all my fault.'

'I'll sort him, don't worry. I'll stay over at yours until I do.'

Before Steph could reply, Peter came out of his office. 'Afternoon, Chief Inspector. I've arranged for Jake to come to the meeting room; he should be here in about five minutes. He'll need an appropriate adult to be present, so you may have to wait until his mother arrives.'

'That's fine. I need to catch up with my emails.'

Hale sat on a sofa and started typing into his phone. A few minutes later Peter reappeared and gestured to Steph to come to his office.

'Jake said he doesn't want to drag his mother away from work and is happy to talk to Hale with you there. Is that OK?'

'I'll get Jane to cover reception.'

She collected Hale and walked into the meeting room. Jake was staring at the floor, looking tired, but he appeared to be managing well with what must have been a hell of a hangover.

'Hi Jake. I think you've met Chief Inspector Hale, and I gather you'd like me to join you.'

'Thanks, Steph. I don't want to bother Mum after last night.'

'Right.'

'Thanks for getting me home.'

'You remember that, do you?'

'Sorry if I said anything rude.'

'You didn't. Not to us anyway.'

Hale placed his phone on the table and settled down opposite Jake. Steph filled a beaker of water from the water cooler in the corner and pushed it towards Jake, who gulped it.

'Right, Jake,' Hale began. 'Are you OK to answer a few questions?'

Jake nodded. Hale continued, 'You're not being arrested or charged with anything. You're helping us with our enquiries into Justine's death. You understand? Are you happy if I record this?' Jake nodded again.

Hale set up his phone, recorded their names, then said, 'When you gave your statement, you told us you didn't see Justine on the Sunday, the day before she died. Would you like to change that statement?'

'I thought you'd come about last night.'

'Really?'

'His hand.'

'Edmund claims it was an accident. That he was solely responsible, after drinking too much.'

Jake said nothing, engrossed in the reproduction of the Monet field of poppies on the opposite wall. Hale spoke loudly; Jake jolted. 'Now, tell me about seeing Justine on the Sunday before she died.'

'I didn't.'

'I know you did, Jake. I've received information that you were there in the evening.'

'It's rubbish. Who told you?'

'Think about this carefully, Jake. We know you were there.'

'Can I have some more water, please?'

Steph re-filled the beaker of water, then placed it on the table in front of Jake. While the boy's head was down, Hale gestured to Steph to take over. They waited. Jake sipped.

'What happened, Jake?' asked Steph.

'I did go there.'

'When?' she asked.

'About eight thirty?'

'Why?'

He turned his shoulder away from Hale and lowered his voice a little as he leaned towards Steph. 'The night before, Saturday night, Edmund had brought Justine a bottle of wine to say sorry for what he did at the concert. From the look on his face, I knew he wasn't expecting me to be there. He'd come to chat up Justine, and he left when he saw me. The next day I had to look after my sister while Mum was at work. Then in the evening I thought I'd go to Justine's.'

'Then what happened?'

'I saw them together—'

'Who?'

'Justine and Edmund. They were sharing a Chinese and drinking wine.'

'That must have upset you.' said Steph, encouraging him to open up.

'His cello was on the floor beside her violin. They must have been playing together. I'd no idea how long he'd been with her. I went in, then he left.' Jake's eyes filled and his head dropped. Steph waited.

'I'm sure it didn't happen quite that quickly, Jake. What did you say to make Edmund leave?'

'I told him to leave Justine alone. She was my girlfriend, and he had no right coming round, and the playing was only an excuse to worm his way in.'

'And?'

'That was it. He left.'

'And Justine?'

Jake lowered his head into his hands as he wept. He grabbed the tissues pushed at him by Steph, blew his nose and looked at her, 'I know – it must have been my fault that she – did what she did.' He sighed and his shoulders juddered in his attempt to stop crying and gain control, but his sniffs punctuated his speech.

'We – we had a row – over him. She said she enjoyed – enjoyed playing with him and he could teach her so much. She told me not to be jealous. I shouted – I shouted at her and told her if she thought he was better than me – to fuck off and that we were over.'

He rubbed at his face. 'It's because of me she did it. Didn't she? It was my fault,' he appealed to Steph. His blotchy face and runny nose made him look like a vulnerable child. She handed him another wodge of tissues. He sighed. 'I shouldn't have shouted – I called her a slag and all sorts – I was so angry. I wish I could go back and – take back what I said.'

Steph leaned towards him. 'I know you do.'

'It was my fault. Wasn't it?'

Steph glanced at Hale.

'We can't say yet, lad. We all do and say things we regret.' Hale looked for once as if he couldn't find just the right words. 'We're investigating it, and anything you can tell us will help us find out what happened. Are you sure you've told us everything now? Anything else you've missed out?'

'No. That's it. That's all.'

'Right. I suggest you stay here 'til you feel better. When you do, just pop over and let Steph know you're going to your next lesson, will you?'

They left Jake sitting, elbows on the table, head in his hands, still weeping, and closed the door. As they walked to the reception desk, Steph called out to the blonde lady behind the desk, 'Thanks Jane. I'll take over now.'

They stood backs to the desk, looking at the meeting room

door, making sure no one could hear them. 'Well?' asked Steph.

'I don't know. He thinks their row could have led to her suicide, but my instinct is that he didn't murder her. He seems to have cared for her so much, but then...'

'But then we don't know.' She finished his sentence for him. 'There's nothing that ties him to the scene.'

'No. But we don't have any other leads. That could all be a big act – we've both seen it before. No. I think we have to keep an eye on him – or rather, you do.'

'I'll do my best, boss.'

Hale grinned. 'We'll see who's the boss later!'

CHAPTER FORTY-TWO

STEPH

STEPH WAS HANGING up her coat when Imogen loomed over the reception desk. 'I need to see the Principal, now!' She looked exhausted, but so did everyone else after a storm, which had pounded Oakwood all night, with winds over sixty miles an hour. On her way to work Steph had been forced to change her route to avoid a fallen tree; she had driven round fences at odd angles and even a shed roof that had landed in the middle of the road. She couldn't recall such a powerful storm, but then, she'd never lived so close to the east coast.

'I'll see if Mr Bryant's free.' Steph smiled and spoke softly to defuse Imogen's fizzing anger. She walked to Peter's office to speak to him, rather than phoning, so she could warn him of the new storm about to hit. Presumably Imogen had come in to complain about the beach party and Edmund's injury. Peter understood her eye movements and followed her out.

'Good morning. Do come through. May I offer you a coffee?'

'No. I don't need coffee.' Imogen's rejection sounded as if Peter was offering her strychnine.

'Steph, will you join us?' asked Peter.

Peter and Imogen sat on either side of the copper art nouveau fireplace, with Steph at the end of the oak coffee table. Imogen sat stiff and upright. Her controlled anger filled the room with an electric energy.

'How may I help you, Mrs Fitzgerald?'

'I believe that Edmund stayed overnight last night with Harriet Weston and I would like to see him immediately.'

For a moment, Peter looked as if he didn't know what to say. 'Sorry?'

'I thought I'd been quite clear. Edmund phoned for a taxi to take him to Harriet Weston's beach house last night. He's not returned home so I assume he is here and I would like to speak to him, please.'

'Steph, will you check Edmund's timetable please?'

On her way to Peter's computer, Imogen's imperious voice stopped her. 'At present, he will be in the music centre in Harriet Weston's Year 12 lesson.'

'Thank you.' Peter turned to Steph. 'Will you go over and ask Harriet Weston and Edmund to come to my office, please?'

Grabbing her coat, Steph left reception and fought against the ferocious wind and horizontal rain. Storm Annabelle, at its peak last night, was still buffeting its way eastwards across the country. What a delicate name for such foul weather.

The criss-crossed blue-and-white crime scene tape prohibited entry to the classroom door where Justine's body had been found and was a constant reminder of the awful tragedy of that poor girl's death. The glass panel of the second classroom revealed the Year 12 students sitting, heads down, working. She opened the door to silent concentration. The teacher's desk was empty.

'Is Mrs Weston around, please?'

The students' heads snapped up, aware that something exciting could be happening.

'Mrs Weston's not here and she's not emailed our work. David Stoppard might know where she is,' said Grace, pulling off her Nike baseball cap.

Steph ignored the provocative insinuation and scanned the upturned faces – no Edmund. Before she could thank the students and leave, Grace continued, 'Edmund seems to be missing too.'

The class stared at Steph, hoping to get more information. 'Thank you so much, Grace.' A pair of socks, one blue and one black, were drying on the radiator closest to her, giving off a strange smell. The students' eyes followed hers.

'They're mine, Miss,' a boy with plastered-down hair said. 'I got wet.'

'I can see that. If you pop over at break, I've got some dry ones I can lend you.'

He nodded and smiled through the strands of hair. As she shut the classroom door, they all lowered their heads and resumed their work. No gossip, no mucking around. 'Bitch Woman Weston' was the name she'd overheard two students calling Harriet a few days ago. Now she'd seen for herself the evidence of her iron discipline. Harriet would never have accepted the racket coming from Sam Griffiths' drama studio, where he struggled to get his students to do anything even when he was there. Pushing her way out into the pouring rain, she wondered why she'd bothered to wear a coat. By the time she arrived at Peter's office, she was soaked.

The silence in the office felt so solid she could have sliced it. Peter was at his desk, head down, working at his keyboard, while Imogen sat up with her straight back not touching the chair and stared out of the window.

'Well?' asked Peter, resuming his seat opposite Imogen.

'Neither Harriet nor Edmund is in the lesson. Both absent.'

Imogen looked horrified. 'What? Well, where is he then?'

Peter sighed. 'I'm sorry, Mrs Fitzgerald, I've no idea. I presume you've phoned him?'

'He doesn't have a mobile phone; neither do I.'

Steph could see Imogen's pride in avoiding the twenty-first century wavering and her angry confidence deserting her as she took in what she'd just heard. From the moment she had thundered into Peter's office, she had made it obvious that she wanted someone to blame for Edmund's absence. Now she had found he wasn't at college she appeared confused and looked unsure of what to do next.

Steph got up and moved towards the door. 'I'll try Harriet's home phones.' She left, relieved to be out of the oppressive atmosphere. She tried all the phone numbers for Harriet held in the college records. There was no answer at her Oakwood home or the beach house, and she left messages on both voice-mails asking Harriet to contact her. Concerned that something was wrong, she phoned Hale and asked him to send someone round to Harriet's homes. There was nothing to do but wait. She made a pot of coffee, and when she took it in into Peter's office, he and Imogen both grasped the cups, desperate for a diversion.

'I've phoned the police to see if they can find Harriet or Edmund at one of her homes.'

'Thank you, good thinking, I—' Peter began.

He was interrupted by Imogen's irritated, 'I think it's rather early to involve the police.'

'Not at all,' countered Steph. 'You said Edmund has been missing overnight and you don't know where he is, and both he and Harriet are missing from college with no explanation. I think it is exactly the right time to involve the police.' Steph poured a cup for herself and sat down to join what had become a silent vigil.

Peter nodded his approval and looked as if he also appreciated her sharp response to Imogen. Steph sipped her coffee, pleased to give him support. There was something not right with Imogen's story. Imogen had said that Edmund had left in a taxi to visit Harriet, but why? He couldn't have played the cello with his injured hand. And she was sure someone had told her that his mother always gave him a lift to Southwold, but she hadn't last night. Maybe they'd had a row.

Looking at his watch, Peter picked up a pile of papers and a notebook from his desk, then moved to the door. 'I'm sorry, Mrs Fitzgerald, but I need to go. I have to teach as I'm covering for a colleague in the maths department who's on long-term sick leave. I hope you understand. Steph, if you hear any news, please come and get me immediately.'

Peter left his office, his back pierced by Imogen's horrified stare.

'We're lucky that Mr Bryant is so good at maths and the students won't suffer from losing their normal teacher,' said Steph. 'He's extremely ill in hospital and it's been impossible to replace him – maths teachers are like hens' teeth. May I pour you another?'

Imogen held out her cup. 'Yes please. I must say I find it odd that Mr Bryant is not giving this his full attention.'

'There is really nothing he or any of us can do until we hear from the police, and I'm sure you wouldn't want the students to miss their A Level maths lesson.'

At that, Imogen's anger subsided. 'Yes, of course.' She paused to drink her coffee and, as she put her empty cup down, her stolid fury appeared to melt a little. 'Sorry, I'm not thinking straight. I'm so worried. Edmund's not done anything like this before.'

Steph nodded sympathetically, not wanting to stop her talking.

'He's such a talented boy, but now he seems to be stubborn all the time. He's so difficult to live with.'

'That's true of most teenagers.'

'But he's never been like that, or wasn't, until he came here. Now I'm really worried after that beach party. I'm sure those boys did it deliberately.'

'But Edmund said it was an accident,' said Steph.

'And you believed him? He told me some story about falling over after drinking red wine and hurting his hand on some bricks. I know he's lying. He's protecting those thugs. They're jealous because he has a future and they don't. I should report them to the police for assault.'

Steph took Imogen's cup and put it on the tray. 'But if Edmund claims it was an accident, there's little the police can do.'

'I suppose you're right... You see what I mean about him being stubborn? He's changed so much. Do you know we had our first big argument last night?'

She had been right. Perhaps Imogen would give the full story now.

'We've never quarrelled like that before. I heard him phone for a taxi; he thought I didn't hear. Then he told me he was leaving and walked out. Now that he isn't here, I'm really worried. What do you think has happened?'

'I'm sure the police will find him.' As Steph reached out her hand to comfort her, Imogen bent down to search for something in her handbag beside her on the floor. Whatever it was, she didn't find it.

Imogen continued, 'He took a ten pound note from my purse. He stole from me! Can you believe that? He did nothing like that before he came here.'

Imogen's glimmer of vulnerability was extinguished. Even in a crisis, she alienated any attempt to support her. She could only blame the college. Maybe she was right: Edmund didn't fit in. The students had tried to include him, and Steph believed the attack hadn't been planned but was a moment of madness by a very drunk Jake. Realising that Imogen was not going to give her anything else but had resumed her stiff back pose, Steph excused herself and returned to her work in reception.

About forty minutes later, a dark car pulled into the parking space outside the sliding doors. It was difficult to see through the ripples of water running down the glass, but it looked like Hale. The car door opened and Hale climbed out, holding his coat over his head as a shield from the torrential rain. Then Harriet and Edmund emerged from the back seat. Steph went into Peter's room and said to Imogen, who hadn't seen them arrive, 'They're here! Edmund's safe!'

Imogen leaped into life, dashed past Steph into reception and threw herself at Edmund. She grabbed him and hugged him. 'Where've you been? I've been so worried!'

Edmund unwrapped her arms and patted her on the shoulder. 'I'm fine, Mother. There's no need for all this fuss.'

'Fuss? Do you have any idea how worried I've been? I didn't know where you were.'

Steph observed the ease with which Imogen lied to her son. She moved to stand beside Hale, who was dripping a puddle on the wooden floor.

Harriet stepped forward and tried to take control. 'Imogen, I'm so sorry if you've been worried. We were talking when out of nowhere the surge tide hit and we were stranded.'

'What? What are you talking about?' Imogen was now shouting. A gaggle of five students on their way to break stopped to enjoy the scene being played out. Steph herded them down the corridor, then turned back and found her old 'don't mess with me' voice.

'Please go into Mr Bryant's room, *now*.' Shocked into silence, the group trooped into Peter's office. Steph shut the door firmly and indicated that they should all sit. 'It's break now and Mr Bryant will be down shortly.'

At that moment, the door swung open and Peter almost walked into Steph. 'What the hell's going on? I could hear the noise down the corridor! Oh, I see.' He looked at the group sitting and looking very tense.

'Chief Inspector Hale found Edmund and Harriet. They got stranded in her beach house in last night's flood.' said Steph as Peter dumped his papers on his desk, pulled a chair from in front of it, inserted it into the circle and gestured that Steph should sit. He then pulled out another one and joined her.

'Thank you, Chief Inspector. Right, Harriet, perhaps you'll tell us why you appear to have spent the night with one of your students.'

'Edmund arrived unexpectedly to ask my advice about his future, following the injury to his hand. Suddenly the surge tide flooded the house, and it trapped us upstairs. There was no electricity and my mobile got lost in the flood so I couldn't contact anyone. We spent the night upstairs – Edmund in the spare bedroom. The flood was receding when Inspector Hale arrived and brought us to college. The sea water flooded my car engine. That's it. I'm so sorry you were worried, Imogen, but I'm sure you can understand this was a freak accident.'

Harriet glanced at Imogen as if challenging her to argue. Imogen sat erect, saturated with silent fury. Steph expected her to explode, but instead she stood and touched Edmund on the shoulder. He also stood.

'Come along, Edmund. I think we should go home now. Mr Bryant, I would like to come in later this week with Edmund to talk to you about his future here at college. Edmund, please thank Harriet for taking care of you last night.'

'Thank you, Harriet.' Edmund, subdued, sounded like a child leaving a tea party. Steph felt sorry for this boy, cowed under such rigid command. Eyes down, he avoided making eye contact with anyone and trailed out of the room after his mother.

Peter's shoulders relaxed after Imogen shut the door. 'Right, thank you so much, Chief Inspector, for your rescue. We are very grateful and sorry to have taken up your time.'

'You're welcome. I'm pleased everyone's safe.' Dismissed, Hale picked up his soggy coat, which smelt of wet animal, and Steph opened the door for him. He winked as he passed her. She was about to follow him when Peter spoke. 'Please stay for a moment, Steph.' She resumed her seat and saw that Harriet had been texting on her 'lost' phone.

'Harriet, I suggest that you spend the rest of the day sorting out your car and the damage the flood has caused. I'd like to see you at ten o'clock tomorrow to discuss the events of last night and also some photographs that have come into my possession. Steph, please phone John Wright and send my apologies for tomorrow's Suffolk Education Officers meeting. Thank you.' Clearly, before she fell, Margaret had carried out her threat to give the photographs to Peter and to tell him of her suspicions.

Harriet marched out of Peter's office, head held high, her stiletto heels clicking as she left reception. As she stepped through the front door, David Stoppard's car appeared. She climbed in and he whisked her away. So that was who she had texted. Steph went back to her desk and uploaded Stoppard's timetable. He was free for the rest of the day. Where were they off to? Her imagination conjured up all sorts of exciting scenes. She watched as they drove off and noticed that the rain had stopped; clouds tumbled across the sky, leaving some pale blue fragments. The storm had passed at last.

She jumped as Caroline dashed into reception. 'What's going on? The students say that Edmund and Harriet have been drowned in the surge tide!'

'That's rubbish! They're both safe. Chinese whispers in this place are amazing!'

Caroline leaned across the desk, lowering her voice. 'Is it true they were together all night?'

'How is Margaret? Any better?'

Caroline's momentary flamboyance drained away. She looked exhausted.

'They're talking about reducing the drugs tomorrow, and she should come out of the coma. But they don't know if she will. I'm dreading it. What happens if she doesn't?'

'Let's hope she does. I'll take Marlene out after college, shall I? You'll be going to the hospital?'

'Thank you so much. Poor Marlene. So neglected at the moment.' With that, Caroline sighed and headed off towards the common room.

Steph glanced at her watch and calculated that there were about six hours left until she could collect Derek from the vet. He had recovered well, and they had flushed the rat poison out of his system with no permanent damage to his kidneys. The flat had felt empty without him, and she realised what an important part in her life he now played. A long beach walk would give him a treat after his confinement and her the opportunity to see the impact of the surge tide.

CHAPTER FORTY-THREE

STEPH

THE HARBOUR CAR park was deserted when Steph parked beside the entrance to the seashore. She was curious to see the impact of the first surge tide she'd experienced since she'd moved near the coast. Unsure what she expected to see after last night, she knew it was much less serious than the horrific 1953 tide that flooded the east coast and took so many lives. The powerful wind made it a struggle to push up the hatchback, and when it was half open, Derek leaped out, sniffing around the car and marking as much as he could with his scent. Marlene posed serenely, a fluffy ornament in the centre of the cage.

'Come on, girl,' Steph urged.

At last she led both dogs through the sand dunes that sloped onto the seashore, only to find there was no beach. The sea crashed right up against the grassy hillocks. She stood on the edge of a small sand cliff, about a metre high, which had been carved out by the surge tide. A chunk – perhaps four or five metres of the land – had been washed away.

With a single bound, Derek leaped down the little cliff and

dashed off. Further along, he had found a tiny strip of beach between the sand wall and the sea and was charging ahead with confidence. She found a slight dip, which allowed her to scramble down to the narrow shingle beach below with Marlene in tow. Derek had disappeared around a sharp corner way ahead of her. She tried to catch up with him, but at each step her feet got sucked into the deep mound of pebbles swept up against the steep shelf.

By the time she rounded the bend, he had gone. Scanning the sea, she panicked, as she knew Derek would have gone in. He was a powerful swimmer, but if he got caught in the treacherous rip tide, he'd be swept out to sea. The waves, well over a metre high, were getting fiercer as the wind pushed them up. She tried to remain calm and searched segments of the swirling grey-brown water, desperate to see the white spot on top of his head as the waves swelled up high then retreated, giving her a view of the valleys beneath. In the distance, the heavy metallic clouds became one with the grey sea and threatened another storm. Derek was out there somewhere, and it was her fault. She had lost him. He had gone, swept away under the sea. She should have kept him on the lead. He would stand no chance of pulling himself out now the tide had turned, and the sea was getting rougher.

'Shit!' She'd left her phone in the car so couldn't even call the coast guard for help. She turned away from the sea, her stomach writhing, and attempted to climb the sand wall. She felt like a demented hamster on a wheel, stepping rapidly but getting nowhere.

Just as she struggled to reach the top, she became aware that Marlene wasn't with her either. Losing her own dog was grim enough, but to lose someone else's was unforgivable. Swivelling round, she saw Marlene on the beach below, looking up at her with disgust. The sudden movement made her lose her balance, and she fell flat on her back on the beach below.

She scrambled to her feet before the next wave whooshed in, grabbed Marlene, tucked her under her arm and started the foot-pumping climb once again.

'Steph! May I help?'

She looked up to see Edmund above her, holding Derek by his collar.

'Oh Derek! I thought I'd lost you in the sea.'

Edmund offered her a hand. 'Here, let me help you up.'

She grasped his hand, found her footing, and at last staggered over the crumbling sand wall. 'Thank you. I thought he'd gone. Drowned.' She grabbed Derek's collar and clipped on his lead. 'Where was he?'

'Walking along the dunes, looking over the edge for you.'

'Thank you. What a relief!' She breathed out and waited for her heart rate to return to normal.

'That's Miss Durrant's dog, isn't it? Do you know how she's doing?'

'Sorry – what?'

'Margaret – do you know how she's doing after her accident?'

'She's still in a coma.' Steph brushed the sticky sand off her legs and back, then swooshed it off her hands. It surprised her to see Edmund at Harriet's house so soon after Imogen had frog-marched him out of college. 'Is your mother with you?'

'She's over there, waiting in the car park. She sent me to say thank you to Harriet for putting me up last night.' He picked up a carrier bag he'd put on the sand by his feet and held it open so she could see.

'It sounded dramatic.'

'It was. You've seen the beach.'

'Yes.'

'We were chatting in the sunroom of her beach house – just over there. The weather-boarded house – you see?' He pointed it out. He must have forgotten she'd been there on the night of the barbecue.

'Yes – lovely, so close to the sea.'

'That's the problem. Last night there was a sudden roar, then the sea forced that door open and flooded the house. No power – it was pitch black. The water got into the car's engine. It was this high.' He held his hand to waist level.

'You said.'

'Look, you can still see the puddles over there, and that damp patch on the wall shows how high the water was.'

He sounded as if he was trying to convince her that the flood had happened. They stared at the tidemark on the concrete, the deep puddles in front of the house yet to drain through the sand, and the darker, damp wood that reached the windowsill. Clearing up the mess left inside that house would be a dreadful job.

'We had to stay upstairs – luckily, there's a spare room. This morning the water still hadn't gone down. We had to wait until Mr Hale rescued us. You wouldn't believe it now, would you?'

'Actually, I would. A great chunk of the land has disappeared – several metres.'

Edmund glanced over the churning sea towards the harbour. 'No way could Grace hold her barbecue down there today, could she?'

'No, no beach left. Your hand looks a lot better than when I last saw it. Good job it wasn't your left one.'

'Yes. But they didn't realise, did they?'

'Who didn't?'

He paused and appeared to be trying to remember what he'd said. 'The students, you know, when they moved the bricks off my hand after I fell over. They thought it would finish my playing, but luckily it was my bowing hand. The doctor said it'll be fine when the bruising goes down.'

They both stared at the plasters crisscrossing his swollen right hand. A blue tinge escaped from the longest plaster closest to his wrist. A car pulled up in front of the beach house.

'Oh look – there's Harriet, in that cab. Excuse me. I must go. Nice to see you, Steph. Enjoy your walk, Derek.'

CHAPTER FORTY-FOUR

EDMUND

HER HAND LAY RELAXED on my thigh. We sat side by side on the sofa and shared a bottle of wine. Through the open door, the sound of the sea's insistent embrace of the shore foreshadowed our lovemaking. We had no need for words. Her expression said it all. She leaned towards me, wrapped her hand around mine and took my glass. She looked into my eyes and drank the last mouthful of my wine. It left a deep red stain above her lips. I pulled her to me and kissed it clean. She raised her left eyebrow and turned towards the steep flight of stairs.

Gently, she took my hand and led me upstairs. There were two doors, one on either side of the tiny landing, and we turned left. She saw me glance at the door on the right and stopped to open it. 'You can go in there if you'd prefer? The guest room.'

I shook my head and laughed. 'No way!'

The bedside lamp threw a pink oval light on her brass bed. She pushed the window open so we could hear the lapping of the sea and feel the light breeze on our skin. The room absorbed the smell of the waves. I undressed her in front of the window. A shaft of moonlight rippled on the waves and created the perfect backdrop for this perfect woman. She allowed me to initiate. Allowed? Did she allow me, or did I take control? I took control.

I felt so powerful. So male, so grown up as I slowly, deliberately took her. Her skin smooth and soft. No wrinkles. No creases. She was passionate. I made her happy. She made me strong.

Above her, I bent to kiss the freckle in the hollow beside her collarbone. My tongue traced the rim of that sensuous curve. She murmured contentedly and moved beneath me. Then she pulled me into her once again. I was complete, triumphant. I wanted to shout out to the world of my love. At that moment I realised nothing else mattered but Harriet. I wanted to hold her, kiss her, touch her, penetrate her. I wanted to spend every moment of my life embracing her. To live and grow and stay inside her, always.

I left her bed as her lover. I went home. I told Mother that from now on I would sleep in the spare room.

CHAPTER FORTY-FIVE

STEPH

Her flat was a mess. How had that happened? It was only the two of them, and one of them was a dog. It looked as if someone had ransacked it. Steph dashed around slotting plates in the dishwasher, collecting her post, some of it unopened, and adding it to the 'must sort out sometime pile' shoved in the sideboard cupboard. As she walked past the bin she sniffed. It was definitely musty. She tugged out the rubbish bag, then the blue re-cycling bag, and hurried outside to the bins by the side of the house. The landline phone's shrill ring penetrated the dark front garden. She ran back in and grabbed the receiver.

'Hello.'

'I'm coming over now. Keep your door open.'

The line went dead. Carter. She felt sick and dizzy and desperate. Telling Hale hadn't stopped him. What did she expect – miracles? She'd got herself into this mess, and she'd have to live with it. Before she could move, the front door smashed open, then slammed shut. Carter invaded her sitting room.

'Been tidying up for me?'

He'd been sitting outside, watching. For how long? She hadn't noticed. She must be losing her touch. He took off his coat, put it over the arm of a chair by the fireplace, sat down, then looked at her expectantly. Derek bounced up at him, wanting attention or treats. Carter pushed him away aggressively. 'Get down, mutt!'

Her temper exploded. 'You shit! You nearly fucking killed him! How could you? A dumb animal!' She ran at him and slapped him across the face, then battered his head. He held up his hands to protect himself from her attack. In one move he stood up and hit her hard, so she fell over, knocking over a side table and breaking one of its legs. He jumped on her and turned her face down, pressed her left shoulder down, grabbed her right arm and pulled it up behind her back. She screamed out in agony. Derek howled, barked, then bit Carter's leg.

'Fuck off!' He kicked back and struck Derek in his chest; the dog cried out and whimpered in pain. 'Keep still, you bitch. If you move again, I'll push it up further and break it. Keep still!'

She stopped thrashing and gave in. Blood dripped from a cut on her face made by the broken table leg, and she slid her cheek on the sticky patch to reduce the pain in the side of her neck. Her breathing slowed and Carter gradually released his hold on her arm. She felt a sharp prick under her left ear. He'd got a knife.

'Good. That's better. Now, I'm going to let you get up very slowly. If you make one false move, I'll slice your face.'

He gripped her shoulder as she struggled to stand, holding onto the chair arm to haul herself to her feet. The sting from the knife grew stronger on her neck. He pushed her towards the other armchair. 'Sit there.' He turned her round and shoved her down. Derek dashed across, licked her hand and sat beside her, whining. 'And shut him up or I'll do a better job this time.'

'Shh! Derek. Stay – it's OK,' she lied in a soft, reassuring voice.

Carter backed into his chair, his knife held out towards her, ready to strike.

'That's better. Now we've got that little drama over, let's get down to business.'

The cut on her face stung as she touched it, but it had stopped bleeding. She sat hating him, feeling nauseous as her stomach churned. She must stop herself throwing up. She felt humiliated enough already. She couldn't give in; there must be something she could do. The jagged wood of the broken table leg would make an excellent weapon if she could distract him. He followed her eyes.

'Don't even think about it.' He bent forward, picked it up and laid it down on the hearth beside him.

From underneath his coat, slung over the arm of the chair, he pulled out a package about the size of a small bag of flour, wrapped in a black bin bag and heavily sealed with criss-crossed brown gaffer tape. He placed it on the chair arm and smiled across at her. Even at this distance she could smell his whisky breath and it was rank.

'What a fuss over nothing. All you have to do is to hold on to this 'til tomorrow evening. Hide it somewhere – a pile of roasting tins in the oven works well. About nine o'clock your phone will ring three times. Don't answer it. When it rings again, leave the package on that small ledge in your porch. Do *not* go out there for an hour. Another package will be left in its place. I'll drop round later and collect it. Simple, eh?'

'Very.' A voice came from behind the flat door. Steph gasped. Carter jumped up, grabbed the package and stuffed it beneath his coat. The knife disappeared into his pocket. The door opened, and Hale stepped in. He towered over Carter.

'What are you doing here?' blustered Carter.

'I came to see you, Carter.' Hale rammed him back into his chair and said, 'Let's sit down and talk this over, shall we?' For the first time he glanced across at Steph and looked horrified as he noticed her face, the broken table and Derek sitting cowed beside her. 'What the fuck's been going on here?'

At last there could be a way out of this mess, and Steph tried to speak with a confidence she didn't feel. 'Just Carter's way of greeting an old colleague, after trying to murder her dog.'

'Don't move. Stay there.' He handed her a box of tissues, strode over to the kitchen and returned with a glass of water and a damp tea towel. 'Hold that on it. It'll help take down the swelling.'

Hale picked up a dining chair and set it down to the left of Carter, who had to turn his neck at an awkward angle to look up at his boss. Now he resembled a guilty child caught stealing biscuits, not the shit who'd attacked and threatened her. The sick feeling had receded a little since Hale had arrived. A shame he hadn't come a bit earlier. Anyway, how had he known Carter would visit her? She hadn't known herself until a few minutes ago.

'What was it you wanted to talk about?' Carter was regaining his confidence. Did he really think he could bluff it out?

'Carter, I could do you for assault before we talk about anything.'

'Yeah, well, she started it.'

'You sound like a pathetic kid in the playground.'

Carter looked down at the broken table leg. 'It wouldn't have happened if she hadn't been so aggressive.'

'So it's her fault you hurt her? She made you do it.'

'And he threatened to cut me,' Steph interjected.

'Did you? Now there's a real bully boy. Hand it over.'

Cater put his hand in his pocket, took out the flick knife and gave it to Hale, who put it in the briefcase beside his chair. Steph became aware of the pain in her shoulder joint and tried to massage it away. It was tender to touch, and she hoped she'd not pulled a tendon or ligament or whatever joined her right arm to her shoulder.

'Now let's talk about your new business idea, creaming off cocaine and blackmailing Steph to be your mule, and then we'll see if she wants to press charges for assault.'

'Blackmail? Cocaine? That's a serious allegation. You have proof – naturally.' Carter's voice was much more subdued than it had been earlier.

Hale bent down and took a folder out of his briefcase. He put it on his knee. 'It's all here.'

'I've seen you pull this one too many times in interviews to be taken in by it.' Carter's confidence was increasing.

'Well, let's look at what's in here, shall we? Yesterday you led a drugs raid in Bungay?'

'You know I did.'

Hale took out three photographs, which he studied as if seeing them for the first time. He re-arranged their order and looked at Carter.

'You recall that Taylor was shadowing you for his training as Crime Scene Manager?'

'Tigger? He got in the way the whole time.'

'Exactly. I'd given him my phone and he was to take photos

of anything he thought was important, then we'd go through them.'

Carter fiddled with his coat sleeve and looked away.

'In this one, you'll see a pile of packages on the coffee table among the usual druggy rubbish.' He passed a photo to Carter, who scrutinised it.

'Now, in this second photo you can see the packages in more detail.' Another picture was passed over. 'And do you know, they look identical to the one there – under your coat.'

Carter said nothing. He glared at the picture.

'Now, here's one of Taylor's photos that shows one, two, three, four – yes, five parcels. Agreed?' Hale tapped his finger on the photo as he counted the packs. Then he passed it to Carter. Silence. He reached into the folder and pulled out an A4 sheet of paper.

'And here's the Exhibit Log, which records the evidence you brought to the station. At the bottom of it – there – I think that's your signature?' Hale pointed to a scribble at the bottom of the page.

'You know it is.' Carter looked sullen.

'Here you claim that you found four packages of coke. No doubt your photos also show four. The fifth is with you, over there.'

Carter inspected the copy of the log as if he could transform it under his gaze. At last he looked up at Hale. 'OK, I'll cut you in.'

'No.' Hale laughed. 'That's not what I want. I want you to add your package to the rest and we'll record five in total. We'll use my photos as evidence. You'll give me yours and I'll shred them, then watch you delete them from your phone. I want this to stop. Understand?'

Carter slumped in his chair. Transfixed by the photos, he avoided looking at Hale.

'Stop this thieving, stop dealing and stop blackmailing Steph,' Hale continued. 'If not, I'll arrest you now on possession with intent to deal a Class A drug. Your choice.'

Eventually Carter broke the silence. 'Some choice.'

'You made the choice when you set this up. You're lucky I don't take you in and throw the book at you, especially after what you've done tonight.'

'You're only doing this to keep her out of trouble.'

'At the moment, it's not too late for you either. You've made a big mistake that you can put right if you choose.' Hale paused. Carter said nothing. His head was down. 'What made you do it? You're a couple of years away from your pension.'

Carter took a deep breath and let it out quickly. He lifted his head and looked at Hale. 'You wouldn't understand. You're a fast-track university graduate – one of the golden boys. I joined the force at eighteen. Worked my way up the old way. No accelerated promotion path for me. I've got stepped over so many times I've lost count. Most of 'em, no better than me... often not as good. You're right. I'm due to retire in twenty months. Not with the pension I deserve, but with the one you lot forced me to take. I do all the work while you take all the credit – I'm one of the grunts.'

A pause. Years of simmering resentment had pushed him to take this enormous risk. He could have lost everything.

Hale pressed for a conclusion. 'We need to wrap this up. Are you going to do as I suggest or are we going back to the station now?'

'That's that, then. No villa in Marbella for me.' Carter stood up and regained his cocky confidence. 'You're as bad as she is, letting her pet crackhead off. We're no different, really, are we? Except she's got away with it.'

'So have you – so far. Look, I'm sorry how you feel about the force, but that's not my fault. This isn't the way to end a fine career.'

'Fine career? Is that what you call it? Knowing my luck, I'd have got caught anyway. Now I can see why you've not turned me in.' He sneered at Hale, made a fist and shoved it upwards in a 'fuck yourself' sign. 'Right, then. I'll sort it tomorrow. I'll be off.' With that Carter picked up his coat and the package and walked out, slamming the front door behind him.

The lump in her stomach dissolved. 'Oh, my God! That was amazing! Thank you so much. I was terrified when that door swung open – but you could have arrived a bit earlier and saved me this. Ouch!' She winced as she touched her face.

'How was I to know you'd take him on single-handed?' He picked up the damp tea towel and wiped away a smear of blood below the cut.

'He'll have a hard time explaining how the coke has disappeared.'

'That's his problem.' He kissed the tip of her nose. 'Now your problem is to look in your fridge and see what's in there. I'm starving.'

He ducked before she hit him.

CHAPTER FORTY-SIX

STEPH

THE NEXT MORNING Caroline's exotic perfume announced her arrival as she bounced into reception. A splash of colour, in a loose purple jacket over a long black dress splattered with white lilies. Not since Margaret's accident had this Caroline existed. It was as if she'd been in mourning, denying herself colour and pattern and style.

'Oh my goodness, what have you done to your face?' she said.

'I tripped over a table and caught it on the edge.' Well, that was almost true. Before she left for work, Steph had blobbed foundation on the cut and the bruise that was developing nicely, but she obviously hadn't used enough.

'Come outside for a moment. I need to talk to you,' said Caroline.

They found a spot in the sunshine, all signs of the storm now blown away. Caroline leaned into Steph and said in a whisper, 'I know you'll hear this from Hale, but I want to tell you myself. Margaret has woken up and she's normal. Well, as normal as she can ever be!'

'I'm so pleased She's OK! Why are we whispering?'

'No one's to know. Hale says we're to pretend she's still in the coma. She's being smuggled out later today to stay with her sister in Norwich. Feels like being in a spy film, doesn't it?'

'She's not coming home?'

'Hale thinks she may be in danger if she does.'

'Has Margaret remembered how she fell?'

'I told you, she didn't fall. Someone pushed her.'

'Who did it?'

Caroline shook her head. 'That's the problem. She's no idea – she was at the top of the stairs and felt a hand push her hard on her back. She didn't see who it was.'

'That's a shame. I'm so pleased she's recovering.'

'I know. I thought I wouldn't get her back. Thank you so much for bailing me out with Marlene. I owe you a lake of wine. Must dash. Students waiting.'

With that, she floated off down the corridor towards her studio. It was so good to have the old Caroline back and fantastic that Margaret was getting better. Now at last Hale knew that Margaret's fall had been an attempt on her life, and somehow it must be linked to Justine's death.

Peter emerged once again from his office, looked at his watch and stood tapping his fingers on her desk as he stared out into the car park.

'No sign of Harriet yet?'

'No. I've phoned both her homes and her mobile and I get the voice mail on all of them. Maybe she's on her way in.'

'She'd better be. She's already an hour late for our meeting. She's making it so much worse. Why does she always have to create a performance out of everything?' Peter stomped back into his office, not wanting an answer.

Steph continued answering the phone, giving out timetables to students who'd lost them and regularly explaining how she'd fallen over and cut her cheek. Just after one o'clock, when there was still no sign of Harriet, a familiar car drew up and parked by the front doors. It was Hale. He signed in and asked, 'Is Peter free?'

'Yes, he's been waiting to speak to Harriet all morning. She hasn't arrived yet and isn't answering her phones.'

'Can we go in and talk with him now?'

Steph knocked on Peter's door and walked in. He was working at his keyboard. 'Has she arrived at last?' He looked up and saw Hale follow Steph into the room. 'I wasn't expecting you this morning, Chief Inspector. Come in and take a seat. You too, Steph.'

He came and sat with them. 'Now, how can I help you?'

'I'm so sorry. I've got some bad news, I'm afraid. Harriet Weston's body was found earlier this morning in her beach house.'

'What? Oh no!' Peter sank in his chair. 'She was coming in to see me this morning. Dead? This is dreadful. Oh, poor Harriet. How did she die? I can't believe it!'

'I'm afraid it's true.' Hale waited for the news to sink in.

'This is awful. She was so young and talented and... now... dead? What happened?' asked Steph.

'Her cleaner arrived at about half-past nine and found the door wide open. She went back to her car and phoned her husband to come in with her as she thought there'd been a burglary. When they went in, they found Harriet lying on the sofa. They thought she was asleep.'

'Like Justine,' said Steph.

'Not quite – no blood – but it looked like suicide. There was an empty wine bottle, and some pills scattered on the table beside her.'

'Oh no! I can't believe it. Harriet wouldn't commit suicide,' said Peter. 'She's so strong. She can't have done. You must have made a mistake. She wouldn't commit suicide.'

Steph looked at Hale. 'What did the note say?'

'There wasn't one. We're treating her death as suspicious and, because of all the events here, possibly murder.'

CHAPTER FORTY-SEVEN

STEPH

STEPH AND HALE took Derek around the west side of the lake for a late evening walk. She had not expected to see Hale again that day, but he'd turned up saying they had done all they could and he needed some air.

They had kept Harriet's death quiet until her husband had identified her body and told her family. The college grapevine was efficient; once news got out it would be trumpeted on social media in minutes, and without doubt the press would descend.

'Peter said that Justine's death has attracted little notice outside college yet, as unfortunately suicides are common in her age group.'

'That'll change after the inquest,' said Hale.

'Everyone thinks Margaret's fall was an accident, but as soon as news of Harriet's death comes out as suspicious the press will have a field day. And the students will be devastated. Those poor music students. They'll think they're in a nightmare.'

'It must be so difficult at that age to cope with any of this.

They think they're immortal, don't they?' Hale kicked a fallen branch off the path.

'Justine's death tore them apart and the whole college was in mourning; well, it still is. Now with Harriet they'll be reeling.'

The path narrowed, and they walked in single file for a while, both reflecting on the tragic events that had darkened the college. Back side by side, Steph held Hale's arm. It felt so good. It was a long time since she'd felt so calm and yes – serene, despite all the drama that was unfolding around them.

'And Carter?' She had not dared to mention it earlier.

'He did as I said. It's OK from our side – not sure how his new dealer friends will take it though.'

She was relieved to hear that, at least for her, it was over at last. Her thoughts turned to the college once more and how the students and staff would react to the news of Harriet's death.

'I can't stop thinking about Harriet. That is so tragic. I know she could be difficult, but she had an amazing talent and was a fantastic teacher. You should have seen that concert. Those kids reached the most incredible standards, and all because of her. She was inspirational and totally single minded. And now she's...'

Hale almost tripped over Derek, who had frozen in his attack mode to growl at an enormous Leonburger, the size of a Shetland pony. 'Can't you train that animal?'

'It's natural for dogs to behave like that.'

Having nodded at the tiny lady who was walking the gigantic dog, they continued walking around the lake, now full after the storm.

'Look at all three incidents – they must be linked and carried out by the same person. We have two deaths, dressed up to appear as suicide. Harriet's PM is not in yet, but the drugs appear to be the same as those given to Justine. Then we have the attempt on Margaret's life. The question is, what links them?' said Hale.

'They're all in the music department.'

'That's high-level thinking!'

'Don't be sarky! You were going to tell me about Harriet's husband.'

'He's been up north visiting an outpost of his empire. He came in to identify her body late this afternoon, and we'll interview him formally tomorrow. The strange thing is, we have his car on an ANPR camera this morning driving out of Oakwood. He was driving on the A1 when we contacted him.'

'Difficult to tie him to Margaret, isn't it?'

'Ignore that for a moment. Let's look once again at what we know. Justine. Who did she threaten? Who would benefit from her death? You heard her say she'd tell Harriet's husband about Stoppard. That's it, all we have. We're going round in circles.'

Steph pulled Hale back while Derek found the perfect spot and squatted. They waited, trying not to look. She bent down to scoop with her doggy bag.

'Ugh! I don't know how you can do that.' Hale shuffled on a little, not wanting to be involved in the necessary clearing up.

They turned away from the common towards the town. The storm had stripped the leaves off the top branches of the trees, which were now black skeletons waving at the dull grey sky. The light soaked away as they walked beneath the grey clouds that were closing in on them.

Hale continued, 'When I spoke to Stoppard last week, he said he always knew it was a fling with Harriet. He wanted nothing more, so Justine wouldn't have been a threat to him.'

'He left college with Harriet yesterday after the flood to sort out her car, so he's still heavily involved with her.'

'I'll see him again first thing tomorrow to find out how he's reacted to her death.'

Steph recalled her visit to the beach house the evening before. 'Stoppard left college with her but didn't bring her back to the beach house.'

'How do you know that?'

Steph bent down to put Derek on his lead as they reached the edge of the common. 'I thought I'd told you. I went to Southwold Harbour to see the storm damage and met Edmund by Harriet's beach house. While we were there, she arrived in a cab.'

'Stoppard could have come round later.'

'True.'

'And Harriet's husband also appears to be playing away. Oakwood seems to be a hotbed of extra-marital affairs!' Hale wrapped his arm around Steph's shoulders.

Steph pulled Derek back before he rolled in some fox poo. 'How does the attempt on Margaret fit into all this? When she took those photos of Harriet and Edmund in the beach house, she said she'd give them to Imogen and Peter to derail Harriet. We need to check if she did. Peter said something to Harriet about photos, but he didn't go into details.'

'We need to know. Ask him tomorrow, will you?'

'Yes, sir! As for Imogen, she came in to see Margaret at break before she fell, and yes—' she hit his arm, 'I asked her why, so stop looking at me like that. All I could get was that Margaret was going to give Edmund additional theory lessons. You're right, we need to find out if she's seen those photos.'

Derek dragged them back to stand by a gatepost while he savoured the perfume at one of his favourite spots. Steph nudged Hale. 'Talk of the devil! That's Imogen and Edmund's house.' The front room was dark. 'Edmund's usually practising when I pass – not tonight though.'

As they stood in the gloom, the window burst into light. Edmund picked up his cello, and through the open window they could hear him start to play loudly and aggressively. It sounded jerky and not as professional as usual. She was surprised that he was able to play at all with his swollen bowing hand. Typical of him to continue practicing even when injured.

'What did I say about the devil? That's a Paganini piece. Do you know, he was so good that people said he'd sold his soul to the devil?'

'What an amazing woman you are! How do you know all this stuff?'

'I had to do something while I was off work.'

Hale took Derek's lead. 'Right! That's enough culture. I'm starving. Let's go.'

As they moved past the house, they heard a scream. Imogen dashed across the bay, hitting the music stand away from Edmund. She grabbed the bow out of his hand and shouted at him. He disappeared from sight as he laid down his cello, then stood up to face her. They appeared to be in mid-argument from the look of it. Her face was bright red, her head thrust forward towards Edmund, contorted by her anger.

She dived towards Edmund, her hand outstretched, her finger stabbing her point, her mouth an ugly gash as she screamed at him. He stepped back against the window. He turned his back to his mother to face the road. Instinctively, Steph and Hale moved to the left, further along the fence, although in the darkness that now surrounded them there was no way that Edmund could see them from the bright room.

They could hear Imogen's screaming accusations – the

sound, but not the words. Edmund appeared controlled. He looked into nothing and ignored the tirade behind him. He might have been the compliant, perfect son, but now it looked as if he had learned how to press his mother's buttons. His stubborn failure to engage was clearly driving her demented. She was screaming and appeared to be oblivious to the fact that their row was on show to the street in the illuminated bay window.

Then she hit him. Again and again she battered him on the side of his head, her mouth shouting with each slap. Edmund cowered. He tried to protect himself by raising his arms above his head. Her screaming got louder. He moved out of the bay and out of their sight. She rushed after him.

Hale dashed up the path and rang the doorbell. One long, insistent ring cut through Imogen's screeching. Silence. He took his finger off the porcelain button. A light appeared in the hall. Through the amber frosted glass, a shadow grew as it approached the front door. A chain was removed, a key turned in the lock, and the door opened. A composed Imogen stood in the doorway, stared at Hale, then brushed down her tweed skirt.

'Good evening, Chief Inspector, Mrs Grant. What a surprise. How may I help you?'

CHAPTER FORTY-EIGHT

STEPH

IMOGEN INVITED them in as if she had been expecting them for high tea. Edmund appeared from the front room. They both looked flushed but calm. It occurred to Steph that Imogen had asked them in without enquiring why they were there. Clearly Hale was also puzzled. She noticed him pull himself up to stand in formal mode in the porch, ready to go through the usual script and state his business, but Imogen had pre-empted him. Perhaps it was because they had caught Imogen mid-row and, despite her calm exterior, she had acted without thinking.

'Come through to the sitting room. May I get you anything?' She gestured down the hallway, setting the tone for a social call.

'No, we're fine, thank you.' Steph answered for them both, not sure how Hale would handle this unexpected meeting.

Imogen turned to shut the front door. 'Would you like to bring in your dog?'

'That's kind, thank you.' Steph returned to the porch and

unhooked the lead from the large rusty nail that must have held a trellis or supported a climbing rose.

They entered the musty sitting room, which could have been a 1950s interior in a museum. A well-worn three-piece suite, with chipped wooden arms and dull orange flowers on dark brown cushions, merged into the swirling mud-brown patterned carpet. Above, a tangerine light shade gave them yellow, liver-diseased faces. Imogen indicated that Steph and Hale should share the small sofa. It was a close fit. Derek lay down at Steph's feet, behaving for once. Edmund and Imogen sat in the two identical chairs either side of the coffee-coloured tiled hearth. They all turned to Hale and waited for him to begin.

'Sorry to intrude on your evening.' He paused. 'I would like to clarify a few points following the incident at the barbecue where you injured your hand.' He looked at Edmund.

'I don't see what else there is to discuss, Chief Inspector. Edmund has explained what happened. We don't plan to sue Grace or her family for building an unstable brick construction on the beach. What else do you need to know?'

Hale paused. Steph could see his jaw tighten. 'What you won't know is that we found Harriet Weston's body in her beach house this morning.'

Taken aback by this sudden revelation, Steph realised that Hale wanted to shock them into a reaction.

Edmund's head suddenly jolted up. 'No, not Harriet! She can't be dead. She can't be! What happened?'

'We're not sure until after the post-mortem. We're talking to all those who may have seen her the evening before she died.'

'Dead? I can't believe it! She was fine when I saw her

yesterday.' Edmund was pale and close to tears. A flash of puzzlement passed across Imogen's face and she looked searchingly at Edmund.

'Yes, we know you were there,' said Hale. 'What time did you leave?'

Imogen turned her head on one side, frowned at Edmund, then gave Hale a hard stare. 'What is this about, Chief Inspector? This feels like a formal interview, and why is Mrs Grant here?'

'This is not a formal interview; as I said, we would like your help with our enquiries. I asked Mrs Grant to join us because she is working with us as a civilian detective. As an ex-member of my team she has a significant contribution to make.'

'So you work for the police?' Imogen made it sound as if it was the worst job in the world.

'No, I work at the college, but Chief Inspector Hale has asked me to help. If you object to me being here, I'll leave.' She hoped this calculated gamble would pay off.

'No, we have nothing to hide and want to help you as much as possible,' said Imogen. 'Now what do you want to know?'

The tension that had spread through her with Imogen's challenge disappeared a little, but Steph decided to stay silent and leave it to Hale.

'As I said, we are trying to piece together the visitors to Harriet Weston's beach house over the last few days. You've never been there, have you, Mrs Fitzgerald?'

'No. When Edmund had his coaching sessions with Harriet, I dropped him in the harbour car park, then collected him about two hours later. I saw no need to go into her house. She never invited me.'

'You'll be willing to have your fingerprints and DNA taken for elimination then?'

'I said we'll help you in any way we can, Chief Inspector. Now if that's all?'

Imogen placed her hands on the wooden arms and was halfway out of her chair when Hale stopped her.

'We've not quite finished yet. I'd like to go through the visits Edmund made to the beach house.' He nodded and turned to Edmund. 'You went to Harriet for help on Sunday night after your accident at the barbecue.'

'You saw me there.'

'You also went there on Monday?'

'Yes, the night of the surge tide.'

'When did you get there?'

'About seven o'clock, I think.'

'Why did you visit her when you couldn't play your cello?'

Imogen stared at Edmund as if it was the first time she'd thought of it. In Peter's study Harriet had said that Edmund had gone to ask her advice after his injury, and she was sure Imogen was there then and must have heard it. Maybe that's what they were arguing about when she and Hale had interrupted. Edmund bent down to pet Derek before he spoke.

'Harriet asked me to come. To talk about the changes to our programme because of the injury, you know. We had to change what we'd planned.'

'You drove him there, Mrs Fitzgerald?'

'No. Not on that occasion.'

'I got a lift with Harriet after college. She said she'd drive me home after we'd finished but, as you know, the flood came.'

'And you knew about this, Mrs Fitzgerald?'

Imogen's eyes moved up to the left, a sure sign that she was trying to think what to make up next. She appeared to have forgotten that she'd told Steph about the row with Edmund and that he'd phoned for a taxi before he stormed out. And why was Edmund lying too – trying to protect his mother? What was going on here?

Imogen lifted herself slightly out of her chair to smooth her skirt beneath her. Now comfortable, she smiled at Hale. 'Edmund phoned me from college. There's a pay phone there.'

'Yet, the next day when you went to college, you said you didn't know where he was.'

Once again, she looked flustered but quickly answered, 'It's none of your business, but if you must know, we had words and I don't quite remember who said what.'

The creation of this tangle of lies was an amazing effort by both of them, and Steph could not see why they were telling such different stories.

'Why didn't you tell your mother where you were going, Edmund?' asked Steph.

He sneaked a look at Imogen and paused. 'Mother was... not pleased with the way Harriet was coaching me. You came to Snape. You heard.'

'Go on,' said Steph.

He paused again, then glanced towards his mother. She sat rigid, her eyes down and her lips thin and clamped tight. His voice became weaker and they had to strain to hear him.

'Well, after that recital, Mother threatened to take me out of college. She was unhappy with Harriet's influence on my playing.' Another pause. He turned his shoulder towards them and away from his mother's glare. 'I'm afraid Mother was... rather... rather upset and cross about it. I decided not to tell her I was going to see Harriet in case she got angry with me again. Sorry Mother, they have to know. I have to tell them.'

His head dropped again. Steph had witnessed Imogen's anger earlier and could imagine the growing tension between them since the Snape concert. He looked young and vulnerable and had been in the middle of a tug of war between two formidable women.

'Then what happened?' Steph prompted.

'You know the rest. We were talking about my future. Then the surge tide came and flooded the house and car. There was a power cut and the phone wouldn't work. Harriet lost her mobile in the flood so we couldn't tell anyone. Then the next morning you came and rescued us. I stayed in the spare room.'

It was strange that he felt the need to keep saying that. Perhaps he was concerned about Harriet's reputation. Or was it important he convinced his mother?

Imogen said nothing. Tight lipped, she looked as if she'd bitten into a lemon. Her disapproval was obvious, but why was she so angry? Could it be she felt guilty for having driven him towards Harriet – the woman she wanted him to reject? Perhaps she suspected something had been going on between them. And then there were all their lies.

'Then you went back later that day?' Steph continued pushing gently.

'That's when I helped you climb up the dunes with the dogs.'

Steph nodded, acknowledging his comment. 'Why were you there again?'

'We wanted to say thank you to her for letting me stay that night, so we took her a bottle of wine – didn't we, Mother? You saw us.' Steph felt as if she was being challenged to support him once again.

Steph turned to Imogen. 'Did you go in then?'

257

Edmund jumped in. 'No, she waited in the car park then drove me home. You saw her.'

Steph said nothing and neither did Imogen, who had turned to observe Edmund. Another pause. Edmund waited. At last Imogen spoke.

'Yes, that's right. I didn't want to see her.' Imogen had regained her frosty tone. 'Now we've clarified all of Edmund's visits, I assume that's it. You have what you need, Chief Inspector?'

'Not quite.' Steph replied for him, and they all turned towards her. 'When you made that visit to Miss Durrant, what did she want to talk to you about?'

Imogen pulled herself up in her chair and spoke to Steph as if to a rather annoying servant. 'I told you that at the time – she offered Edmund additional theory lessons.'

'I didn't know that, Mother. You didn't tell me. I mean, how kind of her.'

'And where did your meeting take place?'

'How much longer is this – this interrogation going to go on? I'm beginning to think I should phone my solicitor.'

'It's your right to do so. But at the moment you're simply helping us to develop a timeline for the events that led to attempted murder,' said Hale.

Edmund looked shocked. 'Attempted murder? Are you talking about Miss Durrant's accident?'

'We now have evidence that someone pushed her down the stairs.'

'That's dreadful! Who'd want to do that to her? She was so sweet. We all loved her. You liked her when you met her that day, didn't you, Mother?'

'You must have been the last person to see her before she fell,' said Hale.

Imogen slumped in her chair. Her eyes darted towards Edmund, then Hale. She closed her eyes for a few seconds, then sat up straight and took a deep breath. 'You're right.' She paused. She looked up and spoke louder. 'I was the last person to see her before she fell because it was my fault. I think I may have pushed her.'

It took several moments for her last sentence to sink in. This shabby but ordinary sitting room felt the wrong place to hear such an admission. Edmund sat, mouth open, eyes wide, apparently unable to speak. Steph opened her mouth, about to ask 'How?', when Imogen continued.

'I also killed Justine and Harriet Weston. I'm ready to confess to it all.'

Dumbfounded, they all stared at her, horrified that this tight, proud woman could be responsible for such monstrous acts. The silence stretched until Edmund's piercing scream made them jump. He flew at Imogen across the room. Kneeling before her, he grabbed her legs, then pleaded with her, shaking her. 'Mother – no – I don't believe you! You couldn't. Say nothing. You couldn't... don't tell them.'

Clearly waiting to see what would happen next as this surreal scene played out, Hale made no move towards mother and son. No way had Steph expected this when they rang the doorbell less than half an hour ago. Was it possible this woman could have committed these crimes?

'I'm sorry, Edmund. It's true. I did it for you.' Imogen's calm, controlled voice made it sound the most reasonable thing in the world.

'For me? Why?'

'You know how many hours, how many years we've worked together for your future. They were getting in the way.'

'What?' Edmund appeared horrified.

'I heard you talking to Justine on the phone about forming a duo and going in early to practise. She'd have been a distraction. That morning I got to the music centre before you.'

'But she committed suicide. Isn't that right?' Edmund appealed to Hale, who said nothing. Edmund continued, 'And Miss Durrant?'

'I had to stop her saying dreadful things about you. She was a threat to us. I followed her to the top of the stairs, grabbed her arm to make her listen, but she fell.'

'How was she a threat?' asked Steph.

'She was trying to get the Principal to stop Harriet coaching Edmund at her house. It would have stopped Edmund from making progress.'

'But that was what you wanted. You didn't approve of Harriet's approach. You should have been pleased,' said Steph.

'If you recall, Miss Durrant fell before the Snape concert.' Imogen patiently corrected Steph as if she was a child making an elementary mistake.

'And Harriet?' asked Hale.

'I had to stop her before she did real damage to Edmund. I thought she'd continue my work, not destroy it.'

Edmund howled. A pitiful scream. Derek hid under the sofa. Steph sat rigid, taken aback by the unemotional, controlled way in which Imogen had explained her actions; she felt Hale tense beside her, about to take action.

'Mother! No! You can't leave me!'

Imogen stood up and unfolded Edmund's fingers from his grip on her arm. She patted his arm and moved towards Hale, who was now standing. 'Chief Inspector, I'll get my coat and we can do whatever has to be done.'

CHAPTER FORTY-NINE

STEPH

THE FRONT DOOR closed behind Imogen and Hale with a decisive click which echoed down the hall. When she and Hale rang the doorbell, Steph couldn't have imagined that they would get a confession. All this death and grief created by the overpowering ambition of a mother for her talented son, who was staring at the front door biting his thumb, looking dazed.

'Can I get you anything? Tea?' she said. It sounded lame offering tea when his mother had been driven away to face the rest of her life in prison. Bad enough for anyone, but for Edmund, whose life had been concentrated only on his mother, it must be devastating.

'No. Yes, please. A glass of water perhaps?'

'I'll get it. You go and sit down.'

She walked through to the back of the house and into the late twentieth century. The beige melamine cupboards with dark mock-wood worktops and orange wall tiles reminded her of her grandmother's pride in her shiny new kitchen about forty years ago. She took two glasses of water through to the sitting room where Edmund sat on the chair recently occupied by Imogen. He held a silk scarf that she'd dropped as she left and was stroking it like a child with a comfort blanket.

'Thank you.' He lowered the scarf and took a few gulps before putting the glass down on the coffee table in front of him. Steph tried to put herself in his shoes and imagine what he would need to get him through the next few days.

'Edmund, we need to think about your immediate future and perhaps phone Social Services.'

'What do they do?'

'They look after people who are left alone by their parents.'

'Left alone? Won't Mother be coming back later tonight or tomorrow morning?'

Steph wasn't sure how much this boy had taken in about the gravity of his mother's confession.

'That's unlikely. What your mother confessed to is serious, and the police will have to look after her until she comes to court for her trial. Social Services may want you to live with another family until you're eighteen.'

He sat up straight. 'I am eighteen.'

'But I thought the Snape concert programme said you were seventeen?'

'I was then, but my eighteenth birthday was the day before Grace's barbecue.'

'Right. Sorry, Edmund but I think it's best if we check.'

She found the number for the duty social worker, explained Edmund's situation, and was told as long as he wasn't vulnerable, and he was over eighteen he could be left alone. Although Steph had suspected as much, she thought it best to double check as rules changed so quickly.

His coming of age changed many aspects of how he could continue his life without his mother. Although he wasn't defined as vulnerable he would need a great deal of support living alone. Edmund looked relieved as he listened to her side of the call, but Steph felt reluctant to leave him alone.

'That means you can continue to stay here, but you'll need help. Do you have any relatives we could contact?'

'No one that I know about. I have a father, but I've no idea where he is or how to contact him.'

Her stomach churned with the familiar tightening. What was she getting herself into? She must remain detached and not take emotional responsibility for him.

As he deliberately placed the glass in the centre of the cork coaster, the realisation of his situation appeared to be hitting him at last. His hands trembled, his eyes filled and when at last he spoke, Steph had to move to the edge of her seat to hear him.

'Do you think she did all that? What she said?' He spread his mother's scarf over his lap, stroked it flat, folded it, then placed it on the table.

'She admitted it. No one made her.'

'But I don't understand. They weren't getting in my way, they were helping me.' He paused. She gave him space. Then his words tumbled out. 'Since I went to college, she hasn't been happy and has lost her temper with me many, many times – I suppose it could be possible she's done all those things she said she'd done. She's always coming into college – you know that. I expect your friend Mr Hale will see that on cameras, will he?'

'I expect so, but let's not go into that now, Edmund. It's late and you ought to get some sleep so you're ready for college tomorrow.'

He said nothing and stared at her as if waiting for something.

'You have eaten this evening, haven't you?' asked Steph.

'Yes, we had cheese on toast earlier before – before you came.'

'Right. I suggest you lock up after I leave and go straight to bed.'

She stood up to signal that their talk was at an end. He didn't move but remained sitting, his head now in his hands as if he hadn't heard her.

'I need to go now, Edmund.' She put Derek back on his lead.

At his name Edmund lifted his head, gave her a look that could only be described as pathetic, then pushed himself out of the chair and moved towards her. 'I don't suppose you would... no, don't worry, I'll be fine here alone.'

'I'll see you at college tomorrow. Pop into reception on your way to lessons and we can talk then. Good night.'

'Bye Steph, bye Derek.' He touched Derek on the head as he passed.

Her walk down the path was lit by the hall light, but it seemed to take much longer to leave the house than it had taken to rush up to it earlier. She turned back and saw Edmund, now a silhouette in the doorway, lifting his arm and attempting a slight wave to her. She slowed down so she could hear the door close and be confident he had gone into the house.

As she walked back to her flat the dark, empty streets of Oakwood suited her desolate mood. This talented boy would have the most challenging time of his life over the next few months. Growing up was hard enough, but now he had to do it alone and cope with the publicity and local gossip of his mother's crimes. She didn't envy him his future and knew she must do what she could to help him without getting in too deep this time.

CHAPTER FIFTY

EDMUND

HARRIET IS DEAD. I feel part of me died with her. I feel numb. The world is grey and the colour will never come back. The night she died I took her the wine to say thank you and sorry. Harriet had red eyes when she opened the door. She took the wine. She shut the door. I stood outside the door, facing the peeling green paint. The wind and salt from the sea had been cruel. Like Harriet. She was angry with me. It wasn't my fault – the flood.

When I got home, Mother screamed at me for going. She was angry with me too. She hit me hard on my head. It hurt. She said she had a headache and needed to go out for a walk. She took the car. Strange, she needed her car to go for a walk. Where did she go? Could she have gone to shout at Harriet?

I practised for two hours until Mother returned, still furious. She wouldn't speak to me. I heard the creaks as she climbed the stairs. She didn't say good night.

Mother's confessed to killing two people and attempting to kill a third. I can't believe it. She's not capable of it. I know.

They've made a dreadful mistake. She said she did it for me. How does killing people help me?

Jealous of Justine and me? Removing Margaret Durrant and Harriet Weston? I gave her no cause. I'm sure I didn't. Mother gets angry so quickly and loses her temper and often hits me, but I can't believe she'd murder anyone.

I sit in the dark. Alone. I think back. She could have been in the right places at the right times. It is possible. I wonder who will get to know about my mother, the murderer. My mother, the murderer. Murderer sounds like a swear word, not a word to use of Mother.

She left to go to the police station in her best camel coat. I sit alone. Now what? I must help to free her. Find evidence that she didn't do what she says she did. I can't live without her. They must understand that I need her.

For ages I have wished that Mother would be like the other mothers and let me grow up. Let me go out. Let me have money or let me earn it. Let college be my place. Now she's not here and I'm by myself, I feel so lonely. This isn't what I wanted. The house is quiet, empty, cold. The heating is on, but I shiver. I miss her. I'm sure she didn't hurt anyone.

I need her now. I need her to be with me in the future. I need her to breathe beside me, to hug me, to hold me and to tell me that all will be well. I need her.

CHAPTER FIFTY-ONE

STEPH

STEPH CHECKED the online attendance register. Edmund was absent. She phoned his home, but there was no reply. She rang three more times and was about to go to his house in her lunch break when Edmund answered.

'Yes?'

'It's Steph. Are you OK? You've not come into college.'

'I overslept and then stayed here today.'

'Are you feeling ill?'

'No. I feel fine. But I thought it'd be better if I stayed here today.'

'Are you sure? You might feel better at college.'

'No, really. I'd prefer to be here. I'll practise.'

'OK. Call me here if you need anything.'

She put the receiver down and felt troubled. It would be grim for that boy every day from now on. Hale had told her they wouldn't make a public statement until they'd checked the details of Imogen's confession and convinced the CPS they'd get a conviction.

He said that Imogen had stuck to her story and would

enter a plea of guilty when it came to trial. She wanted it to be over with as little publicity as possible. There was no hope of that. Imogen and Edmund's life would be nit-picked by the tabloids as soon as her story came out. What would become of Edmund? He'd probably have to change his name and move away.

Hale had asked her not to say anything to Peter or anyone else. Imogen was being questioned at a rural outpost on the border near Diss to reduce the leaks. Gossip travelled at the speed of light in Oakwood.

Once again, the college was in subdued shock, as news of Harriet's death spread among students and members of staff. The music students were stunned by the news, and the counsellor had moved into Harriet's office to support them. Peter had spent a large part of the day over in the music centre comforting the students. He had decided not to put out a press release until Hale gave him the go-ahead.

After college, desperate for some fresh air, Steph collected Derek and they headed immediately to the common. The dull, overcast day threatened rain, and she needed to do up her coat to keep out the wind. She walked along Edmund's road as she wanted to see if the lights were on or if he was practising. The bay window was dark and empty. Poor boy. The impact of his mother's confession would be devastating, and it would get worse as the story emerged. She waited while Derek paused at his usual spot. Aware of someone moving behind her, she took her keys out of her pocket, pushing the sharpest between her second and third fingers, ready to resist, and turned to face the shadow.

'Oh! You made me jump!'

Edmund stood beside her, and Derek leaped up at him, tail wagging.

'Down, Derek!' She tugged him away.

'Sorry. Didn't mean to scare you. I hoped you'd come past. It all feels... empty there. Going to the common?'

She nodded. 'Want to join me?'

'Please.'

They walked in silence to the end of the road. Derek stopped at a lamppost. Edmund leaned down and stroked him. 'May I have a go, please?' He held out his left hand. The right one was still criss-crossed with plasters, but the swelling had gone down. She handed him the lead.

'I'm sorry you didn't feel like college today.'

'I'll come in tomorrow. Does everyone know?'

'Not yet.'

'I suppose I'll have to leave. Live somewhere else.'

Derek crashed to a halt and whined. Around the corner came Marlene and Caroline. Derek's tail wagged like a helicopter blade and he greeted Marlene in the usual manner – nose to nose, then a sniff at the other end, just to make sure.

'Lovely to see you... Edmund, what a surprise!'

When Steph bent down to take Derek off his lead, Edmund, with his back to Caroline, caught her eye and mouthed, 'Does she know?' Steph shook her head without Caroline seeing, and Edmund relaxed.

'How is Miss Durrant?' he asked Caroline.

'Still in the coma.' she lied.

Steph jumped to change the subject. 'Our walks will need to be much earlier soon. This'll be my first winter with a dog. Do you go out in the dark?'

'Afraid so – joys of dogs. Do you have pets, Edmund?'

'I've always wanted a dog, but Mother felt it would be a distraction.'

'She's right. They need a lot of looking after.'

The dogs were playing a complicated game of hide and seek around a fallen oak tree. Caroline clapped her hands. 'Marlene, come! We must go. I've a load of sketch books to mark tonight. Lovely to see you – enjoy the rest of your walk.'

They watched as Caroline disappeared down the path with Marlene trotting at her heels.

'Derek!' For once, he obeyed and arrived at her feet. Steph hooked him up to his lead and held it out to Edmund. 'Want to take him?' He nodded, took the lead and they walked back the long way back through the town.

'It's already lonely without Mother. I suppose I'll have to manage. There's no choice, is there?'

'I'm afraid you're right.'

'All these years we've worked together for my future. Now she's – she's gone. I can't believe it. She said she did it for me. I heard her.'

In the High Street, the squares of light from the shop windows revealed his distress. He looked exhausted and seemed to have shrunk. He was never the most confident of kids away from his cello. Now he looked about twelve.

'If you ever need anything, you know where I am. I mean – if you want to talk or you need help to understand – well – bills or anything.'

He stopped and turned towards her. He looked into her eyes.

'Really? That's so kind of you. I think I can get some money out of my post office savings account.'

Derek pulled on the lead. They walked on past the Pound Shop and the East Coast Hospice window.

'Mother used to control all our money. I've had none of my own. I mean – I've had to ask her for anything I ever wanted to buy. Like Grace's birthday present, the croissants and juice when Justine and I practised – she gave me the wine for Harriet that you saw. It's been difficult to be in college with no money – to have to ask for everything. You'd really help me?'

'Of course.'

Her stomach contracted. Why had she said that? Why hadn't she kept her mouth shut? Look at what happened last time, when she'd become too involved with Sam. Perhaps Edmund wouldn't take her up on it. In one sentence he came across as mature and independent, then the next he was like a child. He knew so little of the world, having been in solitary confinement with his mother. She glanced at him plodding beside her, thrilled at taking a dog for a walk. He'd needed her and Derek's company for a start. Oh well – she'd said it now.

They passed the dark windows of empty shops displaying dusty 'To Let' signs, then into the LED spotlight glare of the new pizza restaurant, where Derek stopped. A child in a family group waved at Derek from their window table. Edmund waved back to the boy, then stood, gazing at the family. Bored, Derek pulled him away.

'When will it come to court?'

'It could be some months.'

'Will she come home 'til then?'

'I suspect she'll be kept on what they call remand. Then she'll plead guilty in court and be sentenced. I'm afraid she'll probably be taken away from you for many years.'

Away from the High Street, they walked across one of the greens at the edge of town. The pavement had become a muddy track across the grass. Deep puddles from the storm sat on the path, unable to soak into the sodden ground. They stepped over them. Derek paddled up to his knees, straight through them. She'd have to hose the mud off when they got home.

271

'Do you often go to the beach with Derek?'

'Yes, he likes to swim.'

'Do you think you could take me with Derek sometimes? I mean – would you mind? Now Mother isn't – I can't drive a car and I love being by the sea.'

Her stomach tightened again. 'I'm sure we could.' Maybe this was his way of coping with the future, creating a safety net, taking control. They reached his gate. His house was in darkness.

He looked up at the empty bay window. He handed over Derek's lead. 'Thanks, Steph. Bye Derek.' He dawdled up the slight incline to his door, his shoulders slumped. He reminded her of Jake after Justine's death. A lad with little hope. Would he ever recover?

CHAPTER FIFTY-TWO

STEPH

DEREK HOOVERED up his dinner and licked the floor around his bowl, searching for the tiniest escaped scrap. Steph settled down with a tuna sandwich and a glass of iced water. Hypnotised by a black vein in the marble fireplace, she struggled to work out what was nagging at her. Something wasn't right and she couldn't work out what it was.

The doorbell rang. Derek bounced up at the door, making another scratch in the paintwork. He greeted Hale so enthusiastically that he was in danger of pulling a muscle if he wagged his tail any faster. Hale looked exhausted, and he collapsed in slow motion into her arms. She held him for a few moments, relishing his touch. 'Tough day?'

'I've had better. I need a drink!'

'Coming up!'

He pulled off his coat, threw it over the back of a dining chair and ruffled Derek's ears, then flopped into his usual chair. She poured him a glass of whisky from a bottle she'd picked up on the way home. 'Thanks. That's so good.'

'Any progress with Imogen?'

'Not really. She keeps saying that she did it, why she did it and that she will sign a full confession, but that's it. She wants to get it all over as soon as possible so Edmund can get on with his life.'

'When it hits the press, he'll have a dreadful time of it. The only thing left in his life will be his cello – poor kid.'

'Not another lame duck! Don't you ever learn?'

He held out his glass for a re-fill. Steph grabbed a tumbler and joined him. Why not? She'd earned it, hadn't she? The deep peat smell hit her as she sipped it. Oh, that was good! 'I saw him earlier. I'm sure he was waiting for me or Derek. He was like a six-year-old, desperate to hold the lead.'

'How was he?'

'Confused. Strange mix of calm acceptance and total disbelief. A little lost boy. But there was something – something he said, or I thought that wasn't quite right... I can't recall it.'

They sat in silence. It didn't feel much like a celebration at the end of a case. Normally when a confession appears like a gift, there's a feeling of excitement, relief and closure. This time it felt unsatisfactory.

Sitting up, she grabbed at Hale's hand. 'That's it!'

'What?'

'He told me he had to ask his mother for money for everything, however small. Like Grace's birthday present and the croissants and juice he took to the rehearsal.'

'And?'

'You remember the crumbs found on the desk behind Justine's body? We assumed they were left over from the concert, but what if they were croissants brought in by Edmund that morning?'

'Go on.'

'Didn't her stomach contents suggest she'd had a breakfast of pastry and grapefruit juice?'

'Yes.'

'Could he?' She got up, picked up the whisky bottle and refreshed Hale's glass. 'No. I can't believe that he'd be involved in any of it. No, forget it.'

Hale placed his glass precisely in the centre of the copper coaster. 'Hang on, let's think this through. Why would he do it?'

'Hold on to the "why" for a moment. Let's see if the "how" works out. Justine – he could have gone to the music centre after Margaret opened it, so no swipe card.'

'That's what Imogen claimed,' said Hale.

'Then Margaret's fall – he was also in the music centre when she was pushed. I saw him in a practice room, not in a lesson, after she was found.'

'But you know Imogen visited her around that time and signed out alone. She—'

'Listen!' interrupted Steph. 'Then Harriet. He was surprised to see me on the beach with the dogs that evening. He told me his mother was there. I didn't actually see her, but I saw him with a bottle of wine. Then Harriet arrived in a taxi.'

'Again, Imogen has confessed to killing her.'

'But didn't she say she'd never been in the beach house?'

'You're right – she did. If we don't find DNA evidence there, we'll know she was lying; if we do then her confession stands.' Hale stood up, collected the whisky from the kitchen island, re-filled his glass and pointed the bottle towards Steph. She shook her head.

'I don't want him to have anything to do with any of it; he's a lovely boy... so talented. Such a strange life. His mother's been both his curse and his strength.'

A door banged in the flat upstairs. Tim, an accountant, had moved in the previous week, but it was unusual to hear anything from him. Derek growled at the ceiling.

Hale ruffled his ears. 'Not used to having your territory invaded, eh, boy?'

'Shh! Something else has been nagging at me too. Last night Imogen said that she pushed Margaret before she knew the damage Harriet was doing to Edmund's playing. So, what was her motive?' Steph bent down to stroke Derek, who lay down beside her.

'You were there. You saw Margaret take photos of them in the beach house and she said she would give them to Peter and—'

Steph interrupted. 'But at that time, Imogen was happy with Harriet coaching him. She even drove him there. Margaret's threat to Imogen was empty. It doesn't make sense.'

'Umm – you have a point.'

Sipping their drinks, they sat thinking it through. Footsteps could be heard from the flat above, then a TV theme tune percolated through the ceiling.

'Perhaps you should phone Margaret and ask her what she and Imogen talked about.'

Hale frowned. 'Isn't it a bit late for that?'

'No. It's only eight thirty.'

Hale got up and pulled his mobile from his coat pocket. He looked up Margaret's number in his notebook, dialled and waited. He stood looking into the darkness outside the French windows. Steph smiled. He always stood up at work when he had an important phone call to make. She'd laughed at him and asked why he did it. He claimed it made him sound more official.

'Hello, Margaret Durrant? This is Chief Inspector Hale.

Sorry to bother you so late but I'm working on the case and would like to check some details with you... That morning when Imogen Fitzgerald came to see you, can you remember what you and she discussed?... I see... And what was her reaction?... Yes, that's helpful... Can you remember anyone else who was in the music centre around that time?... That's fine. Thank you... Yes, very helpful. I hope you're feeling better... That's good... Yes, I'll be in touch. Goodbye.'

'Well, what did she say?'

'Margaret, who's doing well, by the way, said that she showed the photos to Imogen, who refused to believe they were up to anything. So, Imogen had a motive and once again she lied.' Hale reached for the bottle and topped up his glass. 'Anyway, do you really believe Edmund's involved? He's more of a victim, surely?'

'You're right – he is a victim. Not one of my lame ducks! But I'm not convinced that her confession is sound. You said yourself she won't give you details. And there was something not right about him this evening. Too controlled. It's made me uneasy. Last night, Imogen could have spotted that he'd lied and worked out that he was involved somehow. Then she confessed and took the blame.'

She moved to pick up the bottle, but Hale stood up and put his hand over hers and stopped her.

'You could be right. I think it's a good idea to talk to him now. You've not been drinking – well, only a sip. You can drive.'

CHAPTER FIFTY-THREE

EDMUND

THE QUIET HURTS ME. I didn't think it would be like this. I'm not sure what I thought – but not this. Mother isn't here. When I woke up this morning, it felt normal at first, until I remembered what had happened. Then I felt sick.

Now I must get used to being alone. Steph offered to help. She treats me like an adult, not a child. Mother always – no that's wrong – now there will be no always. I must go on, build my future without her. I'm innocent. She's guilty. I wonder what she's saying, what she's saying to them about me.

Who am I? Do I exist without Mother? Do I now become someone different? Perhaps I only existed through her. Now she's not with me, I may dissolve. Is that what will happen? It didn't happen with my cello playing. When I met Harriet and she took over, I changed to her. Now I have lost both her and Mother.

My right hand is starting to unstiffen and move again properly. It'll be fine. It's my bowing, not my fingering hand. I was lucky there. My hand will come back to normal, but will my voice? Perhaps I will find my very own voice that doesn't belong to Mother or Harriet, but to me.

Then the future. The quiet will be everywhere, always. Mother will go to prison... And I? I will struggle to do normal things like shopping, cleaning my clothes and the house and... well, just living. But I suppose at last I'll be free. Free of her overwhelming possession. Is that a dreadful thing to say? After all that she has done for me. Alone now, I see things differently. I now see I was her plaything, her project, her musical experiment. She created me. She made me need her. She was the centre of my life. She made sure she was at the centre. Now I have to grow – grow my own voice, grow my own life without her. I can choose now. I need be different no longer if I choose. I can be the same.

CHAPTER FIFTY-FOUR

STEPH

THE BAY WINDOW was empty once again. No practice. From the road the house was in darkness, but the sitting room was at the back of the house and Edmund could be in there. Where else would he be? The doorbell rang and echoed down the hall. It sounded louder than it had the night before.

'Steph – how good to see you! What are you doing here? Where's Derek?'

'Chief Inspector Hale and I would like to talk to you for a few minutes. May we come in?'

'You know the way.' Edmund gestured to the sitting room and shut the front door behind them.

The room looked as grim and unwelcoming as it had the night before, but there were a few hints that he'd been there alone. Piles of papers covered the dark oak coffee table. Textbooks and black files with the titles of his A Level subjects written on their spines were scattered on the floor in front of his armchair. No plates or glasses. He tiptoed between the piles and was about to sit down, when he stopped. 'Sorry – so rude – would you like tea? Coffee?'

'No thanks, we're fine.' Steph sat in the same seat as she had the night before. Hale moved towards Imogen's chair with a slow, deliberate movement. As he sat, he glanced across the room at Edmund, who gave no reaction.

Hale smiled. 'Sorry to bother you again when you're busy doing your college work.'

Edmund ignored Hale and turned to Steph. 'Why are you here with him asking questions like you're in the police?'

'You know I'm helping the police.'

'I thought you were my friend.'

The sadness in his voice made her feel as if she'd betrayed him. He turned to Hale. 'What did you want to ask me? None of it was my fault. It was Mother. She's confessed to doing it all.'

'She's confessed, but the details are still a little hazy. We think you may be able to help us with that.'

'I'm innocent. I'm sorry that my mother did these evil things, but I'm not to blame. Neither am I involved. Look, I can prove it.'

He leant forward, riffled through the pile of papers on the coffee table and grabbed a shiny red exercise book. He handed it across to Steph. She recognised it as similar to the ones she'd bought from the local newsagent for her daughter's scribbles.

'What's this?' asked Hale.

'It's my daybook. My notes for my memoirs—'

'Your memoirs? At eighteen? Whatever can you have to write about?'

Edmund looked as if Hale had insulted him, then he paused and looked across at the exercise book before continuing. 'I've had an unusual life – home schooled, groomed by my mother to become a professional musician – a very different experience to most eighteen-year-olds.'

'Right,' said Hale.

'After you left last night, I couldn't believe it. So, I looked back at this. Unfortunately, what Mother said could be right. See for yourself.' He gestured towards the red exercise book.

At that moment Hale's phone trilled, and he excused himself and went into the hall to take it. The red book was the one note of colour in the dingy room and it glowed in Steph's hands. Just as she was about to open it and start reading, Hale returned and stood in front of Edmund.

'You are under arrest on suspicion of causing the death of Harriet Weston. You do not have to say anything, but it may harm your defence if you do not mention when questioned something which you later rely on in court. Anything you do say may be given in evidence. Now please get your coat and we'll drive down to the police station.'

Edmund rushed across the room and grabbed Steph's arm. 'Tell him it's nothing to do with me. Mother did it – she confessed. You heard her. She said she did it!'

Hale stepped between them and put his hand on Edmund's shoulder. 'Let's not panic, lad. We'll go down to the station and get this sorted out. Where's your coat?'

Whatever was in the phone call had changed everything, but she didn't know what new information could have triggered the arrest. She followed Hale towards the front door. From the old-fashioned mahogany hat stand in the hall, Steph unhooked Edmund's coat and helped him to put it on. He looked terrified as she helped him into the back seat of her car. Was he an innocent victim? Now she had no idea.

CHAPTER FIFTY-FIVE

STEPH

THE CID ROOM looked almost exactly the same as when she'd last worked there. The unwashed coffee mugs, the piles of paper, the post-it notes stuck around the edge of screens and files spewing out of in-trays. Nothing much had changed. She followed the interview on the monitor on her old desk, now occupied by Janet (Family Liaison Officer), who watched enthralled.

On the screen Edmund, beside the duty solicitor, sat on one side of the table opposite Hale. Alongside him she recognised Johnson, now a detective sergeant, whom she'd worked with when he was a constable. Edmund looked calm. His hands rested on the table. He hardly moved, but often glanced up at the camera in the right-hand corner of the room.

Hale explained the role of the duty solicitor, described what would happen and reminded him he was under arrest for Harriet's murder. Edmund appeared to have regained his calm confidence. Hale had yet to reveal the content of the phone call that had prompted the arrest and was clearly trying to settle Edmund.

While she watched, Steph nibbled on a bag of salt and vinegar crisps, given to her by Janet. She opened the red exercise book and started to read. The crisps clogged in her throat and she couldn't swallow. She coughed the stuck crisp free, then took a gulp of lukewarm coffee to stop choking. She was horrified. According to Edmund, Imogen had exploited and abused him sexually from the age of four and dominated him in the most disgusting way possible, using his talent as the excuse. No wonder Imogen had confessed. She didn't want her abuse to come out in court.

Edmund captured his isolated, controlled life vividly in his writing. She could see him as a young lad desperate for a puppy, and as a student, for a hoodie. Imogen had preserved him in the twentieth century and turned him into an ice man. He had not been allowed to live in real time and was forced to submit to all her demands. Even that had not been enough for her, and she had to kill to clear his path. She was jealous of Justine, envious of his relationship with Harriet and annoyed that Margaret was interfering.

She reached the entries about Harriet. Caroline had told her she had a reputation in the college as a 'bike', but it appeared from his writing that she'd seduced a student! On second reading it appeared that Edmund had seduced Harriet, was convinced he was in love with her and planned a long-term future with her. That was a complex relationship – an eighteen-year-old boy and a thirty year old woman. The image of him playing his cello replayed in her mind. Transformed on stage, he became mature, sensual and highly fanciable. It was credible.

She paused, stared at a coffee ring on the desk. She flicked back to the section on Justine and found that he'd omitted the Sunday evening visit to her house when they'd had their first rehearsal. The quality of their performance as a duo should have been a major area for comment, along with the shared Chinese meal. For Edmund, that would have been a massive deal. Then there was his comment to her about the croissants and juice bought for the rehearsal with Justine, and that also didn't get written up in his book. She grabbed a pad of post-it notes and marked the places where he'd written about the two deaths and the attempt on Margaret's life.

On the screen she saw that there was movement in the interview room. Edmund and his solicitor remained seated, while Hale and Johnson left the room. They arrived beside Steph, who held out the red notebook to Hale.

'The solicitor wanted some time alone with Edmund before we continue. We'll go down again in ten minutes.' He collapsed into a desk chair and scooted with his feet across the aisle towards her to pinch a crisp. Steph pushed the book at him.

'While you're here, look at the places I've marked.' She handed him the exercise book.

'What's this? I don't have time to look at that boy's homework.'

Steph took the book back and opened it at the first marked section. 'It's his memoirs, remember? The book he gave us before we left. The entries incriminate his mother all right, but there's something else you ought to see before you go back.'

Hale took the book and started reading. 'Ugh! Have you read this bit about him and his mother in bed? It's revolting! Disgusting! No wonder she wanted to confess and plead guilty. She doesn't want this to come out in court.'

'And then – there's the affair.'

'Affair?'

Steph showed him the sections about Harriet.

'Wow! Not bad for an eighteen-year-old with – what was she – a thirty-something-woman. The stuff of fantasies, eh?'

He re-read the sections Steph had marked. 'Yeah, I'm right. It's a fantasy – the bits about sex with Harriet read like an adolescent boy's fantasy. Then there's the incest. How do we know that's true?'

'Yes. There are bits that he's missed out but other parts that are true. I wonder how much he's made up?' Steph looked at Hale, who had grey marks under his eyes; his shoulders stooped with exhaustion.

Holding onto the desk, Hale pulled himself up. 'There's one way to find out – let's ask him. Right, Johnson, let's go. Steph, I think you should join us this time.'

The three walked into the room, Johnson carrying an extra chair, which he placed by the door for himself. Steph and Hale sat opposite Edmund and his solicitor. Edmund looked at them, then prompted his solicitor with a nod, which led to his solicitor intervening. 'I suggest you produce any evidence that you have that implicates my client or let him leave, now.'

Johnson got up and passed Hale a blue folder, which he placed on the grey Formica-topped table. Hale lined it up precisely with the wooden-edged corner. He moved his chair closer to the table, pulled the legs of his trousers up at the knees, then noticed a fragment of white cotton on his left thigh. He picked it off, held his thumb and forefinger away from the table and rubbed them together. Hypnotised by Hale's slow, deliberate movements, they all watched the cotton fall to the ground. He pulled the folder from the left-hand side of the table and moved it to the centre, in front of Edmund. He opened it very slowly. They all looked down at it. Inside was a list of what looked like phone numbers, some of them high-lighted in yellow. Hale swivelled the folder round so that

Edmund could read it and pushed it towards him, pointing to the final highlighted line.

'Do you recognise that number?'

'No, why should I?'

'That was the last call made from Harriet's landline in the beach house, the night she died. It's the number of a taxi company in Oakwood. A member of my team has spoken to the driver, who remembers picking up a young lad from the harbour car park, driving him into Oakwood and dropping him three roads away from your house.'

'So what? That could have been anyone. Maybe another student visited her for a lesson after I left.'

'The driver said the boy had several plasters on his right hand. That was you, wasn't it, Edmund?'

Edmund stared at Hale, who held his gaze. Edmund's eyes dropped first. He fiddled with the edge of the largest plaster; now rolled back, it looked like a grey slug.

'Well?' A soft prompt from Hale.

'Well what? You have Mother. She's admitted to doing it. She said she did it for me. Like she's done everything all my life. I'm the victim here.'

No one interrupted him, but they all waited. Desperate to convince them, he continued, 'I've done nothing. I've killed no one. She has. She said she did. You've got no evidence. You have to let me go!'

Silence after his outburst. Hale looked up. 'Now, let's go back to the taxi, shall we?'

'What about it?'

'Why did you lie? A clever boy like you, making a mistake like that.'

Edmund said nothing. He looked down at his hand and picked at the edge of his plaster.

'After all your careful planning, you get caught out by a phone call and a taxi driver. That was one of the lies your mother noticed, wasn't it?'

Silence. Hale let it hang for a few moments longer. He produced the red exercise book from below the folder. Its fluorescent cover glowed in the dull grey of the room. Hale flicked through it, making a performance of searching for a passage he knew was there but couldn't quite find. Stopping at a page, he appeared to read it, then turned the book over, pages down, splayed open on the desk. They waited. What had he read?

'Your mother would do anything for you, wouldn't she? Confess to murder for you. Spend a lifetime in prison for you.'

The pause stretched until it ached. Hale's voice was so quiet it was almost a whisper. 'She knows what you've done, Edmund, and must be horrified by it. Yet she chooses to protect you. But I wonder if she knows about this?'

Hale pulled the book towards him and read out loud the description of Edmund and his mother in bed. The solicitor squirmed and looked down at his notepad, then glanced at his client, who stared up at the camera, his face empty. Hale finished.

'Your mother doesn't know about this little fantasy of yours, does she?'

'It's not a fantasy. She abused me since I was – since I was – I don't remember when she started. She used me in every way possible – you've read it. I'm the victim. She abused me and then killed anyone who got in the way of her plans. She's confessed to it.'

Hale pulled his chair further under the table. The screech on the tiled floor was loud and irritating. 'Let's go back to the taxi. We'll assume it was you, shall we? Earlier that evening you were seen going to visit Harriet with a bottle of wine.'

'You know I did.' Steph felt Edmund's desperate appeal for her support as he turned towards her. 'I helped you up the dunes with the dogs. You saw the bottle I'd brought to say thank you to Harriet.'

Hale interrupted. 'What was it?'

'What?'

'The wine you brought to say thank you.'

'A bottle of red. A rather good Rioja.' He sounded like a middle-aged man with an account at a wine merchant's. There appeared no limit to this boy's confidence, and it was now obvious he was used to drinking.

'And was it?'

'It was better than the rubbish at Grace's party.'

'Did you finish it?'

'I can't remember.' Edmund glanced at his solicitor as if annoyed. His solicitor continued to make notes.

'Then?'

'I went home.'

'How?'

'You know how – by taxi. You know I visited her, that I used her phone and left her house.

'Why did you lie and say your mother drove you home?'

'I was trying to protect her. I knew Mother had gone out again later and I thought picking me up would explain it in case anyone saw her.' He sat rigid, holding Hale's gaze, saying nothing.

Hale continued, 'Did you both have wine glasses?

'Of course we did.'

'We only found one.'

'She could have washed up the other one. Look, I've admitted I was there, that I gave her a bottle of wine and I drank some with her. When I left she was alive. Her death had nothing to do with me. You have no evidence that I had anything to do with it. I can't help it if she used my wine to kill herself.'

'How do you know that she used the wine to kill herself? No one has said anything about how she died. Did I say anything about her using wine to kill herself, Johnson?'

'No, sir, you said nothing about her using wine to kill herself.' Johnson's voice boomed across the room. It sounded so corny, as if it was out of a bad film. Steph had forgotten the performance of scenes such as this. The solicitor raised his eyebrow and cast a warning look towards Hale. But this wasn't a film they were in. It could be the turning point in Edmund's life. If so, he was pretty cold-blooded about it. He sat as if waiting for a train, not being accused of murder.

'Let's move on, shall we?' Hale scraped his chair back noisily, so he was spectating rather than leading. 'I think you have something to ask.' He inclined his head towards Steph. She opened the red book at the first yellow post-it note and started reading out loud. Edmund listened intently and smiled faintly, as if he appreciated his prose style.

'So, you went to the music centre that day to have your first practice with Justine.'

'I planned to, but when I got there it was sealed off. She'd already killed herself.'

'What happened to the croissants and grapefruit juice you took with you?'

'What croissants and grapefruit juice?'

Steph paused and looked him straight in the eyes. They did not flicker. She saw herself in his dilated pupils.

'The croissants and grapefruit juice that your mother gave you the money to buy. It's not here in your book, but you mentioned it yesterday on the walk with Derek.' Was there a slight flicker in his eyes? If so, it was only a millisecond.

'I think you're mistaken. I didn't buy croissants and juice. We were planning to practise, not have a picnic.'

'I'm not mistaken. Remember, you told me you had to ask your mother for the money you needed for Grace's present and the croissants and juice.'

He looked down, examined his plasters and continued to pick at the edge of the largest one until he exposed the start of a line of stitches.

'I'm sure I said nothing about that.' He looked at his solicitor. 'It's your word against mine – unless you'll bring Derek in as a witness!'

This boy was becoming cocky. A good sign. A calm exterior, but underneath Steph could feel that he was wavering slightly. He paused. Was he thinking back to recall whether he'd said anything else that might incriminate him?

The solicitor came to life. 'You've arrested my client, but so far you've only got circumstantial evidence. I suggest you provide some hard evidence and charge him or let him go home.'

Hale's chair screamed across the tiles once again. He moved into Edmund's sight line. Steph leaned back, now the observer.

'Before you go,' he nodded to the solicitor, 'let's go through the evidence you've given us in here, just to make sure that you couldn't have had anything to do with it.'

The solicitor nodded, and Edmund's shoulders relaxed slightly. Hale read out the sections where Edmund had placed his mother at the scene of all three attacks.

'You see. I'd no idea when I wrote that, but now, looking

back, you can see that she must've done it all. Not me. I'm innocent. Can I go home now?'

He shifted in his chair, about to get up. Hale lifted his hand and Edmund sat back with a sigh. 'Now what?'

'I just want to make sure you're happy we can use these notes as evidence for the prosecution when your mother comes to court.'

'But she's confessed—'

'We're obliged to show her any evidence we plan to use. I wonder what her reaction will be when the sections where you describe her abuse of you – the incest – are read out in court and get out into the media.'

'That book is private! You've no right to show it to her. It's mine.' He sat up and tried to seize the book, but Hale got there before him.

'But you wrote this to publish it – you tell us that on page one.'

Hale stood and flipped the book shut. He put it in the folder and tucked it under his arm. 'I'll be back in about an hour after I have discussed these latest developments with your mother. We need to add abuse to the charges against her.'

CHAPTER FIFTY-SIX

STEPH

Even from a distance on the TV monitor, Imogen looked shattered. Her blouse was creased, her cardigan hung on her shoulders and she wasn't wearing make-up. Her appearance was in stark contrast to that of her solicitor, perched beside her wearing a bright green suit, white silk blouse and perfectly applied make-up. Hale went through the formalities, then sat back a little and handed over to Johnson.

'Mrs Fitzgerald, we've some additional evidence that we'd like you to look at.'

'I've already told you. I've confessed and don't want to discuss anything further.'

'We think you may want to see this. It's a collection of your son's writing over the last few weeks, since he went to college.' Hale placed the book on the table in front of her.

'Why should I want to read it?' She stared at the book as if it might sting, refusing to touch it.

'He's been writing it for publication as the memoirs of a home-schooled musical prodigy. You haven't seen it?'

She shook her head.

Hale moved forward and took over. 'In it he implicates you. I think you should read it.' He pushed the book further towards Imogen. Reluctantly, she picked it up, opened it and started to read.

At the end of the first few pages she looked up, visibly shaken. Her face, already pale, lost all colour and she had to clear her throat before she could speak. Hale pushed a plastic beaker of water across the table. She sipped it, then looked back at the first page of the book. 'But this isn't true. Nothing like this – this disgusting – never happened.'

'I suggest you continue reading it, then we'll talk about it when you've finished.'

Imogen sighed, and after an enquiring look from her solicitor, moved the book so she could read it too. As they worked their way through the entries, the solicitor jotted down notes. Imogen read Edmund's writing, her face frozen.

She reached the end. She paused, stared at the wall, then her head drooped for a moment. No one spoke. She flipped back to the beginning and re-read the opening few pages. Closing the book, she pushed it back across the table towards Hale. They waited. At last, she looked up.

'I withdraw my confession.'

She moved her chair back and stood up.

'Sorry. It's not quite that easy. We need to go through the points that Edmund makes, to check exactly where you were and what you remember about Edmund's movements.'

Imogen flopped back into her seat and looked across at her solicitor, who nodded and indicated that Hale was right. Imogen looked hollowed out, and Steph thought she might collapse. Hale re-filled her beaker of water, which she sipped between slow, deliberate breaths.

Hale then took her through each of the incidents, quoting

Edmund's version and checking it with her. Imogen knew that Edmund was planning to rehearse with Justine before college and gave him money for croissants and fruit juice. That morning she didn't drive him to college, as she had an early lesson with one of her adult pupils who was going to take a music exam the next day.

Yes, she had visited Margaret Durrant during break time on the day she fell downstairs. Margaret had shown her the photographs taken at the beach house, and Imogen had assured her she knew all about their lessons and refused to believe that anything untoward was going on. She admitted that she had been angry and vexed by Margaret and accused her of interfering and victimising Harriet. After their conversation, Imogen had told Margaret that she could make her own way out and she went over to reception by herself. Hale did not tell her that Margaret was now conscious and that she had confirmed Imogen's version.

She denied driving Edmund to see Harriet at her beach house with the bottle of wine on the night she died. Again, she had been teaching piano and wasn't aware he'd taken the wine or visited the beach house that evening. Edmund had told her he was meeting friends from college to work on their drama piece. Hale revealed that they had found no trace of her DNA in the beach house, confirming her original story that she had never been there. It was this final lie, after many others in that conversation, that made her realise that Edmund must have been involved in the murders, so she took the blame for him.

After all the formalities were complete, Imogen and her solicitor left. Nothing appeared to be happening in any of the other interview rooms. At last, Hale bounced back into the office. 'Result! His mother's evidence now implicates him.'

'All that stuff in his so-called memoirs he wrote to frame his mother?' Steph was amazed at how she had believed it. How she had believed in him.

'According to his mother, yes.'

'The incest, the affair with Harriet – all lies?'

Hale sat down beside her. 'It was all fantasy – incest with his mother, seducing Harriet. It never happened. None of it.'

'But the drama studio accident, the porn photo, the injured hand at the barbecue – that all happened. We saw the result, the physical evidence,' said Steph.

'Oh, he was clever all right. Much of it was true, which convinced anyone reading it that the rest of it was too. Now we need him to admit it all. Coming?'

Hale picked up the file, opened the door and waited for her. 'Johnson is fetching him up from the cells.'

He opened the door to reveal Edmund, once again with his solicitor, in the same seats as earlier, with Johnson sitting by the door. Steph and Hale sat opposite and Hale re-started the recording. Edmund had a bored expression on his face and appeared calm, but he fiddled with his plaster, most of which now hung off and revealed a long line of stitches across the back of his hand.

'Your mother has read your memoirs and she has withdrawn her confession,' said Hale.

It took a moment for the news to hit Edmund, then he screamed out, 'She can't have. She's guilty! She confessed. I know she did it all!'

The solicitor laid a hand on Edmund's arm to calm him. He knocked it away and stood up. His chair clattered to the floor, the metal screeching on the tiles. As Johnson went to restrain him Edmund dropped backwards, smashing his head on the wall. Unconscious, he lay in a heap, jerking and panting noisily.

Hale jumped round the table shouting, 'Johnson – get an ambulance! He's having a fit!'

Steph rushed over and turned Edmund on his side, making sure he hadn't swallowed his tongue. His breathing became noisier, the convulsions were now rhythmical and he'd become very pale, almost blue. Steph hid the wet patch on his trousers with her jacket until someone brought a blanket. The solicitor hovered in the corner, a spectator. Once again, she felt sorry for this boy reduced to a quivering mass on the floor. Now the initial panic was over and all they could do was wait for the ambulance, she reflected on all he had endured, day after day. Despite the dreadful things he had done, he had suffered too. This fit or seizure, or whatever it was, could be serious and permanently affect his brain or his ability to play his cello.

After what felt like an hour but was only ten minutes, the paramedics arrived. Edmund was still unconscious, but his jerking arms and legs had relaxed. They dressed the open wound on the back of his head, gave him an injection and fixed an oxygen mask over his face. Steph and Hale saw him loaded into the ambulance, which drove away, blue lights flashing and the siren splitting the traffic.

CHAPTER FIFTY-SEVEN

STEPH

STEPH WAS DROWNING. The azure waters became black as she sank deeper and deeper. Struggling up to the surface for air she was pushed further down. She fought to breathe but her lungs filled with water; no room left for oxygen. Her nose and mouth were filled with sand. When she opened her eyes the glaring sun forced her to shut them again. She pulled herself up to the surface, out of her dream but waking to a nightmare.

The sun went out. Squinting, she made out a black shape sitting astride her. A hand covered her mouth and nose, she couldn't breathe and her lungs were exploding. She tried to scream but her voice wouldn't work. A sharp scratch on her neck made her gasp – the tip of a knife. She raised her head, but he pushed her down hard into the pillow. The knife punctured her skin, so she lay still.

'Scream and I'll cut you.'

His hands lifted a little so she could gasp in air through his fingers. She blinked and tried to get her eyes to focus. Whoever it was sat on her, waiting. Through the shutters the streetlight picked out her assailant in strips. Dark clothes, no mask. Those eyes – she knew who it was! He smiled. 'Hello Steph. Now, I'm going to take away my hand, but if you scream, I'll put it back harder and stab you. I'm not afraid to use it. Even on you.'

As promised, the hand moved from her mouth and nose, and she gulped in great lungfuls of air. She was desperate for water to take away the taste of antiseptic left by his hand, but she lay still, saying nothing. She stared into his eyes, trying to convince herself that this wasn't, couldn't be happening. How had he got here? He was in hospital and under guard.

'That's good, Steph. Now put your right hand above your head. I've got this, remember.' A flash of silver passed in front of her eyes – a surgical scalpel. She did as she was told, and he looped a silky tie over her wrist and pulled tight. He must have fixed it to the bars of the bed while she slept.

'Now your left hand – up we go. That's right.'

What was he going to do? Rape her? Both her hands were tied to the bedstead; he checked the knots and pulled them tighter. 'Ow!' Steph gasped as the movement jarred her left shoulder.

'Relax and it won't hurt so much.' He sounded as if he cared.

His hand traced the outline of her body, over her breasts and down to the top of her legs. He stopped, smiled, and moved his weight further down to sit on her thighs. She was unable to squirm or move her legs to kick him off.

His eyes drilled into hers while he stroked the top of her legs under Hale's pale blue shirt, which she'd adopted as night-wear. Without warning he jumped back and spread her legs, grabbing her right ankle and looping another noose over it. As he tightened it, she recognised one of Hale's ties. She kicked out at him with her left leg and tried to resist his attempt to capture her foot, but it was no use. The tie was waiting for her ankle, and she lay captive, spreadeagled across the bed. Only then did Edmund place the blade within reach on the bedside table while he bent down to secure all four knots.

The words of her training flashed into her mind. Surviving is more important than being raped. Keep calm, keep him talking and agree with everything he says to keep alive. Her eyes had never left his as he trussed her up. He showed no emotion; his movements were efficient. Where was Derek?

'Where's Derek? What have you done to him?'

'Would I do anything to Derek? No, he's safe in that coat cupboard, crunching his way through an enormous bag of kibble. Don't worry, he's also got a bowl of water and his bed in there. He was so pleased to see me. Really Steph, you can't believe I'd hurt Derek.'

'But you're hurting me. Why are you doing this, Edmund?'

'I wanted some time with you – alone – to talk. No one to bother us.'

'We'll soon be bothered by Hale. He's due back any time now.'

Edmund drew up the small bedroom chair and placed it halfway down the bed so she could see him without straining her neck. She heard a siren in the distance. It came closer – could it be? For that moment she hoped that somehow, someone would be looking for him and think of checking her flat. But no, the pulsing sound disappeared into the silence of the night.

'Sorry, Steph. Not Hale. But we both know that, don't we? He's at that Norfolk conference and won't be back until late tomorrow evening. Aren't we lucky? We have all that time to be together – just you and me.'

'What conference?'

He smiled, looking pleased with himself. 'The conference

he mentioned when he said goodbye. Your front garden is very dark and wet. I heard your fond goodbyes when he left. It's all worked out so well for us, hasn't it?'

For the first time Steph noticed his wet hair and the damp patches on his shoulders. The rain was now bashing against her bedroom windows, but when Hale had left it was just starting. Edmund must have come in soon after Hale had driven off and she'd fallen asleep, or he'd be soaked. She could hear the rain dripping to her left. It sounded as if it was raining inside the flat. Of course – the bathroom window. That's how he'd got in. She'd opened it after her bath and forgotten to close it.

'Edmund, what do you want and why have you done this to me?'

'I always thought you were my friend. You said you were. You said you'd help me when Mother went to prison. You let me hold Derek on that walk and said one day we'd go to the beach. Didn't you?'

'Yes, I did.'

'But in that police station you changed sides. I couldn't believe it. After all we'd been through together. You joined up with Hale and were nasty to me. Really nasty.'

How was she going to get out of this in one piece? Should she have resisted him? Struggled before he tied her up? But how? No good thinking about that now. He'd held that knife to her neck and she believed he'd use it. He was cold, deliberate, determined. What had happened?

'What's happened to you, Edmund?'

'It's not me who's changed but you, you, Steph. You were my friend and you betrayed me.'

'Look, if you let me go, I won't say anything to Hale. We'll talk and I'll let you walk out and not do anything and you can escape to... to London. You can disappear there. I'll – I'll drive you.'

He turned to the bedside table, picked up her glass of water and sipped it as if this was a social call. As he lifted the glass to his mouth, she noticed the cannula taped into the back of his hand, joggling around as he moved. Smiling, he caught her look and nodded. 'Before you ask, yes, I did walk out of the hospital, and no, they don't know I've gone. That young police officer will get hell when they find out he left to get a coffee and hey presto, I disappeared into thin air!'

He grinned, so pleased with himself. 'All I had to do was unhook this,' he pointed to the dangling cannula, fixed with a plaster into his vein, 'wait for him to move and walk out. They didn't think I could walk, yet here I am spending the night with you, Steph. How risqué is that?' His voice had become a whisper. He was enjoying this.

Here was one manipulative conman. She'd been well and truly taken in for weeks. In the police station she'd glimpsed the cold monster behind his astonishing talent, but to pull off something like this? How she'd underestimated him. The rain battered against the window, followed by the deep echo of thunder in the distance. She flexed her shoulders slightly, as the pain in her arm sockets was becoming unbearable.

'It won't be long, Steph. I'll undo them soon.'

She breathed in deeply, trying to keep calm and to hide the sickening fear in the depths of her stomach. 'Why are you doing this to me, Edmund?'

He took another sip of water. 'In the police station you wanted to know what happened. Well, I'm here to tell you before I—'

'Before you what?'

Her shoulders were throbbing, and she wanted to go to the

loo. She ached in all her joints – her hips, her knees, her elbows – everywhere. She wanted to move but the knots were tight, and she was stuck, flat on her back. 'Tell me what happened if that's what you want.'

'I thought it was what you wanted too, Steph. You said it was. It's quite simple. It was Mother. Mother confessed, didn't she? She was behind it all.'

'Behind it?'

'She made me do it. She's controlled me always – turned me into what she wanted me to be. When people started getting in the way of what she wanted, they had to go.'

Blaming his mother was the obvious move. Yet there was enough truth in it to sound convincing. Steph had seen Imogen's controlling behaviour only too often at college, and she'd heard her say something similar the night she'd confessed. She decided to push him. She had nothing to lose, had she?

'What do you mean, "in the way"? Justine never got in your way. Your mother wasn't threatened by her.'

'She was. After the concert, Mother was really annoyed when she heard Justine play so well and I'm afraid – well, it didn't help when I told Mother I wanted to form a duo with her. You see, I'd already told her that Justine kept demanding Harriet's time. We'd be practising, and Justine would appear at the door with that spaniel begging look. I mean, I'd only just found Harriet, and Justine wanted to take her away from me.'

His calm speech with its confiding tone horrified her. He made it all sound reasonable and perfectly normal. All the more shocking as he sat beside her bed while she was trussed up and so vulnerable. Now he'd launched into his explanation, he spoke rapidly.

'Justine said we'd share Harriet's time. Share? No. I

realised then she wouldn't leave Harriet alone, so I suppose in the end, it was her own fault. That morning she looked so pretty – her curls bounced in the sunlight and she smiled as she came through the door.'

He spoke as if in a dream, re-living that warm autumn morning. He talked to himself, not to her, and seemed lost in the memory of that moment, a moment to relish. It had become his story, not his mother's. Her stomach clenched as his voice chilled her. She was afraid he wouldn't let her go. She had to get out of this. They both jumped as a flash of lightning lit up the room, and the crack of thunder made the house tremble. While he wasn't looking at her, she moved her wrist and folded her right hand over the knot. It was slippery material – perhaps she could work it loose.

'I remember asking myself – perhaps it would work, the two of us? She was so pretty – her hair smelled of rosemary. But it wouldn't have worked, would it? She wouldn't let go of Harriet. Mother gave me the money to buy grapefruit juice and croissants on the way to college. I'd even got napkins and glasses.'

He smiled, recalling the treat he'd prepared for Justine. His words in their everyday tone made Steph's flesh crawl. How could she ever have admired him? Her second finger forced its way into the core of the knot. Any movement shot electricity up her arm, but she stopped herself from crying out by biting hard on her tongue. Lost in his story, he didn't appear to notice.

'We ate and drank and planned our futures together. As we talked, she became drowsy. The drugs didn't taste in the grapefruit juice. She yawned, shook her curls and tried to keep awake, but very slowly her head went down to her chest. At last, she slept—'

'Where did you get the drugs?' Steph kept her eyes on his so he wouldn't get distracted and look at her right hand.

'Mother's bedside drawer. The doctor gave them to her when she couldn't sleep.' Clearly, he was annoyed that she'd interrupted his story. He frowned at her; she held still. He tutted and continued as if he'd been interrupted by an irritating child. 'I like to think her last thoughts were happy, as she dreamed of us playing Mozart and Bach together.'

He stopped and looked down at Steph. Her hand froze and she held his gaze. 'She was good, but not as good as me. Mother was afraid she'd get in the way because she wanted Harriet to spend time with her – time that should be mine.' He looked into Steph's eyes, expecting affirmation. Even in this appalling situation he needed and expected her support. How had she not seen this before?

'I see.' She nodded and hoped that would be sufficient. She had to keep him talking to give her enough time.

'You do, don't you? I was right, wasn't I?' Not waiting for any response, he continued, 'I took the craft knife. It had a new blade – she wouldn't have felt it – she was in a deep sleep when I ran it along her veins. I hardly touched her – she started bleeding. She wouldn't have felt it, would she?' Again, there was that look. The look of a child needing approval, or Derek desperate for a treat. She felt sick and all her joints were throbbing. Was he going to do that to her? 'It wouldn't have hurt, would it?' His voice grew louder.

'No.'

'No, it wouldn't have hurt her, and in the long run it was the best thing. Underneath she knew she wasn't good enough to get to the very top of the pyramid. The music world's tough, you know, and she would have been second or even third class. I saved her all those years of failure.'

Horrified by this easy justification of his actions, she struggled to keep her expression neutral. It was surreal – Edmund was chatting to her as if they were sitting over a coffee, when he was calmly describing the vicious murder of a beautiful young woman. She felt bile moving up her chest and swallowed hard, trying to keep it down. She must keep control and not panic. Was her arm coming out of its socket? It felt so taut, and once again as she fiddled with the knot, the pain was excruciating and it felt as if she'd torn something. She took a deep breath and tried to keep her voice level to reflect his.

'Right – and Margaret?'

'Margaret? Now Margaret was jealous of Harriet, who was a much better teacher. One day Margaret nagged Harriet so much she cried – sobbed – real tears. Harriet didn't deserve to have that old woman interfering all the time.'

He wriggled, sat up straighter on the chair and took another sip of water. The bins clattered outside as they were blown over. Steph winced as she tried to hold out against the relentless pain that shot through muscles she didn't know she had. Even through the pain she noticed how the influence of his mother was slowly disappearing from his account.

'One evening, I saw Margaret taking photos of Harriet and me in the beach house. You were there too. She threatened Harriet. She was going to say we were doing vile, dirty things. All lies. She said she'd tell Mother, who knew anyway, and the Principal, who didn't. I had to do something before she limped to Mr Bryant.'

'So, you—?'

'I didn't push her hard; it was more of nudge and she tumbled down the stairs.'

The unemotional, factual way in which he described these attacks turned her stomach. If he could do that to them, what could he do to her? He didn't appear to have emotions at all. He'd disposed of these women as if they were inconvenient objects, not people.

'And then?' Exhausted, she held onto his eyes. Her finger was now inside the knot, and she rotated it, making the hole at the centre larger.

'I went back to my practice, of course. Anyway, she hasn't died, has she? She's asleep, in a coma. She's not in pain, is she?'

'Is that important?'

'Yes – of course it is. I didn't want to hurt her, but to keep her quiet. Now she's asleep. No more shaking, and her Parkinson's won't stop her from playing the piano, will it?'

'I suppose not.' She tried to smile, approving his kindness to Margaret in cutting short her pain. Keep him talking. Agree with him. Don't judge or criticise.

'She would have hated not being able to play her piano, not walking on the beach with that little dog. It was only a few moments, not years of pain and shaking and her life closing in on her. Now she'll sleep, until one day when she stops.'

He paused and looked down at Steph once again. She nodded, pushing down the revulsion she felt, and dragged up positive thoughts, which she hoped would appear on her face. Re-assured, he sat back, cleared his throat and fiddled with a toggle on his navy hoodie. For the first time she noticed the logo across the top: 'Edinburgh Medical School' beneath a blue St Andrew's cross that mirrored her spreadeagled position. So, it wasn't only the scalpel that he'd stolen? A second finger was now working away at the inside of the knot, but it was such slow progress. She was not sure how much longer she could tolerate this pain. She must carry on, keep him talking.

'And Harriet?'

'Harriet... I loved Harriet. She was my first love. So special.

On the night of the flood, I thought we'd sleep together but Harriet laughed at me. She opened the door to some pokey spare room – smelly, damp, with a stained camp bed – I thought we'd be in her bed together. But she stood outside her bedroom door and laughed. She laughed at me! Told me I had a crush on her and that she didn't sleep with students and to be a "good boy" and go into the spare room. She called me a "good boy" like you tell Derek.'

'You must have been upset.' Her sympathetic tone almost choked her but prompted him to reveal more.

'I was. So upset, I was awake all night. How could she laugh at me? She hurt me. The next night, when you saw me, I took her a bottle of wine. We drank a glass together, then I left. I slept very well that night, but she drank the rest of the bottle and never woke up. I left the beach door open so she could hear the sea. I thought it was a kind thing to do after what she'd done to me. She'd spoilt it all.'

'I see.'

'I hope you do.' A hint of aggression had crept into his voice. He turned to her and searched her face for a reaction. Shocked, sick, horrified – she wasn't sure she could find a word to describe the pit that his story had pushed her into. The dispassionate way he talked about such vile acts was repulsive. No remorse, but he justified his acts as necessary and blamed his victims for forcing him to kill them. She hid it all and fixed her face while he frowned and appeared to be thinking about what to say next.

'You know, I did all of it because of Mother. She wanted me to be a great cellist and made sure nothing and no one got in my way. I deserve to be pitied, not to be punished for what she drove me to do. Don't you agree?'

She didn't reply quickly enough, so he prodded her left

arm; she winced and cried out loud. 'Don't you agree?' he said, about to shove her again.

'Yes,' she screamed out. The pain made her feel faint. She didn't care what he did; all she wanted was for the pain to stop.

He stood and grabbed the knife. 'Now you agree. But you didn't, did you? Not in the police station. You didn't agree there. You betrayed me. You know what happens to traitors, don't you? They used to hang, draw and quarter them.'

He moved the scalpel closer to her, ran the tip up her stomach towards her neck. Clearly, he was enjoying his power over her, and she was terrified that he would go through with it. There was another blast of thunder and a car door slammed somewhere outside.

'I won't say anything, Edmund, I promise. Please. Please let me go. I'll drive you wherever you want.'

He rotated the blade in the air over her left breast, getting closer to her on each circuit. It sliced through the blue cotton of Hale's shirt, and her nipple, then her breast, emerged through the hole. He ran the sharp tip around it and grinned at her. She wanted to throw up. He stood back a little, admiring her breast as if considering what to do.

'But that would be silly, wouldn't it, leaving you here to tell Hale?'

Once again in slow motion he moved closer, the knife moving up towards her throat. She tensed, closed her eyes, waiting to feel the bite of the knife.

CHAPTER FIFTY-EIGHT

STEPH

'Drop that knife!'

Hale! As Edmund swung around, Hale smashed his right arm and the knife clattered to the floor. He grabbed Edmund's wrist, twisted him round, pushed him to the ground and handcuffed him to the bed post. Edmund sat on the floor, shocked. He looked up at Hale puzzled, clearly not sure what had happened. 'But you shouldn't be here – you're at a conference.'

Hale moved to the top of the bed and with great care undid the knots that tied Steph's hands. She gasped as she moved her arms down to her chest, covering up her exposed breast. Hale freed her feet. 'Look at the weather, lad. The storm is even stronger in Norfolk. The River Yare burst its banks and I was turned back. Decided to go tomorrow morning early. Good job I did, eh?'

As gently as possible, Hale put his arm around Steph's shoulders and supported her as she struggled to sit on the side of the bed. Pins and needles made it difficult for her to stand and impossible to walk, but with Hale's support she shuffled to the sitting room away from Edmund, now manacled to the bed.

On the way, Hale grabbed her bath robe and wrapped it around her. She shook and shivered as the shock of what could have happened hit her. She stumbled into Hale, who carried her to the armchair and lowered her down. A frantic scratching from the coat cupboard prompted Hale to open the door, and Derek bounced out.

'Derek?'

'He's fine. Look at him.'

With difficulty she turned her body, as she couldn't move her neck, to see him wagging his tail. He put his head on her knee, waiting for her to stroke his ears. She winced, as any touch was hell, and she couldn't stop shaking. Hale tucked a duvet over her and handed her a glass of whisky. She sipped it and gasped as she lifted her hand to her mouth. Every move was excruciating.

She sat, numb but racked with pain and shock. How could she be numb and in pain at the same time? The torture she'd been through was just starting to hit her. She could have died. Another minute and he would have cut her throat, she was sure. He would have slaughtered her like he had the others. She could hear Hale on his mobile, calling it in.

As usual she started to blame herself. How could she have prevented what happened? No, stop! This time she was not going to take emotional responsibility for Edmund's cruelty. What he did was hatched in his own warped mind. She was the victim and had been helpless against his brutality. Although she should have seen through him earlier, shouldn't she?

Phone call finished, Hale came and sat on the arm of her chair, draping his arm over her shoulders. Her sharp intake of breath as he jiggled her shoulder prompted him to move.

'Sorry.' He sat in the armchair opposite. 'You've been through hell. If that storm hadn't happened, you might...'

'Don't. What could have happened is starting to hit me. I thought he might let me go, but when he cut your shirt, I knew there was no way out.' She sipped the Scotch, wallowing in the warmth as it hit her stomach.

'Look at you – shaking. It's the shock. Would you prefer a hot drink?'

'No, this is fine. Thanks.'

Hale had pushed himself halfway out of his chair but sat back again. 'You should have heard me curse when I had to turn back, but when I came in and heard what was happening... Oh Steph! I can't bear to think what might have happened – should I get you to A&E?'

'No way. I'll be fine.'

His head on one side, he looked across quizzically, then nodded.

'How did he get in?'

'Typical policeman eh, Hale?'

She held out her glass. He leaned forward and topped it up. At last the alcohol was working, relaxing her stressed muscles and taking away the pain in her joints. 'If you must know, I left the window open after my bath.'

'What? I don't believe it! How could you be so stupid?'

'Come on, it's at the back of the house.'

'Oh, burglars only come to the front, do they?'

'Stop it!'

'Honestly, I'm—'

Their bickering was interrupted by the arrival of a car outside her house. Hale went to the door and had a mumbled conversation with two uniformed police officers, who went through to the bedroom and re-appeared holding both arms of a handcuffed Edmund. He looked across at her in desperation. 'Tell them, Steph. I wouldn't have hurt you. You do know that, don't you?'

She lowered her head and couldn't bring herself to look at him. As the door clicked shut, she felt safe at last. Hale stood beside her and stroked her hair, taking care not to jolt her. 'Are you really all right?' He bent down and kissed her on the top of her head.

'He confessed to it all, you know. It was horrific. He killed Justine and Harriet and pushed Margaret down the stairs, and made it sound as if it was all their fault. It was amazing – he expected me to be on his side and agree that he had no choice. How could he?'

She placed the empty glass on the table to her left. Hale immediately topped it up, while she rubbed her right arm joint, trying to sooth the electric shocks. Another sip helped.

'And all that talent wasted. Even now I can't believe how manipulative and ruthless he was and how I was taken in by him.'

'I can't begin to imagine what goes on in the twisted mind of the lad. Stop thinking about him and concentrate on you.' He bent down and kissed the top of her head again.

'His mother's had a massive influence, but he's really clever, isn't he? Blaming her might help his case. Do you think he's worked that out too?'

He sat in the other armchair and faced her. 'It'll be interesting to see how that plays out with a jury. No doubt his brief will stress the pity they should feel for him and the extent to which his mother was behind the murders. She may not have held the knife or put the drugs in the drinks, but he'll claim she made him.'

'I've lost all sympathy for him. Let's hope the jury does too. He won't get away with it, will he?'

'Not with his confession and what he did to you. No, he'll be put away for a very long time.'

'To think I felt sorry for him! I shall think twice before falling for another lad's sob story. They must think I'm a real soft touch.'

'Stop beating yourself up – you weren't the only one taken in by him.' He looked at his watch. 'Look at the time! No conference for me. I'm not leaving you until I'm convinced you're as normal as you'll ever be!'

'I'm fine.'

'No, you're not. Don't argue. I'm staying here. Edmund can sweat for a while and I'll get Janet over to take a statement from you later. You need some sleep first.'

'No way can I go back in that bedroom yet. I'll stay here. I'll be fine.'

'See? That's why I'm staying. No, we'll have a quiet day here and maybe take Derek out for a walk later if you feel up to it.'

Derek sat up at the 'W' word and dashed to the door, then back to Steph.

'Some guard dog you turned out to be.' She ruffled his ears.

'That's not fair is it, Derek? You knew him so didn't bark.'

'You sound as if you're becoming a dog lover at last.'

'I wouldn't go that far... Perhaps I'm beginning to appreciate Derek's finer points.'

BLOOD LINES

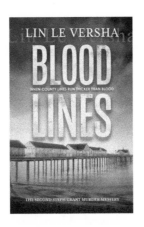

'This wonderfully fresh take on a crime fighting duo, expertly explores dark, contemporary themes brought to life by a fabulous cast of characters who will stay with you long after the last page.' **GRAHAM BARTLETT, AUTHOR OF** *BAD FOR GOOD*

Eighteen year-old Darcy Woodard appears to have it all –
intelligence, good looks and artistic gifts. His teachers adore
him, as does former policewoman Steph Grant, who is now the
receptionist at Darcy's college.

But beneath the surface - all is not as it seems.

Darcy is convinced he doesn't fit in with his peers and tries to
ignore their online taunts.

There's Darcy's dysfunctional mother Esther who is trapped in
a literary time warp.

Then there's his sister Marianne, who Darcy desperately wants
to protect from the dark forces that surround her.

Then tragedy rocks Darcy's life when a drugs gang forces its
way into his life and all the people he cares for.

What can Steph and her former boss DI Hale do to protect the
local community? And can they really trust Darcy to help
them defeat the county lines gang?

'Exceptional' Monika Armet

**'A gripping, fast-paced, dark and twisty murder
mystery.' Michelle Ryles**

'A highly excellent read!' Jude Wright

ACKNOWLEDGMENTS

Thank you

Henry Sutton, Julia Crouch, Nathan Ashman and Tom Benn, my tutors on the Creative Writing MA (Crime Fiction) at the University of East Anglia for their challenge and support in improving my writing and enabling me to become a novelist at last!

Bridget Burgoyne, Denise Bennett, Lucy Dixon, Mark Hankin, Helen Jones, Melissa Pelzer, Amanda Rigali, Paul Stone, Mandy Slater, Emma Styles, Martin Ungless and Lucy Wood, my wonderful 2018 *Crimies* MA group at UEA, for being true critical friends and for the wine and laughter at *The Murderers* and other hostelries throughout Norwich.

Kay Dunbar and Stephen Bristow for tempting me to Italy for *Ways with Words* writing courses, where tutors Blake Morrison and Mark McCrum's stimulating workshops and encouragement convinced me I could do it.

My children, for their love and always being there during the course and the re-writes.

Jo Barry, for reading and discussing everything from the start and for her amazing generosity, encouragement and for asking the right questions.

Helen Jones, for her tireless support and invaluable comments on the drafts and re-writes.

Jayne Camburn, Debby Hurst, Freda Noble, Bob Noble,

Ivor Samuels, Gerry Wakelin, my first readers for their enthusiasm and critical appreciation.

Caitriona Vulliamy, for confirming the role of Social Services in Safeguarding.

Sue Davison, for an outstanding edit and Jayne Mapp, for a stunning cover design.

Rebecca Collins and Adrian Hobeck, for their leap of faith in inviting me to join the Hobeck family and for their excellent, constructive feedback and inspiration.

All my friends, for putting up with me banging on about getting published!

ABOUT THE AUTHOR

Lin Le Versha has drawn on her experience in London and Surrey schools and colleges as the inspiration for this book, her debut crime novel.

Lin has written over twenty plays exploring the issues faced by secondary school and sixth form students. Commissioned to work with Anne Fine on *The Granny Project*, she created the English and drama lesson activities for students aged 11 to 14.

While at a sixth form college, she became the major author for *Teaching at Post 16*, a handbook for trainee and newly qualified teachers. In her role as a Local Authority Consultant, she became a School Improvement Partner, working alongside secondary headteachers, work she continued after moving to the Suffolk coast. She is the Director of the Southwold Arts Festival, comprising over thirty events in an eight-day celebration of the Arts.

Creative writing courses at the Arvon Foundation and *Ways with Words* in Italy, encouraged her to enrol at the UEA MA in Creative Writing and her debut novel was submitted as the final assessment for this excellent course. *Blood Notes* is that debut novel.

Lin is now working on the second title in the series which will be published in 2022.

HOBECK BOOKS – THE HOME OF GREAT STORIES

We hope you've enjoyed reading Lin Le Versha's debut crime novel.

Lin has written a short story prequel to this novel, *A Defining Moment.*

This story, and many other short stories and novellas, is

included in the compilation *Crime Bites. Crime Bites* is available for free to subscribers of Hobeck Books.

Crime Bites includes:

- *Echo Rock* by Robert Daws
- *Old Dogs, Old Tricks* by AB Morgan
- *The Silence of the Rabbit* by Wendy Turbin
- *Never Mind the Baubles: An Anthology of Twisted Winter Tales* by the Hobeck Team (including all the current Hobeck authors and Hobeck's two publishers)
- *The Clarice Cliff Vase* by Linda Huber
- *Here She Lies* by Kerena Swan
- *The Macnab Principle* by R.D. Nixon
- *Fatal Beginnings* by Brian Price
- *A Defining Moment* by Lin Le Versha
- *Saviour* by Jennie Ensor

Also please visit the Hobeck Books website for details of

our other superb authors and their books, and if you would like to get in touch, we would love to hear from you.

Hobeck Books also presents a weekly podcast, the Hobcast, where founders Adrian Hobart and Rebecca Collins discuss all things book related, key issues from each week, including the ups and downs of running a creative business. Each episode includes an interview with one of the people who make Hobeck possible: the editors, the authors, the cover designers. These are the people who help Hobeck bring great stories to life. Without them, Hobeck wouldn't exist. The Hobcast can be listened to from all the usual platforms but it can also be found on the Hobeck website: **www. hobeck.net/hobcast**.

Other Hobeck Books to Explore

Silenced

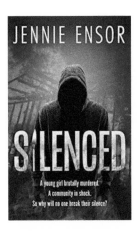

Silenced is the compelling and gritty new thriller by British author Jennie Ensor. A story of love,

fear and betrayal, and having the courage to speak out when the odds are stacked against you.

A teenage girl is murdered on her way home from school, stabbed through the heart. Her North London community is shocked, but no-one has the courage to help the police, not even her mother. DI Callum Waverley, in his first job as senior investigating officer, tries to break through the code of silence that shrouds the case.

This is a world where the notorious Skull Crew rules through fear. Everyone knows you keep your mouth shut or you'll be silenced – permanently.

This is Luke's world. Reeling from the loss of his mother to cancer, his step-father distant at best, violent at worst, he slides into the Skull Crew's grip.

This is Jez's world too. Her alcoholic mother neither knows nor cares that her 16-year-old daughter is being exploited by V, all-powerful leader of the gang.

Luke and Jez form a bond. Can Callum win their trust, or will his own demons sabotage his investigation? And can anyone stop the Skull Crew ensuring all witnesses are silenced?

The Genesis Inquiry

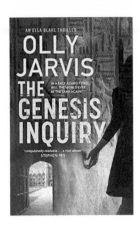

'What a treat it is to read Olly Jarvis's THE GENESIS INQUIRY: a compulsively readable crime and legal thriller that pulls off the trick of being both satisfyingly traditional and supremely up to the minute. In the attractive, cussed and charismatic person of lawyer Ella Blake Jarvis has created a hero that we can hope to see again. A real winner.'
STEPHEN FRY

'I'm approaching the final pages of The Genesis Inquiry and I don't want it to end. A phenomenal achievement by Olly Jarvis – highly, highly recommended.'
THE SECRET BARRISTER

Is there one last undiscovered, great truth?
A moment zero, a place in time that links all cultures and creeds?
A revelation that will unite us all and change the way we see history forever?

Brilliant but burnt-out barrister Ella Blake accepts an apparently simple brief: investigate the mysterious disappearance of an African American polymath from his rooms at Cambridge University. The Inquiry quickly becomes the greatest challenge of her life – solving the mystery of Genesis.

Facing danger at every turn, can Ella find the answers to the riddles and clues left by the missing genius?

Reunited with her estranged daughter, the Inquiry sends them on a quest across the world and through ancient texts. What is the secret that binds us all?

Who is behind the dark forces that will stop at nothing to prevent the world from knowing the truth?

The Genesis Inquiry **is an epic and gripping thriller by the brilliant Olly Jarvis which asks a key question – what can our shared past tell us about humanity's future?**

Lightning Source UK Ltd.
Milton Keynes UK
UKHW040633030323
417973UK00007B/690

9 781913 793524